THE BARGAIN

HENRIETTA VINCENT

Stories find us when we need them most.

Sometimes we don't even know why we pick up a certain book—only that something calls us to it.

The Bargain is a story about love. But not just the easy kind.

It's about the kind of love that makes you choose.

That asks something of you.

That stays with you, long after the last page is turned.

This book won't pretend to have all the answers.

But perhaps, in the quiet between chapters, it might stir something in you—a memory, a question, a longing you hadn't named before.

So settle in.

Let the words take you somewhere unexpected.

And if they stay with you after you've finished reading,

then maybe—just maybe—the story was always a little bit yours, too.

-Henrietta

PROLOGUE

"*W*hat is your name, girl?"

"Lenora MacLeod."

"MacLeod?"

"Yes, mum."

It was odd that the earl had chosen this girl out of the sea of possible candidates. With all the fine upstanding White governesses to choose from, he instead chose her.

"I trust there will be no issue with your attending church services with the children."

"No, mum."

"And how old are you, Miss MacLeod?"

"Nineteen, mum."

The Honorable Mr. Michael Chesterfield silently observed the slip of a girl his half-brother intended to hire on as the new governess. One hand draped carelessly over the arm of his Rococo chair, the other arm bent at the elbow, his long caramel-colored, manicured fingers supporting his head. A head crowned by an unfashionable amount of auburn ringlets. He was the sort of handsome that tiptoed treacherously close to pretty. He presented a well-staged and painfully familiar portrait of *les s'ennuyer riche*. The bored rich.

He studied the girl. She was slender. Not terribly tall. Dressed plain, but meticulously neat. Her skin a rich cocoa brown. Not quite as dark as his father's 'n. Her wide, almost black, eyes were framed by thick lashes and her dark curls pulled back into a stern bun. She was not quite pretty, not in the conventional sense, though she had rather appealing lips.

She faced her interrogation from Mrs. Hennings, the Chesterfield housekeeper, with great dignity for a girl of nineteen; her spine as stiff as a broomstick, her face determined, and her slender fingers linked protectively before her.

Everything in her demeanor, her carriage, and her deportment fairly screamed, *I won't be crushed by you!*

Three months. That was precisely how long it would take to entice her to his bed. And by the looks of her curving hips, it would be worth the effort.

Chesterfield slid lower in his chair with an idle sigh, his mind drifting with well-practiced ease to what he planned to wear to this evening's rout. Perhaps the pale blue vest with gold piping. How could one be expected to think too deeply on any one subject when there were so very many trivial things to rot one's brain upon?

"Don't even think of it." This, from the earl.

"Think of what, dear brother?" Chesterfield turned to the earl with a smile.

The Earl of Walpole eyed his younger brother with an air of fatigue. "I know you, Michael. And after what happened with Lily, I would ask you to keep your hands off my staff."

The men spoke in whispers, as only a carved Indian Mahogany screen shielded them from the view of the two women beyond it. Though their view was slightly obstructed, Chesterfield and his brother were mere shadows at best from where the women stood.

Of course he would bring up Lily. Chesterfield's face darkened at his brother's reminder. Was it not enough he had behaved as a monk for the last six months? Was that not penance enough for his slight indiscretion?

The earl himself had two bastard children to care for. So, he now had his first, a boy of three months. Of course it 'n idiocy to have bedded that upstairs maid. Lily 'n a silly girl without the slightest notion of care. She still to this day thought herself in love with him.

Him, the half-savage. He knew that's what the women called him as they tittered behind their fans. At once fascinated and terrified at the thought of bedding him. Bearing a child they could not so easily pass off as their husband's. And yet, still they came to him. The nobler ladies in secret. The others more openly. He may be a half-savage, but he was decidedly a handsome one.

He thought back to Lily. What had gotten into him that night? And the other four?

"Are you at all disinclined to leaving London?" Mrs. Hennings continued her questioning.

"No, mum." Simple enough of an answer.

"You understand you will be moving with the children to Waverly, His Lordship's country house."

"Yes, mum."

A woman of few words. Chesterfield raised a brow in admiration.

"Your family has no objections, then?"

"None, mum."

"Very well then, Miss MacLeod." Mrs. Hennings rose from her seat. "On behalf of the Earl and Countess of Walpole, I welcome you."

"Thank you, mum."

The girl neither smiled nor altered so much as a lash. She was as stiff as before. Perhaps it would take five months, but no more. Chesterfield eyed the newly appointed governess with a slow, purposeful smile.

CHAPTER 1

*L*ight!

Too much light! More than his aching head could bear. Enough to drown the senses. Somehow, they had captured the sun from the heavens and pressed its ponderous mass into his room. He turned his head away from the blaze chasing after elusive shadows created by the bed's heavy brocade canopy.

Mr. Michael Chesterfield, younger half-brother to the Earl of Walpole, turned over in his bed, his head still pounding from the previous night of hellraising, seeking the cool comfort of black satin sheets. "What time is it?"

"Half past two, sir."

Chesterfield blinked his eyes open. Half past two? Dare he make the effort to rise? Had Christ himself found it such a dashed chore after three days in his tomb?

Chesterfield decided to hazard it and rose to his elbows with a pained groan. His brain swam from the spirits still thick in his bloodstream. He had to rise. Yes, he had something to do.

But what, exactly?

Ah yes, he was to have tea with the charming widow

Rebecca Stanley. And of course there was always hope for afternoon delights. Chesterfield swung his long tan legs to the side of the bed. Langley, his butler of four years, held up his robe.

"Coffee, sir?" Langley didn't raise a brow at his master's long naked body. Chesterfield shrugged into the silk robe without thought.

"Yes. Strong." Chesterfield lurched forward toward the bathing room. *Yes, something more than tea was needed... as always.*

"And for the lady?"

"Lady?" Chesterfield froze in his steps. He turned toward the bed, causing his brain to spin like a top. Certainly enough, there was a sleeping form in his bed with a surprising shock of ginger hair.

He took a step forward before realizing he had little time to get ready and sober up. He turned to the two Langleys pulling back the last of the heavy green curtains that covered the bedroom windows. Even more sunlight flooded the room eating away every last remaining shadow like a hungry golden beast.

Instinctively, Langley turned to his employer. Chesterfield gave a half-hearted beckoning wave. The butler approached his master with a firm face.

"Sir?"

Chesterfield took a breath before speaking. He was already fatigued by the labor of waking. Damn it to hell! If he couldn't perform this afternoon, he was going to find Freddie and shoot him.

"Whatever I promised when I brought her here, see that she gets it."

"Yes, sir."

Chesterfield took another precarious step toward the bathroom. Then a thought struck him. "And Langley?"

"Sir?"

"Promise to never let me go drinking with Lord Frederick again."

"Yes, sir." Langley tried to hide a smile as he remembered that not less than twenty hours ago, he had reminded Mr. Chesterfield to not go drinking with Lord Frederick Warrick again. A warning he "n giving since he first came to Chesterfield's employment four years before.

Of course, in those days Langley "n scandalized by his new master's behavior. The young man was a rakehell at best. Drinking and whoring with a reckless abandon that was afforded to only the very rich and very indolent. The man was already supporting two natural children and from the pace he was setting, there was bound to be a third. And, of course, each one was well cared for. That was the Chesterfield way. But Langley had not known it then and many were the sleepless nights he had spent praying for his master's soul. Yet his soul never appeared to be getting any brighter. In fact, quite the opposite.

Chesterfield groaned as he lumbered toward the bathing room. He raked a hand through his curls, worsening the disarray. Langley held a breath as Chesterfield negotiated the door. Would he make it? It didn't look promising.

"More to the left, sir."

Chesterfield swayed to the left, narrowly missing the doorframe.

AN HOUR LATER, Chesterfield was feeling vastly better, if not fully recovered. His lover for the night had discreetly been removed from his chambers, allowing him the freedom to pick precisely the right ensemble for tea and an afternoon of bedding.

"What do you think Langley? The green or the black vest?" His butler had just that moment entered the room.

Langley eyed his master from head to toe. The young man was handsome by all accounts and of strong build; more well-muscled than was considered typical of a London dandy. His curls were trimmed along the side, though a little overly long on top. They were still wet from the long bath he had taken, giving his ringlets the perfect definition. Women adored his hair and his master knew it.

But what he knew to be his master's prize possession were his hazel eyes. Eyes the precise shade of blazing emeralds, woven through with golden sunlight. No one had ever seen the kind before, and it seemed rather a shame for a man so blessed as he to have one more unneeded piece of good fortune.

But Mr. Chesterfield was indeed so blessed with ethereal eyes, curling hair and a charming smile. More than one lady of high or questionable standing had complimented him on one of his many attributes, all before plopping shamelessly into his bed.

"The green, sir. They bring out your eyes."

Chesterfield smiled in agreement. Yes, his eyes were his lure. That and deep pockets of course. He gave a silent prayer to his maternal grandmother for saving him from the vicarage with a generous bequeathment. It was already rough business being the second son but add to that being the product of a scandalous second marriage and having a father of African heritage should have doomed him to the lower classes. Imagine, actually having to work! Chesterfield gave a shudder.

"Sir, there is a young woman at the door who insists upon seeing you."

"Can you see what she wants?" Chesterfield donned the green vest with Langley's help. He nodded at the result. It was always tough business being in the first stare of fashion. But by heavens he did it well!

"I believe it is your brother's governess."

Chesterfield froze at his words. She was here? Lenora? At his

8

townhouse? There was a sudden quickening to his pulse. His mouth suddenly felt dry. Michael looked around nervously. His hands moving absentmindedly to the vest he had just moments ago lavished with admiration. He couldn't possibly let her see him in this piece of fluff.

"Shall I send her away?"

"No!"

Chesterfield quickly removed the vest as he tried to think of the possible reasons Miss MacLeod would have to make the trip over. His brother had brought the children to London just three days ago, so he was aware the group was in residence at Halley House on Upper Grosvenor. But never before had Miss MacLeod called upon him. Hell, she barely acknowledged his existence. Bloody hell, was he perspiring?

"I need a vest."

"You had a vest, sir."

"No! Something simple. More respectable." When Langley met his request with a blank stare, "Surely I have something more respectable."

"No, sir. You do not." Langley looked at his crestfallen master in befuddlement. Surely the man was not... nervous? No, of course not.

"Is she alone?" This asked as Chesterfield searched his armoire, pulling out possible replacements, then casting the rejected garments to the floor. Langley quietly stepped forward to gather them.

"Yes, sir."

"Where is that grey vest?"

"At the modiste to get mended."

Chesterfield nodded absentmindedly as he continued his search. "Did she give you any clue as to what she wanted?"

"None, sir. She is a very quiet woman."

Quiet?! The woman was made of pure marble. She was like a graceful statue of a goddess, guarding the entrance of an ancient temple. He cringed in near pain at the thought of his early attempts to seduce her. What a cocky prick he "n—so devoid of discernment. Lenora MacLeod was a superior sort of woman. A woman above reproach in all things.

When she had first started with the earl, Chesterfield had attempted a lighthearted flirtation and when that hadn't provoked a single flutter of a lash or semblance of a smile, he had conducted a short but valiant assault rivaling Waterloo. He "n an idiot.

She had given him a scalding set down and sent him running for the hills with his tail between his legs. It was more mercy on her part that she had done so in such a quiet fashion. Chesterfield smiled as he shook his head. He would meet her without a vest. Better she think him careless than a fop.

"Show her into the salon."

"She preferred to meet in the study, sir. She said it's a matter of business."

Chesterfield raised a brow. His pulse once again quickening. Had he perhaps offended her in some way? He had done his best not to cross her path and always to be deferential when it couldn't be helped. But perhaps there "n some slight. Some unintentional insult.

"Very well. Show her to the study," Chesterfield heaved a sigh. Whatever his offense, he undoubtedly deserved the lashing she was about to give him.

MISS LENORA MACLEOD had taken a seat across from his work desk, which was sufficiently uncluttered except for the few obligatory unanswered invitations. Chesterfield entered his study with masked apprehension. Her back was to the door and thus to him. He took a steeling breath before moving forward.

"Miss MacLeod."

"Mr. Chesterfield." She hadn't even turned around. He must be in some real trouble. But what had he done to her?

"Please don't get up." He came around to take a seat at his desk.

"I hadn't planned to, sir."

So, she *was* upset with him. There was nothing more to it, but to apologize profusely and to offer amends. Then suddenly he noticed it. Something amiss in her cool façade. She was trembling.

"How may I be of service to you, Miss MacLeod? I hope I have not wronged you in any way."

She looked surprised by his words.

"No, sir. And I assure you it will not take long."

"Very well." Chesterfield relaxed with a relieved breath and leaned back into the high-backed leather chair. The wood creaked with the shift of his weight. The two were silent for a painfully long moment. Chesterfield watched Miss MacLeod, while Miss MacLeod stared at her hands. Was she wringing her hands? It could not be.

"So, who have you killed?" He asked in a tone that danced between jest and trepidation.

Her eyes shot up in shock.

"You didn't actually kill someone, did you?" He eyed her in approbation until she shook her head. Did she just smile? No, but there was a hint of a smile.

Chesterfield kept silent, watching her. Mastering his own features so as not to reveal his nerves. She had gotten prettier over the years and when admired from certain angles, she was really quite beautiful. It was a shame he had made such a mess of their acquaintanceship. But even if they were friendly, what more could there be between them. She really was a pillar of moral rectitude. And he? He was what he was, the half-savage trying desperately to maintain his precarious position in society.

"Miss MacLeod..."

"I am sorry." She attempted to still her hands. Her eyes finally rose to meet his. Now they were getting somewhere. "This is rather unaccustomed territory. My coming to you."

"It certainly is." He tried to infuse a sense of warmth in his words. While they were not friendly, they had a connection, did they not. Some shared ancestry that dictated at the very least some form of civility.

She took a breath. "I am in need of twelve hundred pounds."

Chesterfield's brows lifted. "Twelve hundred?" He studied her with growing curiosity. It wasn't a trifling amount, but it also wasn't an impossible one. He could lose that much in a night at the gaming tables without so much as a blink. "That's no small request, Miss MacLeod."

"I know." Her answer was almost a whisper.

It took him a moment to realize what this was. "And you're wishing me to provide it?"

"I know of no one else—"

"Surely my brother—"

"No." Her fingers curled into the polished wood of his desk. "I cannot ask it of him. And I beg you not to reveal this... visit to him."

Chesterfield watched her carefully. She was always so composed, so rigidly contained. Yet now, there was something raw beneath the surface.

"Can you at least tell me what you need the money for?"

She simply shook her head.

"I see." Chesterfield once again leaned back in his chair. This was quite unexpected. And very confusing. "And how do you intend to repay this loan?"

She hesitated. "I do not wish it to be a loan." She met his gaze steadily. "I could never, in a lifetime, earn that sum honestly."

"You wish me to give you this money."

"No. Of course not."

Were they somehow speaking at a cross-purpose? She could not repay him, yet admitted she must repay him.

"I apologize, Miss MacLeod. My intellect is not my strong suit."

"No apologies needed, sir. I..."

She stopped speaking. Her eyes suddenly darting nervously about the room. She certainly was not making this meeting any easier. What could she need with such a ridiculous sum? And why come to him of all people?

"What would you... ask of me?" She finally spoke, once again raising her eyes to him. They were filled with determination. Her words floated between them like a hazy specter attempting to take shape. It took a long moment before he realized what she was offering, before he saw the picture her words were forming.

Chesterfield let out a long breath. She was offering her body —for twelve hundred pounds.

He hadn't realized he was shaking his head until she rushed forward, "I know I am not... experienced, like the women you frequent. But I am clean. And you would be the first —"

"How long?" His voice cut through the words, rougher than intended.

She blinked. "How long?"

He could see the confusion on her face. Then he was equally confounded.

"Yes, how long would I have you for? Or did you mean this as a one-time occurrence?"

She looked down in clear embarrassment, her eyes blinking, desperately trying to discover the error in her calculations. But good heavens, the woman had meant it to be a single encounter!

"A week?" Her words came out more as a question than the statement she surely intended it to be.

Chesterfield frowned just before his head started to feel light. He felt as if he had suddenly become unmoored from solid ground and was floating away into the ether. Surely this was not real. This entire situation was a fever dream from which he would wake. Was he truly negotiating for Miss MacLeod's virtue? Then the thought struck him—he would finally have her. All these years of longing would end. His desires would mercifully be satisfied.

"A week for twelve hundred pounds? That's hardly fair, Miss MacLeod. No, I would need at least six months... for that sum."

Her eyes opened wide with shock. "I couldn't... no... that's far too long!" A little of her defenses crumbled at the very edges. Revealing hints of the fragile young woman it protected.

"Miss MacLeod. I assure you six months will hardly be long at all." His pulse quickened as a malignant fear crept in. He was at once filled with the dread that she might change her mind.

"One month. It is all I can bear."

"Bear?" Her words immediately humbled him and brought him crashing back to Earth. His ego bruised by the careless insult. "Miss MacLeod, you wound me. I can assure you my lovemaking is not something a woman simply bears."

"I'm certain you are quite... skilled, but that is of no importance to me. I only wish to arrive at a set time." There was a glimpse again of the stalwart Miss MacLeod. Her back was stiff again with that ever-present broomstick. One month for twelve hundred pounds.

"Please, sir. I know it is much to ask," she looked up at him, her eyes glassy with unshed tears. His stomach sank. Don't let the woman cry. Please God, do not allow her to shed so much as one solitary tear.

"Do we have a bargain, sir?"

Chesterfield studied her for a long moment before giving a small nod. "One month is fine."

"Thank you," she answered quietly. "And it cannot be in England. I couldn't allow anyone..."

"Very well. The continent then?"

She nodded.

"And when shall this month begin?"

"I will need time to make arrangements for my absence."

"Of course, Miss MacLeod. Take all the time you need."

"I will, however, need the money today." She looked at him waiting for his response. Waiting for him to laugh in her face and say forget it. Waiting for him to come to his senses and realize that bedding her wasn't truly worth twelve hundred pounds, even if it were for a lifetime.

"Very well. I'll have my secretary give you a note for the sum." He pulled pen and paper from the desk and began writing. "You need only present him with this letter." She neither smiled nor relaxed at the news. Not his Miss MacLeod. "As for our month, I will make preparations. I think I may have the perfect place. Away from prying eyes."

Lenora watched as his long perfect fingers made pen waltz over paper. He wrote the short missive with graceful easy strokes. She would soon feel those hands against her skin. She closed her eyes, immediately banishing the thought away. There would be time enough for such ruminations later. For now, she had to focus on the task at hand.

Was he really giving her the money? No, not giving. She had bargained for it.

"Mr. Chesterfield, concerning our bargain." He looked up at her as he sanded the note. "I do have one demand."

"Demand?" He was immediately curious and wary.

"Yes." She gave him a stern look. Certainly, she could make a demand or two. Was she not the one prostituting herself? "I ask that we exercise the greatest caution." She stared at him to see if he understood. Already the man had two children. She did not wish to provide him with a third.

"Yes. I quite agree."

She nodded in relief.

Chesterfield folded and sealed the letter. He then held it out to her. She reached for it, but he did not release it.

"Do we truly have a bargain, Miss MacLeod? You don't intend to cheat me?"

His eyes were sharp upon her, with a small hint of uncertainty. In his hand he held the means to her family's salvation.

"We've a bargain, sir."

Chesterfield released the letter.

Lenora rose. Looking far more composed than she had earlier. She had done the thing, she told herself. She had saved her family. There was no need to think of the cost now. This was not the time for naivety.

Chesterfield rang for Langley. The butler appeared immediately to usher Miss MacLeod out of the study.

When the butler returned moments later to confirm the young woman's departure, Chesterfield instructed him to send his regrets to the lovely widow Stanley. Damn, he hated to miss an afternoon of delight, but his head was still reeling. What had he just done? Had he really paid twelve hundred pounds for Miss MacLeod's virtue? Would they truly go through with this bargain, or would some twist of fate reveal this all to be a cruel jest? Only time's quiet turning would uncover the answers to his questions.

CHAPTER 2

The channel crossing was Lenora's first. It should have been a pleasure, but instead, it was utter misery. It had rained torrentially for four days prior to her sailing and even now there was little promise of respite.

Gray mist haunted the white cliffs behind her like brooding ghosts. This would be her last glimpse of England for an entire month.

Few of the travelers ventured onto the outer decks, preferring to remain where it was warm and dry. They were a sensible lot.

Lenora, however, preferred to brave the elements. Her wet hair shrinking into a puff after all her efforts to brush her curls straight. Large drops pearled onto her eyelashes, blurring her vision. Lenora shivered, yet would not go in. What was the use? What was the point of seeking shelter when she felt so utterly cast out to the elements? Confined indoors she would be dry, yes, but she would suffocate. No, she needed the air. It was the only thing that prevented her from slipping into inexorable wretchedness.

Her mood was just as gray as the heavens, Lenora mused, pulling her dampened cloak more tightly around her. She had made a bargain with the devil and now came time for her to pay. But she had saved her mother from debtors' prison for the foolish mistakes of her late father, the drunkard. The drunkard and the gambler.

By what means a penniless man could gamble was beyond her. But after years of mounting interest, the debt had grown enormous. And worry had eaten away at both her and her mother for the last two years. The questions plagued her ceaselessly. Like an unending nightmare, they haunted her. *Where would her mother go with four children to feed, the elder two having already left home? What would they eat next week? Tomorrow? What would become of them all?* Such worries burned in the pit of her belly until she was nearly mad with it.

She and her brother Aubrey's salaries had barely been enough to feed and house her mother and four younger siblings. Lenora knew there could have been no other way. Had there been, without doubt she would have thought of it. Surely the answer would have made itself known by now. She had not taken the easy way, had she?

Truly, Chesterfield "n an answer that came to her at her lowest point, when she had seen her mother fall ill from worry. How could she have guessed there was such a thing? No cold, no fever, no influenza. Simply worry. Worry so great, so deep, so overwhelming that a healthy woman could be reduced to a mere shell of her former self.

The last straw could have been the landlord's threat to cast her poor siblings out onto the street. But it had not been. The last straw "n twelve-year-old Susanna confiding to her that a man had approached her about selling her body for money. Lenora "n terrified. Poor Suzie, still only a child, forced to consider such a barbaric course!

And Suzie had considered it, poor lamb.

But where to get a thousand pounds? Never mind that she could not even create a mental image of such a sum. It was like speaking of angels and fairies. A thousand pounds.

Then she had remembered her employer's younger brother. The reckless bon vivant. That cockerel who she had lain eyes on no more than a dozen times in the last five years. Their early encounters "n marred by some insolent flirtation or other. Until the day she had set him straight.

It had not been courage that made her speak that day, but frustration. And not even at him really. But at everything in life; the lack of choices, the lack of freedom and the constant worry. She barely remembered what she had said, but it "n brutal. She had stunned him. Her words cutting to the quick. Though her rage "n too high to show it, she had felt immediately contrite. It was not like her to lose her equanimity. But moreover, the look of utter devastation in his eyes had thrown her. She had expected rage. Anger. Perhaps an equally cruel set down. But instead, he had looked utterly devastated. The memory of his face had haunted her for weeks.

But her words had their desired effect. He avoided her. He no doubt hated her. Of course he did. No servant can speak to a man of breeding and hope for anything less than hate. For years, she feared his revenge. She could have lost her employment. She could have been thrown out to the street. What on earth made her think she could speak to her employer's brother with such unveiled superiority? Such disdain?

But she had not been fired. He had said not a word. Choosing instead to simply avoid her. And in time she hardly thought of him at all.

Until she found herself at her lowest point—until she remembered he was spoken of as a seeker of pleasure and free with his money. He bought women for enjoyment. Why could he not buy her? Why not? Why not, indeed. And why not ask for a little bit more beside? To give her family some meager comforts once the debt 'n paid. Two hundred pounds was a fortune!

Like a beacon shining through the darkest night, Lenora had held onto the thought—salvation. Salvation at the hands of Mr. Michael Chesterfield.

She never imagined how easily he would acquiesce when she told her mother of her plan. Her mother had warned her against it. Just because he was a playboy did not mean evil didn't lurk behind that smile. And just because he was half African did not mean he was anything like them. His grandfather had not been born into slavery like Lenora's grandfather had. He was a man of privilege, accustomed to getting his way.

In time, Lenora had placated her mother with assurances that Michael Chesterfield was truly of the harmless sort. He behaved in the fashion of a footloose playboy, but no whispers of mortal danger had ever followed him. And with one stroke of his secretary's pen, debts that would have taken a lifetime and beyond to repay were forever banished.

But Lenora was now to pay the proverbial piper. She bit her lip in worry. *What had she gotten herself into?*

"Papa, what have you done to me?"

TRUE TO HIS WORD, Chesterfield had made all the arrangements. A simple carriage 'n sent to await her at the end of the channel crossing. The driver was polite and respectful even with the sorry state she presented.

Despite its simplicity, the carriage was surprisingly comfortable—and painfully new. Lenora busied herself by watching the countryside slide by her window. Her nerves pulling tighter with every mile they covered.

The rain had receded into a dull mist that clung to everything it touched.

At last, the carriage turned down a pleasant drive bordered by violas. Soft lavender blooms gave the drive a burst of spring. Lenora looked out the carriage in surprise at the country house they were heading toward.

Whatever she had expected, she had not expected this. The French cottage was breathtaking, the garden and drive were blooming with late spring flowers. It certainly did not look like a place a gentleman took a young woman with whom he was having an illicit affair. It looked more like a home. Warm and inviting.

The carriage stopped before red double doors and a young man bounded out to greet her. He was a tall child with curling black hair and thick sooty lashes. He rushed forward to open the carriage door with a brilliant smile.

"Madame Chesterfield."

Lenora held out her hand for him to take it. Behind him came a robust older woman with a remarkable resemblance to the young man.

"*Bon jour, bon jour*, Madame Chesterfield. Welcome. *Bienvenu.*"

"*Bon jour*," Lenora answered the woman's greeting hesitantly. She immediately felt contrite. These people had nothing to do with her debt to Chesterfield. They seemed authentically genial. Lenora tried to widen her smile. It would have been easier to have asked her to swim the channel in her gown and pelisse.

"I am Madame Louparet. The housekeeper. Come, come inside," Madame Louparet waved her in. "Phillip, take the Madame's bag to the room."

Phillip threw himself into the task with all the boundless energy of a coltish youth.

Lenora longed to reclaim her pitiable bag, but she allowed herself to be led inside by the smiling woman.

The entrance was small and intimate. The cottage's interior was far more elegant than the rustic exterior had promised. Marble flooring spread out in all directions like a white and gray sea. The foyer led immediately into a large open salon. A sparkling chandelier held court over the entire room. The furnishings were simple yet elegant—seafoam green upholstery paired with rich, polished oak. The walls were painted white up to the chair rail. The rest was wallpapered with a detailed pattern of green leaves with small gold flowers.

The furnishing was dainty and very feminine. Delicate French figurines and gilt-trimmed gewgaws adorned every nook and corner. It was evident that the same hand that had decorated the Earl of Walpole's London home had a hand in this room's appointments.

"I am so pleased to have you and Monsieur for your wedding trip."

So, was that what he had told these people? That they were newlyweds? Lenora pulled her attention from the room and back to the housekeeper.

"Is Monsieur joining us this evening?" Madame Louparet asked in excitement.

"I'm not entirely certain," Lenora answered truthfully. She had followed Chesterfield's secretary's instructions to the letter. She arrived at the ferry on the day they settled upon. And now she was here.

She had not laid eyes on Chesterfield since their brief meeting nearly two months ago.

"Then we'll make you comfortable until he arrives, yes?"

"I would like that very much," Lenora nodded with a smile that most probably lacked warmth.

According to the housekeeper, the first order of business was to take Madame's coat. Then they were to serve her tea and cakes in the salon. Lastly, Madame Louparet escorted her upstairs to the beautiful master's chambers.

Lenora released her breath when she stepped into the cream and burgundy confection. From the walls covered in a rich patterned cream fabric, to the large, canopied bed, to the parquet and white marble floors, the room was sumptuous. Two bedside tables, a high-back winged chair, an escritoire and armoire. All of Indian mahogany, like the bed. At one end of the room, a white marble fireplace burned with an inviting fire.

This was her room?

She was hesitant to admit her heart beat a little faster. She had never had such lovely quarters. If she did not remind herself just what her purpose was here, she would almost have smiled. Almost.

A vase of white roses sat on one of the small bedside tables.

"It's beautiful," she gave an efficient nod to the housekeeper who was apparently waiting for such a response.

Madame Louparet gave a proud smile. "You'd like to take a bath now." A statement, not a question.

"Certainly." Lenora turned to the bed where she suddenly noticed three flat boxes.

A young woman with golden olive-toned skin, dark curls and features that hinted at Eastern ancestry entered the room carrying Lenora's valise. "I sent Phillip to get more wood for the fire. I will unpack your things, Madame?" Lenora's thoughts immediately went to the two dresses and nightgown in her valise. She turned red.

"No. It's quite all right." She made a move to retrieve her property.

"Oh, it's no trouble, Madame." The girl had already opened her bag and was pulling out her clothes. She gave no apparent reaction to the two dull serviceable gowns she pulled out. One faded gingham and one modest navy wool. Her two best dresses.

She unconsciously ran a hand over the grey gown she was wearing. What was she doing here? She felt ugly in these elegant surroundings—a brown duck among lovely swans. She had certainly not considered this aspect of the bargain.

The maid moved efficiently about the room, casting smiles in Lenora's direction whenever their paths crossed. Never before had Lenora felt more out of place and in the way. It was a feeling she was not accustomed to. Lenora decided she didn't like having servants take care of her while she did nothing.

She thus floated to an unobtrusive corner of the room.

The girl opened the armoire, and Lenora was interested to see a dressing gown and robe already inside. She eyed the pale pink ensemble with veiled fascination. They were beautiful confections trimmed with white lace. The lady of the house must have left them behind. Or perhaps they belonged to one of Chesterfield's mistresses.

Lenora's attention went back to the boxes on the bed. They were each tied with velvety dark pink ribbons. Perhaps a gift for their supposed wedding? She moved toward the bed and cautiously fingered a box before daring to open it. But once she lifted the lid, she praised the heavens she 'n given skin dark enough to hide her mortification.

Silk drawers and chemises—each adorned with delicate ribbons and lace.

She threw another glance to the maid who was now hanging up her own plain wool nightgown next to the lovely pink one. She immediately felt her heart sinking. What was she thinking? Had reason completely deserted her?

She was a woman of wool and calico, not a lady accustomed to silks and lace. How could she possibly hold Chesterfield's interest for an entire month? Lenora's nerves began to thrum. She attempted to take a calming breath, trying desperately to remind herself that he was a man full grown and had willingly entered into this bargain. He could have easily turned her away, could he not have? He surely knew what she had offered him.

He could not expect her to be the sort of woman that wore crimson silk drawers.

But that was the rub. For one month she would have to be any woman he wanted her to be. Even one who wore such outrageously scandalous attire.

Lenora turned her attention to the next box. Stockings and handkerchiefs. She fingered the fabrics. Smooth and cool.

"Your bath is ready, Madame." Lenora had forgotten the housekeeper's presence in the adjoining room. "Lorette will help you from here. I will see to dinner."

"Thank you, Madame Louparet."

"It's my pleasure." With that the housekeeper exited leaving her in the hands of the little French maid.

Lorette was an efficient young woman, divesting Lenora of every stitch of clothing in no time at all. And though Lenora was truly mortified with embarrassment at having her body viewed naked by eyes other than her own, she made great effort to appear outwardly calm. After all it would not serve for her to behave like a shy wallflower when she supposedly was to act the part of bride to the rather rich Mr. Michael Chesterfield.

Once Lenora was satisfactorily soaking in the tub, Lorette left her for a moment. She returned a quarter of an hour later carrying the sumptuous pink gown Lenora had spied in the armoire.

"You must be mistaken, that isn't mine."

Lorette looked at her in confusion. "But they are Madame. They came with the rest of your things. In fact, Monsieur explained that most of your things have been lost and the modiste will be here any minute to measure you for your new gowns."

"New gowns?"

"Yes. And he has told her to spare no expense for *la belle Madame*." Lorette gave a brilliant smile showing her approval at such a dedicated and well-trained husband.

"I see."

Without further protestation Lenora slipped into her new gown. It was slightly large, but Lorette was certain the modiste could make the alterations. In any case, Monsieur would be pleased.

Lenora wondered if he would in fact be pleased considering the expense he was going through for her. The twelve hundred pounds were dire enough. But this beautiful cottage and a new wardrobe. She hadn't even thought of such things. And of course he would have to feed her. The money he was spending! The repayment he would demand!

When had breathing become a conscious struggle?

He was getting something out of their bargain, she had to remind herself. But what was that exactly? Neither had discussed the details of their arrangement. *Would her being his mistress for a month mean she never leave the bed? Would they have moments outside of the cottage?* Or perhaps it meant wherever they were she would have to submit to him at a moment's notice. *Would he be cruel? Would he be gentle? Would he be demanding?* It was not as if she could have gone to his past lovers for references. She couldn't guess. She didn't know. She hadn't cared to know. The knowledge would have served her no good, especially if it would have veered her from her course.

Lenora had to resign herself to the fact that she simply had no idea what she had gotten herself into. But in a month's time, it would all be over and life would once again be livable.

The modiste came one hour later with her minions in tow. Lenora was poked and prodded, measured and re-measured. When the tempest was over, the modiste promised a gown in three days and two more by week's end.

Afterward Lenora was left to her own devices, which found her speculating when Mr. Chesterfield would make himself known. *Perhaps at dinner*, she wondered. In any case, today counted as one of the days. That meant there were twenty-nine to go. Then she would be free.

Mr. Chesterfield did not make an appearance at dinner.

Donning her navy wool gown, Lenora took her meal alone in the small dining room that adjoined the salon. She did not mind it terribly. She was never much of a conversationalist in any case. A solitary meal with Mr. Chesterfield would have proven awkward at best.

After dinner she took a walk in the garden under the evening's fading light. It was so peaceful, so quiet away from the Lord of Walpole's spirited children. This would almost seem a holiday were it not for the specter of Mr. Chesterfield looming in the horizon. *Where was he? Perhaps he wouldn't show?* She told herself again. Her spirits elevated for a few brief moments, but then she reminded herself this would mean she still owed him, body and all.

Lenora awoke to a brightly lit room. It took a moment for her mind to place the rich creamy furnishings and polished woods. *Where was she?* She was in the pretty cottage in Calais. Now she remembered.

The French doors leading to the balcony were wide open, letting in a surprisingly temperate breeze. Had she left the doors open? She did not remember doing so. Perhaps Lorette had already visited her chamber and having found her in a deep slumber, opened the doors and left.

She sat up in her bed looking straight ahead. The doors were toward the foot of the bed and with them open she enjoyed a full view of the countryside. She drew a deep breath and smiled. Slipping from the bed, she stepped toward the inviting scenery without placing on her robe. It was the first morning in years that she had awakened mistress of her own movements. No children to attend to. No morning church service. No duties whatsoever. Save one perhaps.

She stepped out onto the cool stone and leaned against the iron railing. She drew another deep breath, spreading her arms out wide. The early morning sun gently caressed her dark skin. Lenora drank in the rare, radiant moment like a woman starved of sustenance.

"My sentiments exactly."

CHAPTER 3

*L*enora's eyes flew wide as she turned to the man already seated on a wrought iron chair. His feet rested casually on the railing. He wore buff-colored breeches that disappeared behind well-polished Hessian boots. A deep navy coat with its usual proliferation of detailed stitching, a matching buff vest, crisp white shirtsleeves and a white cravat held in place by a solitary diamond pin. She took in every detail of the well-tailored and very posh looking outfit in a single glance. For everything was as it always was on Mr. Chesterfield. Perfect.

"Sir, I did not know you had already arrived!"

Lenora immediately became aware of the painfully thin gown she now wore. Of course she could dash into the room for her robe, but she thought of the futility of it. What was the point in playing the shy virgin when she was in fact this man's whore? She thus stood her ground.

Chesterfield's eyes raked over her body.

The pink gown was a little too large on her. He had remembered her a bit more filled out than she was presently.

Had she lost weight? The thought caused him some concern. Still, in a word, she looked lovely.

"Yes, I've only just arrived this morning." He rose, but did not move any closer to her. "I hope Madame Louparet has treated you well."

Lenora was immediately aware that he was keeping a respectable distance. And yet, she swore she could feel the heat radiating from his body. *Had he always been so large,* she wondered with some surprise? *Were dandies not supposed to be thin and effete? Leave it to Michael Chesterfield to be so contrary even on this point.*

"Yes. She has been most kind, sir." Lenora finally answered. Chesterfield rewarded her with a warm smile that caused her to frown. *What game was he playing?*

She attempted to school her features, to remain calm though she felt a hundred emotions at once. The greatest of them being the call to run from him.

Twelve hundred pounds.

Twenty-nine more nights.

"Mr. Chesterfield, we never did speak on the parameters of our bargain."

"Perhaps we can do so tomorrow? It has been a long journey and I'm quite weary."

"Oh."

"Is something the matter, Miss MacLeod? Something perhaps not to your liking?"

"No. Simply, I thought you would want to get started today."

"While I appreciate your eagerness, I am only human and would very much like to rest today."

Lenora stood confused.

"I hope you can understand."

"Yes, of course."

"So very kind of you. Would you mind terribly calling for Lorette so we can request breakfast?"

Lenora was uncertain for a moment. "Yes, certainly." Chesterfield responded with a smile. Lenora retreated into the room in evident confusion. Chesterfield shook his head. It had taken everything in his power to not pounce on her like a green schoolboy the moment she had stepped out onto the balcony. He wanted her. This much was clear. But he needed to make this good between them. He therefore needed to be patient and measured. He had an entire month to make love to her. There was no need to rush.

He shrugged off his coat and loosened his cravat as he stepped into the bedroom.

Lenora had made her way to a side chair where her robe laid waiting. He smiled as she quickly placed it on. She then pulled the cord to summon the maid. Lorette came immediately with a cheerful smile. It made Lenora wonder if the girl "n standing just outside the door.

Chesterfield ordered their breakfast and when it came, he ordered that they not be disturbed for the rest of the morning.

Lorette had curtsied with a knowing smile. Chesterfield had only to give her a boyish grin and Lenora had not missed the obvious look of envy the little maid had given her. Women would consider themselves fortunate to capture such a husband as the handsome Michael Chesterfield. Unfortunately, he wasn't really her husband but her patron. Lenora let out a sigh of frustration.

The days ahead stretched out like a slow, crawling eternity.

Chesterfield ate with great gusto. He made no comment on how little Lenora was eating, though he was keenly aware. No doubt she was nervous about bedding him. He would have to play the next few days wisely.

After filling his belly, he decided on a bath. The road from the port "n dreadfully dusty.

"Now, I think I could do with a good bath."

"I can run it for you if you like."

Chesterfield raised a brow at her offer. "That's very kind of you. But you needn't —"

"I don't mind. Truly." She seemed a little desperate to have something to do. Or was it that she wished to escape him? Either way, he simply nodded. Lenora rose and quickly fled the room.

Lenora bent down to turn the porcelain handles. The hot and cold water poured out freely. She stared as the water began to fill the tub. She need only separate her mind from her body. A thing she had done many times before. When her father "n drunk and abusive. When the neighborhood children had teased her because of her brown skin and the ill-fitting rags. When Mr. Grace-Martin had come to her with roving hands during the six long months she had worked for the banker and his plump wife.

This would be more of the same. More of struggling through an ugly life. This certainly was no different.

Lenora's stomach contracted when he came into the small room. She chastised herself for reacting like a skittish colt around him.

He had indicated that he had no plans to make use of her today. But what did it signify? What did it matter? Today or tomorrow. She had best get used to the idea.

"Not too hot, we would not want to burn my delicate skin," Chesterfield joked. He cast her a glance as he spoke. The woman was absolutely petrified. Chesterfield shook his head. He turned to cast a casual glance at the rest of the small bathing room. White tile spread out like a wintry landscape, flanked by rich wood walls with a carved railing. The ceiling was more carved wood. The claw foot tub and basin were a simple rich creamy porcelain. It "n years since he had visited his grandmother's cottage. Now his cottage.

Chesterfield smiled at the memory of visiting the place as a child. It "n one of the few bright spots to an otherwise cold, lonely childhood. He wondered if Lenora understood the significance of his bringing her here. And if she did, perhaps she would be considerate enough to explain it to him. He could have taken her to any number of places. Places far more appropriate. But this was the only place that had seemed... what was the word? *Fitting.*

Lenora turned off the flow of water and rose to stand beside the tub. She looked away from him in clear discomfort. But at least now it seemed she was trying to school her features.

"Thank you," he stated and waited.

"You wish me to leave?" She turned to him in confusion. Why had she never noticed he was so tall?

"Please."

She stared at him with a frown, as though trying to read his face. Trying to calculate her opponent's next move. To uncover some hidden agenda. He found her piercing eyes unsettling. For a moment something flashed in them. Some hurt. Some ancient wound he had accidentally uncovered. He should have questioned it. But his male ego cautioned him against exploring this woman's deeper emotions. The search would likely reveal truths he could not hope to understand and so he remained silent when she simply nodded and left the room.

He sighed in relief. But there was also some disappointment in himself. What would these next coming days look like? Whatever had given him the idea that he was a match for Miss MacLeod? He clearly was already blundering this. He had thought to give her a bit of a reprieve. To start things off slowly. But perhaps that "n a mistake. Perhaps it looked instead as if he didn't want her. He didn't desire her. Chesterfield undressed himself and stepped into the steaming water and leaned back against the tub. He let out a small curse. He would have to rethink his approach entirely. Leave it to Miss MacLeod to make even his kindest gestures seem malevolent.

. . .

"Oh." Lenora turned to find Chesterfield staring at her. In the time he "n in the tub, she had donned her grey gown and was at the mirror trying valiantly to coax her curls into a bun. It was then she had seen his reflection in the mirror.

He stood in the doorframe of the bathing room in his shirtsleeves and breeches. His damp hair in perfect ringlets. He stared at her, his hooded gaze unreadable, unmoving—as if granting her one final chance to flee.

She did indeed wish to—but she could not. She dared not. She waited, like a soldier expecting orders.

Something dark and smoldering began to blaze in his eyes. Lenora had never seen him like this before. Even during the worst of his flirtations, he had never felt predacious. She remained silent, feeling her pulse quicken. *Was this some sort of witchcraft?* She frowned.

"What are you doing?"

Chesterfield smiled just then. He knew he was affecting her. She pulled her shoulders back in response, her expression indignant. He was immediately transported back to his childhood with his old governess. A certain Miss Rothtrend. A nasty piece of womanhood, who was none too fond of the darker races and made no effort to hide it.

A governess like Miss MacLeod would have been a godsend. He had seen her with his niece and nephew. They were good children, though high-spirited and certainly demanding. She was kind and patient with them. Perhaps not warm or loving. But even simple kindness would have won his fragile heart when he was Bertie's age.

"Miss MacLeod," he began with a soft tone that caused her frown to deepen. He took a slow step forward and she unconsciously stepped back. "I had erroneously thought to give you time to grow accustomed to my company before bedding you." He continued his slow prowl forward.

Lenora watched him approach, eyes wide and mouth agape.

"But I realized as I sat in that tub that such an approach was utterly foolish. And the simple truth is, I have no wish to wait." Chesterfield closed the distance between them. Her eyes frozen on him as he pulled her to him, one arm snaking around her waist while his other hand cradled her chin tilting her face toward his. He stopped a moment, just enough time to give her fair warning of what was to come.

She watched his mouth make the slow decent toward hers. Their lips touched softly like a teasing wind. He made a sound deep within his throat. It was a pleasant sound that reverberated through her. His kiss deepened, and she parted her lips for him. His other hand came up and captured both sides of her face, guiding her into position. She followed, allowing him to deepen the kiss even more.

Her eyes closed and she was suddenly lost in that kiss. And it was more than a kiss. It was as though a fragile silk thread connected her lips to her breasts and down further, to deeper parts of her womb. She felt the energy radiating outward from the point where their bodies connected. Her body fairly hummed with it. When their lips disconnected, it took her a few moments to regather the fragments of her thoughts.

"Are we to begin?" She asked breathlessly.

"Yes, Miss MacLeod. We are indeed."

He released her and she looked up at him in confusion. "Undress me," came his quiet command.

Lenora blinked up at him. Her body was at odds, torn between fleeing and uncovering the mystery of what was to come. He had commanded her to undress him. She frowned as if deciphering an unfamiliar tongue. She took a deep breath and moved forward.

Lenora struggled against his height on tiptoes to pull his linen shirt over his head. Why had she never noticed he was so tall?

After she finally managed to remove the stubborn garment,

she hesitated. Mr. Chesterfield stood before her shirtless. He was, in a word, beautiful. His expanse of chest only lightly dusted with dark curls. He was well formed with unblemished bronze skin. Well-muscled throughout his broad shoulders all the way down to narrow hips. With his hair slightly disheveled from her struggles in removing the shirt, he presented the perfect picture of the rake. This was no doubt how he looked after bedding his mistresses. Beautiful.

How she hated herself for admitting this.

Michael watched her in fascination. Her eyes darting to him then away in shame. The little governess had more than likely never stood this close to an undressed man. She suddenly frowned and returned to undressing him. Her hands hesitated at the buttons of his breeches.

Chesterfield was reluctant to admit his heart pounded in his chest. His breathing turned shallow with anticipation.

Her fingers slowly released each button like a well-trained courtesan. The torment was so sweet. Made sweeter because it was she. It was Miss MacLeod's hands that unfastened his trousers. How was it even possible?

The libertine had worn nothing beneath his breeches.

The thought should not have shocked her, yet it did. The thatch of dark curling hair had immediately been unveiled by the release of the second button. But like an actress forced to continue with her lines, she had to finish her part. So, she removed the last of his clothing. Sliding his breeches down impossibly hard thighs covered in auburn hair.

His erection sprang free, and Lenora's breath hitched. The skin there was darker than the rest of his body and it was impossibly large. How could something that size be expected to fit inside of her?

He stilled her head by placing his fingers on her chin. She hadn't known she had even been shaking her head.

Lenora stepped away, straightening her body. She watched

him as he stepped out of his breeches. His eyes bore into hers. She found their beauty terrifying and looked away.

"Don't I please you, Lenora?"

"I do not receive pleasure from the sight of the male form," she whispered. *Was a lie still a lie if spoken quietly?*

"Look at me," came his soft command. When she did not obey, he gave a firmer "Look at me."

Her eyes turned to his. When her gaze did not waver, he nodded.

"I'll undress you now."

They were simple words, but their effect upon her were immediate. Her mouth suddenly felt impossibly dry. Her heart pounded in her chest. She nodded, no longer able to speak.

His eyes raked her body, taking measure of her gown and calculating how to efficiently divest her of it.

She reached to remove her gown, but he stilled her with a raised hand. She immediately stopped. "I assure you, I'm quite good at this." And so, he was.

Lenora hardly knew where to rest her eyes as Chesterfield worked to remove her gown.

Chesterfield took his time and spoke not a word. He occasionally looked up at her with a knowing smile that sent frissons of electric energy spiraling up from her core.

He finally removed her stockings, then stopped to admire her in her shift.

"Why do you keep stopping to stare at me?"

"Growing impatient, Lenora?"

"No, sir."

He smiled down at her. "Sir? I don't think calling me sir will do, will it?"

"Michael." Something tight and uncomfortable roiled in her stomach. To call him by his Christian name felt too unnatural.

"Now, that wasn't quite so terrible, was it?"

Yes. Yes, it was. "No."

He stared at her for a few more painful minutes before saying, "You've the most beautiful breasts I've ever seen."

She stared at him with cold hard eyes. He was making fun of her.

"You needn't be cruel, sir. That was not in our bargain."

Chesterfield's eyes flew wide. His mouth opened and then closed. "You, my dear, are the most contrary woman I've ever met."

Instead of being chasten, her shoulders straightened just a little more.

"I was paying you a compliment, Lenora..."

"I am not beautiful. Nothing about me is beautiful. I know you to be a rake. Are you also a liar?"

Her eyes flared to life as she spoke, her fist clenched at her side. For a moment, yes, a mere moment he had seen a glorious goddess made of passion and feeling. Then like a whisper, she was gone. But he had seen it. Life in those unfeeling eyes.

"You wound me most terribly, Madam. I am a man of great feelings, Lenora," he slowly bent down to reach for the hem of her shift. "More feeling than is perhaps prudent for a man, so I've been told. Lift your arms."

She obeyed, too distracted by his words to question his command.

"I will never lie to you, Lenora. I'll never speak words that I don't mean. Not to you. Is that understood?" He stood staring down at her from a towering height.

She nodded with much reluctance. It was only then that she realized that they stood bare, facing each other. Lenora felt a flush of color coming to her cheeks. She looked to the ground, her mind unable to make sense of how she had come to this moment.

She could sense him looking at her. All of her. She hazarded a peek and her fears were confirmed. He was indeed looking down at her. Her body. His eyes hooded and a small, pleased smile on his lips. They stood like this for what seemed an eternity.

His eyes were fixed on her body. She was beautiful. Sheer perfection!

He never could have imagined that the pious Miss MacLeod hid such a body. Her breasts were full and pert, crested by perfect dark nipples. Her waist was high and narrow to flare out to flawlessly rounded hips. The hair at the juncture of her legs was as dark as her crown of curls. Her skin impossibly smooth and unblemished.

He took in a deep breath, closing his eyes for just an instant. He immediately opened them as if afraid this was all some strange dream, and she would disappear at any moment.

"Would you have me on the bed?"

"Patience, dear one."

"It's simply that —"

"How often have you done this, Lenora?"

"You know I've never..." she barely spoke the words when his lips were on her again. Giving her deep languid kisses.

"Precisely."

They kissed like this for what seemed another eternity. And her body, the treacherous turncoat that she was, began to soften under his ministrations. Molding her form to his. Drinking in the heat of his bare skin against hers.

It was moments before she realized he had spoken to her between kisses.

"Say it," she heard him speak before his mouth worked over hers again. She tried to decipher his meaning before plunging once again into the building passion of their kiss.

"Tell me your breasts are beautiful."

She frowned at him and wanted to pull away, but he held her in place.

"Say it," he coaxed.

"No," she made her best attempt to shake her head. What an

absolutely silly thing to have a woman say. Bargain or no bargain, she would not participate in such foolishness.

His invading lips drowned out her protest, and her nerves sang in hunger for the energy he had awakened. It wanted more. More of this connection. More of his kisses. And as if in answer to this desire his tongue invaded her body, sweeping in bold dominant strokes, flaring her singing nerves, drawing then tight.

"Say it," he whispered. "I want to hear you speak the words."

She could not think. She no longer remembered why she wouldn't do as he asked.

Her mouth moved to speak those impossible words.

"Yes..."

How was she to speak? He barely gave her a moment to breathe.

Her stomach clenched in fear. She didn't like this—losing control, becoming this mindless, craven thing.

She was first to break the connection. She stared up at his languid face.

"Please. Can we not just simply do the thing?" She had not meant to sound so desperate. But she had not known there could be such feelings in what happened between a man and woman. She had made a grave miscalculation, one for which she would soon pay dearly. "Please?"

"With the utmost pleasure, Miss MacLeod."

CHAPTER 4

*W*as it her imagination, or had the room suddenly become wintry and cool? Her eyes flickered to the still open French windows. Clouds had gathered in the distant horizon promising rain. Even now the faint scent of rain danced in the air, mixed with the perfume of spring flowers and fresh growth.

She thought he would have placed her on the bed, but instead, he touched her. Tentatively at first. His hand stroking the downy texture of her cheek. Then gliding down her neck to her shoulders. The skin was cold there and he raised gooseflesh where he touched. His hands then became bolder, more searching.

She watched as he slowly fell to his knees. His touch tracing down her waist to her thighs. He reached around to the globes of her buttocks. He weighed, squeezed and caressed them.

Lenora closed her eyes and swallowed down her mortification. He hadn't even bedded her yet. What had she done?

His touch was not terrible. His large hands were as soft as they could be. Indicative of the life of a London dandy. What was the use? Disparaging him didn't make what was happening any less mortifying.

Then he touched her there! Her eyes flared open, and her breath caught. She whimpered as he cupped her woman's mound. His thumb flickered over a sensitive spot and her body shuddered.

"No."

He looked up at her through lids heavy with desire. A small smile played at his lips. "No?"

She looked away from him. They both knew her *noes* amounted to less than nothing.

"Open your legs," he commanded gently, before placing a chaste kiss on the swell of her belly. "Open for me Lenora."

She did as he asked, though she was loath to. But what was the point in refusing?

His fingers slid between her nether lips and Lenora sucked in a quick breath. This was utter wickedness!

"Why do you do this?" Her voice was tight with mounting fear. Unshed tears suddenly burned in her eyes. She did not want this! Not anymore! She wanted to undo the bargain she had made. Foolish, foolish girl!

"To enjoy you, Lenora." His tongue jutted out to give her belly the faintest of licks. He was enjoying himself, the fiend!

"I do not like this. It gives me no pleasure." She looked at him with hard eyes. Eyes burning with anger and fear. "You mustn't be very good at this if I don't enjoy your touch."

She struck out to hurt him like a viper. To crush his ego. And her aim was sure.

His fingers froze, then abandoned her altogether. He rose silently to his feet. If he was angry, she couldn't quite tell.

"On the bed," came his quiet command.

Lenora immediately felt terrible. She wordlessly complied, climbing onto the bed. She lay still on her back. Waiting. Why must she antagonize him? What was wrong with her?

Because you're afraid, her mind answered her. Because you feel powerless.

Chesterfield climbed onto the bed over her. He looked down, studying her. And as if he could read her mind, he reassured her, "There's nothing to fear, Lenora." Chesterfield shook his head. "I'll never hurt you."

Foolish man. She knew he thought she feared bodily harm. This she had suffered all her life. There was something greater to fear here. There was desire. There was need. There was the possibility of losing her heart to him.

"Then do it," her voice was weary. She had thought she could hold the fragile edges of her sanity through this. She had thought she could wear her superior morality like a mantle, shielding herself from him—from his touch. But she "n wrong. So very, very wrong!

She had not understood what it was to be his. To have him over her. To suffer his touches and kisses. They had not even begun, and she was already unraveling.

He moved lower on her body.

"Spread your legs."

She complied. *Yes. Yes. Have it done with.*

"Wider."

"I cannot..."

She did not have an opportunity to finish her words when she felt his hot mouth on her center and her spine bowed.

Lenora cried out some animal sound as a surge of electric heat shot through her. She writhed beneath him, but his grip held firm.

"No, no. This isn't proper," she protested to deaf ears.

He was merciless. Feeding on her like it were his dying feast.

"Dear God, help me!" She clawed at the sheets, her head shaking from side to side. He suckled now, tormenting that one exquisitely sensitive point. It was too much!

She opened her mouth to scream when the stimulation

receded like a retreating wave. His mouth remained at her core —kissing, suckling—but he had moved off that spot.

Her body relaxed despite herself, and she was reluctant to admit that his mouth brought her pleasure.

Twenty-nine more nights—and then, freedom. She could endure it. Yes, she could bare it—if only she tried.

His mouth moved away, and she felt a mere moment of frustration. He was kissing her belly now. His teeth intermittently grazing her skin. He made telling sounds deep in his throat, which spoke eloquently of his pleasure.

It took every ounce of effort within his body to keep from plunging into her.

His kisses were languorous now. He appeared determined to cover every inch of her body. She lay quietly watching him as though it were not really her body he was kissing. Lenora felt too many things at once and was suddenly too tired to muddle through her jumbled emotions.

He came to her breasts, saving them for last. He kissed along the curve of the underside of one breast. The skin was so very fine there and a little moist with perspiration. He moved closer to his target and hesitated. Her chest rose and fell just a little more quickly. He glanced up at her pleased to find her watching him.

His tongue flickered out to touch one nipple. Her breath caught. She was so responsive. That pleased him very much.

He ended one torment and began another when his mouth finally closed over one breast. Lenora let out a whimper as every nerve ending flared to life!

He suckled and kissed her. Lenora had never known a person could lavish such attention on one singular breast. She had also been wholly and completely ignorant of the blinding power his lips could have. She almost forgot who he was. Almost forgot she did not want to be here.

His campaign was one of ruthless possession. Even her own

limbs betrayed her to her enemy. Her hand was suddenly stroking his hair of its own volition. *Judas*, she called out to it, pulling it away from him as if she had touched fire.

But she still needed to hold onto something as he moved to give the same attention to the other breast. She let out a sibilant hiss. Her hands wanted to reach for him. They begged to touch him!

Lenora clawed at the sheets, balling a fistful in each hand as she held on for dear life. She could not remember what it was like to draw normal breath. Her throat released sounds unfamiliar even to herself. She needed something—something more.

She needed him!

Lord in heaven he had made her want this! Truly want this.

"Please," she whimpered. Even as she spoke, she knew she would later burn with shame at pleading with him.

"Yes," he prompted her. How could he be so cruel? How could he force her to say it?

"Please." Had he no mercy?

The answer was a painfully resounding no. "What is it you want Lenora?"

He knew. He knew!

"End this torment." Satisfy the hunger you've awakened.

She feared he would not heed her plea. She "n begging him to finish it since the moment it began. But as he moved higher over her, she knew he would finally get it over and done with.

His hips settled between her thighs, and she immediately felt his straining manhood at her entrance. He balanced himself on one elbow as he guided himself into her opening with his free hand.

Lenora shut her eyes, willing the pain to come.

"Look at me," he commanded, his breath ragged.

Her eyes opened in abeyance. His hand came to cradle her

face—not as a sign of affection, but to keep her from turning away.

"You've no idea how long I've wanted this." His smile was pained as he thrust forward.

Lenora let out a pain filled cry as he broke through her barrier and came to rest deep within her. It was a long moment before her eyes focused again on the man above her.

His eyes were glazed as she stared at him. He looked in no better shape than she.

Chesterfield took in a quick breath. He shut his eyes, squeezing out the moisture that was distorting his vision. When he opened his eyes again it was to find her staring up at him with a frown on her face.

He gave a surprised chuckle. How was he supposed to explain it to her when he did not understand it himself?

He began to move within her. She was so tight and so very wet. And it was glorious. Far better than he could have imagined. God help him, he should have demanded a year!

His movements were slow and languorous. Her gaze had fallen away.

She had turned her head because she could not bear to watch his face. She had not expected such need. She had thought he would be heartless or at the very least aloof. Was that not how playboys treated their lovers?

Suffice it to say, Lenora had not expected a tender lover. This was most cruel indeed.

He reached for her face, and she allowed him to kiss her. What was she to do? It took all the fight out of her to see him like this. And it truly wasn't terrible.

And it no longer hurt to have him moving inside her. If anything, it was rather pleasant in an odd way. She perhaps wouldn't care to perform this act very much, but once in a while with one's husband would be sufficient.

His movements quickened and she sensed he was nearing

something. His lips released hers as his breath came in more raged pants.

"So beautiful," he was whispering.

She watched him, thinking perhaps the words applied a little to him. Her heart lurched. No—she would not concede, not even a little.

His pumping became more determined. He pulled out of her almost completely only to plunge back deep into her.

She felt too good. There "n no chance of his lasting. "Wrap your arms around me." She obeyed, like a good little soldier. His Lenora was not a woman for whom intimacy came naturally.

The embrace, though entirely artifice, was sufficient. In mere seconds the feel of her pressed close to him sent him into oblivion. His climax crashed over him like a raging storm. And for a mere moment he wanted to pump his seed into her, to fill her. But wisdom won and he released himself from her spilling onto her belly.

Chesterfield collapsed beside her and wisely did not attempt to take her into his arms.

Now that the thing was done with, she felt absolutely nothing. She was not in the least impressed. Well, perhaps a little by the things he had done before he entered her.

Lenora let fall a sigh of relief. It had not been so terrible. She could last the next few weeks. It was not knowing that "n the most dreadful. Now she knew and she was suddenly no longer afraid.

The beginning of the end at last!

CHAPTER 5

The rain receded, leaving in its place a sweet, heavy mist. It was still early evening, and the sun had never returned.

Chesterfield stood on their balcony, staring out at the countryside.

Stout gray clouds hid the firmaments from view. Neither moon nor stars could be seen for miles. The air had turned decidedly cold and still he stood like a fool with nothing on but his breeches.

He had to think. Lord in heaven he had to think!

She lay in the bed. Quiet as death itself. She "n there since after Lorette brought up dinner and lit the fireplace and a few lamps.

He would have given anything to be privileged to her inner thoughts. But she had said nothing since their lovemaking. That "n hours ago.

They had at first fallen asleep. At least he had. Something he rarely did after a daytime bedding. He usually put on his clothes and made his escape. Not this time.

They cleaned up and made themselves presentable and he then rung for an early dinner.

Now he stood out here, afraid to go in—yes, afraid!

Damn her!

He did not plan on using her again tonight. So, what did one do with a mistress one felt entirely uncomfortable with? Dear lord, only he would be fool enough to find himself in such a situation.

Could he stand a month of this? Perhaps he could send her home and consider her debt paid. That would be the kind thing to do.

Bloody hell! It wouldn't be kindness that sent her away. The truth was simply that he feared something. What was it? A feeling perhaps? Yes, it was something that she made him feel. And yet, he did not want her to go. Tomorrow. He'd make a decision on whether or not to end their arrangement tomorrow—not now.

He turned to the bed where she lay under the sheets. She had even pulled the blankets to her chin. She lay there, curled on her side like a wounded animal.

Chesterfield finally went inside. The cold and damp had won. He closed the French doors upon entering and shut the curtains.

"I never particularly liked the rain," he threw over his shoulder as he busied himself straightening the curtains. She did not respond. He had not known if he really expected an answer.

He took in a deep breath.

"Get up."

She turned to him.

"Up."

"Why?"

"It's far too early to sleep."

"I was not sleeping."

"Precisely."

She huffed but decided to rise. She sat up and threw the covers off her body. In moments she was on her bare feet, clad only in her pink nightgown. He, as usual, was standing far too close.

"Now what?"

"Can't we at least be friends? Is the thought so repugnant?" He tried to give her his most charming of grins. A practiced smile to set the fairer sex a twitter. But leave it to Miss MacLeod to be completely immune to his charms.

"Friends?" She asked suspiciously as she reached for her robe. The thing was just as pink and silly as the nightgown, but Lenora would not quibble when it added another layer of clothing.

"Yes, friends." He said with something close to a sigh. "You do have friends, do you not Lenora?"

"I've no need for friends, sir."

"Michael," he corrected.

"I've my employment," she went on ignoring his correction. "The children. I've my family." She dared him to mock her. "And I have God," she added with a tilt to her chin.

"The Godly Miss MacLeod." He stared at her a long moment before shrugging. "We would make interesting friends if you would but allow it."

"How so?"

"You could teach me to be good. And I could teach you to be wicked."

"I don't wish to be wicked," she stated in her cool crisp manner.

"I think you wish to be very wicked."

"I don't!"

"Well, you should," he ended with a shrug.

She stared at him like he had entered the room wearing his pants on his head. He chuckled out loud.

"You're a very odd man," she said with some exasperation as she crossed her arms and moved toward the fireplace. No, he would not let things stand as they are. They would be friends. He followed her, determined to settle things between them once and for all.

"What is it?" he began.

She turned to him.

"What is it that makes you so cold and unfeeling towards me?"

"I am not unfeeling, sir."

"Then why can we not be friends?"

Lenora examined his face, wondering where this foolish talk of friendship was coming from. Once this month was over, would he still claim to desire her friendship? Her? His brother's governess.

"Are you still cross with me for my ill-mannered flirtations earlier in our acquaintance? I was an egotistical prick."

"And now?"

"Now? Well, I'm an older but wiser egotistical prick," he said in an attempt to bring levity to the situation. She nearly smiled. He saw it. But she quickly schooled features. She didn't trust him. If he could but be honest with himself, he could not blame her. He had never before this moment given her a reason to trust him or to expect friendship from him.

Her gaze returned to the fire. For a long moment they listened to the logs crackle as they were consumed by the flames of the golden fire. Their shadows danced against the wall like natives in the jungle.

"Can we at least not be enemies," he asked in a quiet voice. He was barely one step away from pleading. "The offer stands Lenora. That is all I will say on the subject for now." With that he left her side. In minutes he had dressed and quietly left the room.

Imagine them as friends. Lenora shook her head. No woman

of her class had ever emerged unscathed from a friendship with a man like him—no matter how beguiling his smiles were.

THE MORNING USHERED in another tempestuous day. It had rained mercilessly through the night and showed no signs of ceasing.

Chesterfield had not slept in the bed with her that night, thus Lenora was quite surprised to open her eyes to the sensation of feathery kisses on her shoulder.

"It's raining again," she heard his petulant voice.

"Yes."

"Yes?" She felt him rise higher on his elbow as the mattress sunk a little beneath her. "Is that the sum of all you have to say on the subject?"

"I like the rain, sir."

"You would, you contrary girl."

She almost smiled at the grumbling tone of his voice. He rolled away from her and she hazarded a glance over her shoulder. Chesterfield lay on top of the covers completely dressed. He gave a gargantuan yawn as he lethargically scratched his scalp.

He almost looked innocent in his actions. She shook her head. Innocence was hardly an accusation she would level upon Michael Chesterfield.

"What?" Chesterfield raised a regal brow.

Lenora shook her head again before pushing off the covers and stepping out of the bed.

"I dislike this habit of rising early. There is something quite unnatural about it," he voiced as he watched her don her robe. Ignoring him, she headed for the bathing room.

"Lenora?"

She stopped at the door and turned to look at him.

"Where is my morning kiss?"

"Morning kiss?" She stared at him blankly.

"Yes, my morning kiss." He crossed his arms beneath his head and smiled most devilishly. "After all, it's customary when one awakens to greet one's lover with a morning kiss."

"Is it as you say? Is it customary?"

"Quite."

She regarded him for a moment. He almost thought she would resist. But like an obedient girl she made her way back to the bed. There was another brief moment of consideration before she bent down and kissed him.

On the lips. Bravo, Lenora. Well played!

They both regarded each other after that innocent kiss.

"May I go now, sir?"

"Yes." He frowned as he watched her retreat. She entered the adjoining room and quietly closed the door behind her.

Michael remained where he lay for a few minutes more as he considered the events of the previous day. It all seemed like some odd dream where the players and places made absolutely no sense and yet the mind feverishly attempts to make some story out of random parts. He had bedded Lenora MacLeod. She was here with him now, in his grandmother's house.

Michael stared at the bed's canopy with unseeing eyes. Why had it been so good with her? She clearly did no relish being here with him. She was untried and without even a hint of seductive skills. Yet he wanted more of her. He wanted to drown his senses in her.

Michael rolled to his side in frustration. He had barely slept all night. It was different with her. It was peaceful. He could not guess why. Nor did he want to think too deeply on it.

Was he in love with her?

Chesterfield immediately frowned at the errant thought. No! Perhaps a tad obsessed with her maybe. Likely due to her tenacious resistance! But not in love. God in heaven not in love with Miss MacLeod!

He rose to stand. Needing immediately to shake off the ridiculous suggestion. Where in heaven had such a foolish thought come from? He had never before given haven to such thoughts after bedding a woman. What was wrong with him? The room felt all at once hot and suffocating.

LENORA STARED at her reflection from the small looking glass above the basin. She looked fatigued and far too thin. Even she could see it.

He had paid twelve hundred for this?

But he thought her body beautiful. She remembered the look he had given her just before his release. How can a man who had bedded so many women have the ability to give such an unconcealed look of longing... of need?

It should have been impossible.

She shook her head deciding it was best not to think too deeply on it. She took care of her needs and exited the room ready for whatever this day would offer. And indeed, she was ready. She knew the worst of it. This she could do. This she could suffer through.

Chesterfield ordered their breakfast. Lorette smiled shyly as she wheeled in the cart. She and Chesterfield exchanged some light banter as Lenora looked over the offerings. She was pleased to find her appetite restored after months of worry.

She quickly reached for a croissant before even properly taking her seat.

"Glad to see you waited for me, dearest."

Lenora froze with a mouthful of warm croissants.

"It's quite alright," he smiled. "This bounty is ours to enjoy."

Lenora gave an embarrassed smile to the retreating Lorette before returning her attention to their feast. Chesterfield took a seat across from the little table he had had brought into the room the evening before.

Lenora spread a liberal helping of butter and marmalade on the remainder of her croissant before placing it in her mouth. *When had the woman last eaten?* he wondered. She had barely touched her food on their previously shared meals.

They ate in silence for a long while. Neither daring to speak. Chesterfield knew what he needed to say. That if she wanted to end their bargain here and now, then he would let her. But his mouth would not let him. And so, he continued in silence, selfishly refusing to grant her her freedom. Maybe just a few days longer. Where was the harm in that? Surely, he could avoid falling in love with her for a few more days. Chesterfield must have frowned just then, for Lenora stopped eating to stare at him.

"What shall we do today?" He mused as he picked up the last of the croissants. "I daresay it will rain for the rest of the day and inactivity does make me temperamental. What would you suggest Lenora? Clever girl that you are."

"I do not know, sir."

"Michael," he chimed in easily.

"Michael." She popped the last of her pastry in her mouth and washed it down with a sip of thick hot chocolate.

"We could make love all day." He looked over the contents of the tray, eggs, cheese, ham, kippers and a few slices of toast. "I've spent my hours in less... amusing pursuits." Michael finally looked up at her.

She stared at him with wide eyes. "But all day?"

"Then it's decided."

"Decided?" She straightened in her chair.

"I think perhaps you'd better have this." He placed his croissant on her plate. "I think you'll need the energy."

Lenora looked at the tempting croissant on her plate and somehow her appetite had fled. Chesterfield apparently suffered from no such ailment as he served himself a liberal helping of all that remained. He suddenly felt absolutely ravenous.

She watched him as he made work of his meal. Was it possible for two people to devote an entire day to bedding? Surely, he wouldn't…surely, she couldn't…

She reclined into her seat staring at him very much as the bird must stare at a nearby cat. Suspicious and watchful.

Her eyes raked his face following a strong jaw line that led to a generous mouth. He was far too pretty, she thought with a frown.

No not pretty, but beautiful.

She could feel her frown deepening. She pulled up her legs and hugged them to her, making certain to adjust her nightgown so that it covered her completely.

Why was she so prejudiced against his beauty? Her eyes noted the thick lashes that surrounded his eyes. Such eyes! She had never seen the precise shade of green before. Green should have been cool, soothing. It should remind one of growing things and mother earth. Green most certainly should not glow with a gentle radiance. Nor should it remind one of a blazing fire that warms one minute and consumes the next.

She did not realize she had sighed until his eyes were suddenly on her. It was as if he could now see deep within her to places she believed she had firmly locked away.

Lenora immediately turned her attention to the French doors. He must have pulled back the drapes while she was in the bathing room. Beyond the glass the world was indeed a mass of differing grays filtered through weeping clouds.

It would rain for the rest of the day. And they would make love. No, not make love. He would bed her. Such a word as love was ridiculous to use in this instance.

"I wonder what thoughts you turn to when you have that look on your face."

She turned back to him a little more confident that her

secret places were well hidden. She met his gaze unflinchingly. He sat relaxed against the high-backed chair, his fingers laced over his stomach. His lips curled ever so slightly when he noticed where her eyes had strayed.

Lenora's back stiffened just a little more at his knowing smile. She was certain she was up for whatever challenge he had in mind for her. His next words proved her wrong.

"Tell me, Lenora—what do you fantasize about?" He slowly leaned forward, his voice having gone low and velvety, caressing her like a warm blanket.

"Fantasies?"

"I'm certain even a governess must have one or two."

"I assure you I do not." Lenora pulled her robe closer around her. "Such wickedness."

"Wickedness?" Chesterfield considered her a moment. He chuckled to himself. "I am sorry, Lenora. I did not mean to embarrass you. I know all too well the stings suffered by an unwelcomed teasing."

Lenora shook her head with a scornful laugh. He should have let it pass, but with her he was always acing at odds with what he should or should not do.

"What do you find so amusing?"

She shook her head as if to say it was not worth broaching, but to his detriment he insisted.

"Clearly I must have said something."

She considered him a moment before speaking, "That you believe yourself to have ever suffered." She went on, "Were the other privileged and pampered boys cruel to you in your fancy school? Did they not share their sweets with you?" Then more to herself, "Suffering." She shook her head in disbelief.

Chesterfield remained silent. His face calculating his next words. He did not look angry, but more uncertain. Then finally…

"You're right, of course. What do I know of suffering?"

"Precisely," she offered in vindication.

He suddenly stood with a serious look. Lenora felt the first pangs of worry. Had she angered him? Would he call off their bargain and send her away. Damn foolish mouth of hers. She had too much pride for a woman of her station. Countless were the times her mother had warned her of this.

She stared at him wordlessly. He was angry, she was sure of it. He took a step forward and held out his hand to her.

"Come," he spoke the one word as a command, and she was powerless but to obey.

For a bare moment she regretted antagonizing him. What purpose did it serve? Foolish woman.

"Shall we amuse ourselves?"

HE LED her to the bed and Lenora could feel her heart beating through her chest. She was surprised to feel him lift her onto the bed. Once there, he quietly removed his shirtsleeves all the while staring at her. He still did not speak, but a small smile now played on his lips. A smile that promised some retribution. Would he hurt her for speaking so freely? She hadn't feared him before, but now she was truly worried.

Once he divested himself of his shirt, she had a full view of the firm planes of his broad chest. She had never known a man could be so well formed. Why had she antagonized him?

She expected for him to remove his breeches next, but he did not. He climbed into the bed beside her, forcing her to move over to make room for him. He turned on his side, facing her, supporting his head with right hand.

She whimpered when she felt his left hand reach under her nightgown to make its way up her thigh. His hand slowly roamed her body kneading her cool flesh. She could sense whatever anger he may have had drain from his body as lust replaced it.

Her skin was so incredibly soft it was paradise. He placed a tender kiss on her neck. God, how he wanted her. He had wanted her for so long!

Michael gave a satisfied groan as he reached the curls at the juncture of her legs. The portal to his personal paradise.

He looked over to find her eyes on him. They locked gazes and she frowned, too afraid to speak. Without thought he leaned forward to kiss that frown as a finger delved between her nether lips.

She gave whimper as his fingers began a slow dance. Back and forth. Like a snake charmer he beckoned her moisture with a practiced hand.

Lenora bit her lip against the blossoming sensation.

His lips found hers and they were so gentle. Lulling her into acquiescence. Lenora was suddenly drowning in sensations that she felt powerless to fight. The assaults were on too many fronts and in the end it appeared so much easier to give in.

Michael felt the very moment Lenora surrendered. Her lips became pliant beneath his, spurring him to increase the pressure he applied. His mouth opened over hers and she responded allowing him to dip his tongue in.

She opened for him willingly her breath catching as he adjusted the movements of his hand. He had found her secret button and gently circled it with his thumb as he penetrated her with his finger.

She moaned with the invasion but did not run from it. Michael took it as a good sign and increased the level of their mouth play, kissing her, suckling her tongue, exploring her mouth as if it were a rare delicacy.

Lenora was drowning. She had succumbed to the enemy and her mind could not quite recall why she had fought at all. Her hips lifted—seeking, needing, aching for more. And she now knew what that more was. It was him. Her traitorous body wanted him inside her.

Without thought she found her legs opening just a little more hoping he could somehow reach that part deep within her that called out for completion.

How could she have known she would succumb so easily? Her sentence had barely started and already she felt the need. Everything she had previously thought of herself evaporated under the harsh light of reality. She was a wanton. It had simply taken her being here in this cottage, in this bed to show her.

She wanted.

She needed him.

She kissed him back now—tentative at first, so faint he barely noticed. Then she began feeding on his mouth. Raising her head from the bed as she pushed back with the force of her kisses. She was devouring him, and it further fed the flames.

She whimpered beneath him attempting to pull him over her.

"Yes… yes…" she needed him. She needed him in that part of her that had known so much hunger far too long.

He covered her with his body. And she welcomed it wanting him with a savage craving that went beyond thought and propriety. She needed him there, filling her.

She barely heard him shuffling with his breeches in some distant part of her consciousness.

Her eyes fluttered then closed as his length slid effortlessly inside her. She sighed in relief as a tension she did not recall eased from her body. Michael watched her response, his mind devoid of all thought save one.

Mine.

He had never thought of his previous lovers as his before. Even the two who had born him children. But this woman he knew unequivocally was his. She had always been his.

Lenora belonged to him, and he would keep her. Long past this month.

She was still so tight but so very wet. Her body hugged him to her as though he were a long-lost part of her.

"Lenora," he whispered her name, kissing her still shut eyes.

Lenora refused to think. She refused to acknowledge who it was above her, around her, inside her. She released herself to the feeling. The mating dance. As old as time itself.

Had she thought it merely pleasant? It was wondrous this second time.

With each stroke he reached closer to that something that needed releasing. She sensed it like a large sleeping cat, finally waking deep within her.

He reached a hand between them and her eyes immediately flew open, fighting to focus on him. He stared down at her, face contorted with concentrated effort.

Sensations ripped through her and her body buckled as his fingers once again found her bud. She shook her head denying the overload to her senses. It was too much.

"Don't fight it, Lenora."

She turned to him searching for guidance.

"Yes, yes. Release yourself to the feeling."

"Michael…"

"Yes, love. Yes."

No sooner did she release when she was assailed by a frenetic storm. She cried out as the great sleeping cat tore through her body leaving her a bundle of raw nerves. She convulsed with the power of her orgasm.

Michael groaned as she tightened around him. He fought to catch his breath, to keep from spilling his seed inside her.

She stared at him through glassy eyes, her breathing quieting. Her lids growing heavy. He placed a tender kiss at the peak of one breast. She shivered in response. Closing her eyes, squeezing out a solitary tear.

"You've had your first release. How do you feel?"

She shook her head slowly. "I never knew." She licked her parched lips and sighed. No one had ever told her.

"You were wondrous, Lenora."

She looked at him again trying to decide if he were teasing. His face told a different tale. It held a certain wonder, colored with his still unquenched desires.

"You were a goddess, Lenora—golden and magnificent. I should worship at your feet."

Silly words, she thought, but she was too tired, too depleted to speak.

Still, they had their desired effect. She did feel a little like a goddess. Perhaps a minor one.

She was boneless when he began to move within her again. Her cat 'n well fed on thick rich cream and now lay warm and content.

Michael cursed beneath his breath. He could not last. Her wetness and the image of her release played havoc on his endurance. A few more strokes were his undoing as he pulled out from her to spill over her belly.

Moments later he crumbled to her side, trying to catch his breath. God help him this would not be an easy month.

CHAPTER 6

The man's appetite was inhuman!

It went against the very laws of nature. If this had perhaps been another time or place, where he would have had the common day distractions that one experienced, perhaps she would have had some hope of respite. But as it stood, there was no immediate hope of rescue and so they made love to while away the hours.

As the heavens had promised, it rained for the rest of the day and for two days more. Lenora feared it would continue to rain, and the world would wash away leaving only her and Chesterfield and this little cottage.

After yet another bedding, she lay crumpled on the bed, her body covered in a fine sheen of sweat. Her legs ached. Her back ached. Her mind ached!

He had bedded her three more times the day of her first climax, but now on their fourth day together she had lost count of the number of times they had made love.

She was saturated in the man. The scent of him and their lovemaking hung around her like a fog, filling her lungs with each breath she took.

She had long given up wearing any clothing and thus lay naked watching him move about the room.

Why wasn't he tired? she groaned inwardly. *Inhuman—simply inhuman.*

He paced the floorboards like a prowling tiger, dressed in his shirtsleeves and breeches. He cast glances at the French doors watching the glass weep its endless tears. More rain, more rain, they cried. Always more rain.

"I am convinced this rain will never cease!" Michael raked a hand through his already unruly curls. He looked like a wild man, Lenora thought with amusement.

"Heaven help me if it doesn't," she moaned from the bed.

He threw her a dark look and belatedly realized she was jesting. He approached the bed not intending on getting any closer, but her naked body tempted him, called him to touch her. He gave in readily and climbed into the bed behind her.

"Entertain me, Lenora."

She threw him a look. "Have I not entertained you until this very moment?" She asked with a sleepy yawn.

"Of course you have. And quite well I might add."

That comment earned him an elbow to the ribs.

"Oof!" he shook his head. "Dearest you have the elbows of a New Gate laborer."

She smiled despite herself. But his next words chased that smile from her face.

"Have you ever pleasured yourself, Lenora?" He touched her to illustrate his words.

She immediately pushed his hand away. "Why must you always speak such wickedness?" she frowned as she shook her head.

She attempted to pull away, but his hand on her shoulder stopped her. "There is no wickedness in self-pleasure, Lenora. These are things lovers discuss freely."

"We are not lovers, sir."

Damnation, but she could frustrate a saint!

"Would you rather we entertain ourselves in our usual way?" He asked with a touch of annoyance.

She turned to him, distress written across her face. If she did entertain him with this wicked talk, he would not use her, was that it? She really was too tired for another go.

"No, I do not... touch myself," she spoke just above a whisper.

Chesterfield did not know quite how he felt about the fact that she had answered him. It was evident that the thought of sex with him was viler than this "wicked" talk.

When had bedding him become a thing a woman avoided?

She stared up at him watching his face. "Do you... touch yourself, sir?"

"Michael," he corrected, irritation creeping into his voice. He stared down at her. "And yes, I do." He watched her eyes run from his. *What did she plan to do with this information?*

"I confess I don't understand why you're so fixed on this one subject." She gave a heavy resigned sigh. "Why do men think of joining so? Why do they race to amass women? Why do you?"

Michael blinked in surprise. He hadn't expected such a question.

He thought of his answer for a mere moment. There was really nothing to consider really. "It gives me pleasure."

She looked over her shoulder at him, a thoughtful frown on her face. "Pleasure?"

"Yes. It may come as a surprise to you, but men find the act of mating quite pleasurable, Lenora. If someone has told you otherwise, they have been lying to you."

"I know that men find bedding pleasurable. I mean only to ask if that is all you seek out of life? Pleasure?"

"Of course. Why would one seek misery?" He asked in all honesty. He snuggled closer to her, reaching a hand to cup her breast. "I think only idiots waste their time being miserable in this world."

She didn't reply to his last comment for a very long time. And he had begun to think she may not answer at all.

"I think a man of worth should seek more in life than pleasure."

He flicked a thumb over the peak of her nipple. She shivered in his arms.

"Why must you always insult me, dove?"

"I didn't insult you."

Chesterfield rolled away from her coming to a sitting position. "And what do you seek out of life? Are you one who enjoys running toward misery?"

Lenora turned to face him. She knew she had hurt his feelings. He was sensitive when it came to the subject of his indolence. Yes, but he was sensitive on an endless number of topics she reminded herself.

"There is more to life than forever seeking pleasure. There is work. There is the pursuit of knowledge. There is charity. There are endless other labors one can pursue in life."

"All you speak of is drudgery."

She sat up and stared at him. Chesterfield turned back to her at that movement.

"Why look so serious?" he quirked a brow. "Do you fear for my soul?"

"You take nothing seriously, sir."

"Michael."

"Life is not so easy for the rest of us mortals. For most people I think it is not. We all of us must toil and labor for our bread. Some must toil harder than others."

"And what comes of my indolence, do you think?"

"I think it serves only to weaken your character."

"Somehow I'm not surprised by your answer." He turned

back around with a sigh. "So much for being entertained. All this talk is as depressing as the rain."

"Do you never speak seriously with your friends?"

"I assure you that serious talk is not their purpose," he answered frankly. He could well image the tragedy that would result of talking seriously with Freddie, or worse yet Bella. No, his friends had their use. Weighty conversation was not one of them.

Chesterfield rose again and walked to the doors. "Why did you need the money, Lenora?" He turned his head to her. "Why did you enter into this bargain that you so evidently detest?"

"That is my affair."

"Yes, it is." He waited for her to say more. When she didn't, he continued, "Had you not been in need of my money do you think you would have ever succumbed to my... whiles."

"Never."

An honest answer. Michael chuckled. He had never had such a candid mistress.

She would probably answer any question he asked with her unique brand of brutal honesty. He had yet to decide if this was a curse or a blessing.

His gaze returned to the seemingly permanent twilight outside. In the distance a flock of white birds rose up from the trees in coordinated flight only to melt away into the horizon.

"Do you find me handsome?" He spoke without turning to her, but at her hesitation he hazarded a glance in her direction and found her seated, her back to the headboard. She avoided his gaze. "Am I to take that as a 'no' then?"

"Surely you must know the answer." There was definitely a hint of annoyance in her voice.

"It doesn't matter what I think. I want to know what you think of me."

She heaved a heavy sigh. "You know that you have a pleasing form. I'm certain all your mistresses have told you as much."

"All save one," he spoke under his breath.

She turned to him saying, "Do not be vain, Michael."

"Alas, music to my ears! You've called me by my name."

She frowned. "I also told you not to be vain."

"But it's not vanity my dear that makes me question you." As he spoke, he leaned against the cool glass of the French doors, crossing his arms before him. It made his shoulders appear broader.

The effect was pleasing if one found pleasure in male beauty.

"Then what is it if not male pride?"

He thought for a moment. "I never know where I stand when it concerns you. It's evident," he continued "You don't care for me. And though you may find my form pleasing, you've never desired me."

"Are all women to desire you then?" Lenora pulled her legs up and hugged them to her.

Michael's breath caught at the sight of her open to him. She was not accustomed to her nudity just yet and therefore could not know that the position she placed herself in was so inviting. He shifted his eyes away for fear of alerting her to his interest.

"I didn't say as much." It was a miracle he could continue this conversation. A testament to his fortitude.

"And yet it bothers you that I do not desire you?"

Michael froze, giving her question serious thought.

"Yes." He was as surprised by the answer as she.

"Has there been no one before me to spurn your attentions?" She asked in evident amazement.

He frowned as much from her question as from the effort not to stare at her. "Of course there has," he answered honestly. "Not every woman cares to lay with a half-savage."

"Half-savage?"

"Have you not heard that charming moniker? You can hear the ladies twitter it whenever I walk by."

"Then what does that make me? A full savage?"

"No, never. Not you Lenora."

"But others like me?"

"I can't speak to what they think, nor would I give them much thought. But I do wonder if perhaps I'm not dark enough for you?"

Lenora suddenly laughed. "What?"

When he did not join in her laughter, Lenora hesitated. Was he really concerned about the fairness of his skin? That his dearth of pigmentation was somehow correlated to her lack of desire? Surely, he was joking. But the earnest look on his face told her otherwise.

"I assure you, your skin color has nothing to do with my desire for you. And if, as you say, there have been others who have spurned your attentions, why does it vex you where I am concerned?"

"I do not know," he lied. He knew why her rejection stung more acutely. Because her rejection of him flew in the face of the dictates of society. She was of a lower station and should therefore have been grateful for his attentions. He was handsome, wealthy and not an ogre. She should have welcomed his advances. But she had not.

Lenora shifted, stretching out her legs. He studied her movements. She was lovely nude. Long brown limbs, curved in just the right places. Her curling hair in lovely disarray. She stared back at him, her face once again its usual placid mask. Had it been another woman, any other woman, he would have thought she sat naked before him to tease and beguile him. Offering up her undressed loveliness to tempt his lustful appetite.

But he knew better. Miss MacLeod had simply grown tired of dressing and undressing and thought only of practicality.

Why indeed did her opinion matter to him? It had to be more complicated than his being master and she servant. It had to go deeper, and if he were just a little more courageous, he would certainly unearth the truth.

"Perhaps it is because I respect you where I have never respected the others." She frowned at him, and he gave a Gaelic shrugged. "Then again perhaps not."

Lenora shook her head. Respected her? Her eyes searched the room for her discarded nightgown. She didn't believe he respected her or anyone. He was a selfish seeker of pleasure and now also a liar.

She rose, her gaze landing on the nightgown draped over a chair.

"You needn't bother."

She turned at the hollow sound of his voice. Chesterfield approached the bed removing his shirtsleeves. She gave a barely perceptible sigh as she reclined back on the bed.

Had she truly considered the possibility that he respected her? If she had it "n momentary foolishness. The last complete thought she had as he climbed atop of her was that no man ever respected his whore. She would be no exception.

CHAPTER 7

*S*un!

Glorious sun. Like a beacon in the storm, the clouds shattered, spilling rays of light upon the sodden earth.

Sun! Bird and beast both sang a chorus in praise of the golden light that rescued them from the weary and ceaseless storm.

Ah, sun, sweet sun alas!

Chesterfield burst through the doors just as Lorette attended Lenora's bath.

"Monsieur!" Lorette squealed in surprise.

"A picnic!" Chesterfield proclaimed like a town heralder. "We shall have a picnic." His eyes settled on Lenora rising from her bath. His gaze raked her still wet form just before Lorette rushed to cover her mistress.

"Monsieur, you must allow me to get Madame ready."

His eyes locked on Lenora's. She looked back at him unwaveringly. In that moment he realized he was far more entranced by the sight of her than she was of him. But more than that, she knew it. The three days they had spent in ceaseless lovemaking had somehow crystallized their positions in their somewhat odd relationship.

"Very well," Chesterfield finally answered with a nod. "I shall go make all the preparations."

Once Chesterfield had departed Lorette clucked her tongue in playful disapproval.

The dresses the modiste had promised finally arrived on this the first sunny day since her first morning. And the gowns had all come. Lenora stared at her gowns as Lorette cleared the dishes from their petit déjeuner.

"They are so lovely Madame," Lorette threw over her shoulder as she tidied up.

Lenora nodded somewhat uncomfortably. The gowns were indeed lovely. Too lovely for the likes of me. But what would she be expected to wear? Her plain, serviceable dresses?

"The blue one will be wonderful for a picnic," Lorette said with obvious approval. "I shall return to do your hair tout de suite." With that the little maid was out of the room.

Lenora had not moved from her spot when the maid returned ten minutes later, ready to help with the dressing and coiffure. Lenora thought to protest. She did not like dressing in a manner so alien to her. But she had to remember the part she was playing.

She allowed Lorette to dress her in the powder blue silk. A white ribbon tied around the high waist. And white lace edged the rather low neckline. The dress was simple, yet elegant. Far more elegant than she was accustomed to.

Lorette braided her hair into two braids and pinned them neatly behind her ears. Lenora stared at the stranger in the looking glass. She nodded to Lorette as the girl stood back expectantly. The maid smiled in approval.

· · ·

THE DAY WAS breezy and drowning in sunlight. The ground was too wet for a picnic. But she would say nothing to discourage him. They were both far too relieved to be out of doors to let moist soil discourage them.

Lenora observed the countryside with a somber expression. It was lovely. Green and lush. She glanced at Chesterfield leading their horse with an expert hand. If only she could have been here under more pleasant circumstances.

She turned her attention back to the landscape. It reminded her a little of home when the summer was still quite young and untried. The sun heated her skin, and the air smelled clean. When she closed her eyes, Lenora could hear the wind racing headlong through the trees.

If only this were a different time. She could release herself to enjoying the moment. And perhaps she still could a little.

They drove on for nearly an hour. Passing hills and meadows, farms and fields.

"Where are we going... Michael?" she finally braved a question as the day became warmer. They had already passed many suitable spots for a picnic. Spots where full trees framed rich green grass in just the perfect setting for a picnic. Yet he led them onward.

He turned to her and smiled. "Finally, she speaks."

She gave an exasperated sigh and turned away from him.

"We are going to the ocean."

She turned to see he was staring at her. An odd look on his face. Chesterfield was glad she could not read his thoughts. For she would know that at that very moment he thought her lovely. The modiste had done a superb job. The powder blue gown suited her exquisitely.

"The ocean?"

"Yes. A particular spot. We picnicked there when I was a child. Ah, here we are."

Lenora turned her head and the trees that had lined their path fell away to reveal a long sloping stretch of beach.

"We'll have to leave the carriage here. But the walk will not be difficult."

She simply nodded and followed where he led.

Chesterfield carried their basket and blanket as Lenora trailed behind him. Her eyes casting glances around her. He finally turned to her with a brilliant smile. Her stomach contracted at the sight of him, and she frowned. Apparently thinking the frown was for him, his smile dimmed a little.

"Just over here," he said turning back.

He led her to a little cove, protected from the wind on three sides. It was calmer and cooler here.

"We shall set up our blanket here."

She came forward and helped him set up their blanket and basket with her usual efficiency. Michael tried to suppress the smile that threatened to spill over. His efficient Miss MacLeod. The thought made him hesitate in his movements and she looked up at him expectantly. He shook his head, and they continued with their task.

His Miss MacLeod. He did want her. He gave furtive glances in her direction, not wishing to ignite her suspicions. What he wanted to do was stare at her. And had she truly been his mistress, he would have. But this prickly woman was not his mistress. Not in a way that was typical.

What would it mean to have her beyond this month? He liked her. She was intelligent. She was honest. It amazed him to realize that was important to him. There was no one he trusted to tell him the truth. Chesterfield ran through the tally of his nearest and dearest. No, not a one. Perhaps save his half-brother, but even the earl rarely spoke of deeper feelings.

No, there was not a single soul. Save Miss MacLeod.

He turned to her then. Lenora's head was tilted back to the sun. Thankfully her eyes were shut. He respected her. Thus, her opinion mattered to him. He shook his head. He was going to fall in love with her. He let out a curse between his lips.

Lenora turned to him. "What is the matter?"

"Nothing," he answered turning away from her questioning eyes. He frowned to himself. Idiot that he was, he would fall in love with her and the best he could hope for was that she no longer despised him.

"Are you hungry?" He finally asked after a few long minutes of silence.

"No, I think not." She would perhaps be hungry in an hour or two, but not yet. She had eaten very well at breakfast.

"Then let us walk." He began to pull off his boots and stockings.

"What are you doing?"

"There is nothing comparable to the feeling of sand beneath one's bare feet. I highly recommend it."

"I think not," she answered in her clip governess tone.

"Come now. It will surely set you free."

"I have no wish to be set free," she gave him a superb haughty look.

"I daresay, Lenora, looking as you just did, you might have been a duchess."

"Ridiculous."

"Yes," he answered quietly. "I am ridiculous." He stood and stretched out a hand to her. "Come."

He could see that she rose reluctantly. If she did not wish to remove her shoes, he would allow that. But that was all the quarter he would give her today. He meant to enjoy himself.

She took his hand and Michael lead her out near the water's edge.

"My boots will get wet," she admonished him as if he were a naughty boy.

"Then remove them," came his simple answer.

She released his hand, moving away from the shore. "Standing at a farther distance is a far more suitable solution."

"Very practical, Miss MacLeod. As always." He gave her an eloquent bow and she recognized immediately he was mocking her.

Michael walked a little further out. The waves lapping at his feet. He began to trace the shoreline, enjoying the feel of the cool water.

Lenora was forced to follow, though she watched him dubiously. He would occasionally walk a little deeper, his breeches hungrily soaking up the seawater. Though his movements were carefree, his face appeared reserved.

She had a sense that she somehow ruined the party. And guilt began gnawing at her. But she did not have a playful nature. And he should not have anticipated her to suddenly have one. It was unfair to expect it.

Why the seawater would ruin her dress. She was certain it had cost an exorbitant amount of money. All to be ruined on the first day of wearing.

Ridiculous!

And yet watching Chesterfield play alone seemed somehow distressing. She had a sudden glimpse of him as a little boy playing along this very beach. Alone.

Chesterfield reached down through the receding water coming up with a stone smoothed to perfection by the unceasing waves. He ran a thumb over its smooth wet surface.

He had collected them as a child. Once gathering nearly one hundred. He had called that pile of worthless stones his treasure. Perhaps even saying it aloud once to his grandmother.

He pulled back his arm and hurled the missile out to sea. It disappeared beneath the building waves with an unceremonious splash.

A sudden movement to his left snared his attention and he turned to where Lenora sat upon the sand, removing her boots.

A smile burst on his face. In that moment she turned to him and time slowed.

Lenora looked up to catch him smiling. He was pleased. Beyond pleased in fact. She returned his smile tentatively.

His smile grew impossibly brighter, and her stomach once again clenched. Her own smile wavered as the call to flight nearly screamed at her. But she would not run from him. She set on removing her boots.

With the task done she rose and approached the waves. "The gown will get wet."

Michael laughed at her as she held her dress high above her ankles. "I shall buy you another. Perhaps ten more."

She shook her head at his teasing. "I don't want you to buy me ten more."

"Ah, you're the best mistress I've ever had, Lenora. Perhaps I shall keep you long after our month ends."

She gave her usual disapproving frown.

He approached her where she stood, his smile turning tender. "Would it displease you if I kept you, Lenora?"

"I am not a thing like a sturdy shoe or pretty parasol to be 'kept'." She looked at him fearing he was no longer teasing.

Michael reached for her chin, stroking one soft cheek with his thumb. "Then that is a terrible shame indeed." He leaned slowly down to kiss her, and she opened immediately for him.

There was nothing comparable to kissing Lenora. She was an odd mix of innocence and worldliness. He could spend an entire day, nay an entire lifetime kissing those lips.

Lenora leaned her body against the hard planes of his chest. He was so solidly built. So alive! She nearly drowned in him. She wanted to be alive too. She too wanted to hold the world in her palm like it were her plaything. But she could not.

She pulled away, feeling her envy of him poison the moment. He did not notice for he smiled down at her.

"Your dress is getting wet."

Lenora screeched when she looked down and found her dress floating above the waves. She had released her hold of the gown to kiss him. And somehow the fiend had brought them deeper into the water.

She screeched again, attempting to head for the shore when she felt strong arms clasp around her waist. He laughed at her as she attempted to seek dry land.

"Let go of me!" She tried to hit his arm to force him to release her. But he merely laughed louder.

"Give up, Miss MacLeod. Your goose is well and truly cooked."

"What on earth do geese have to do with a ruined gown?"

He laughed louder at her words and futile struggle.

"Release me this instant!" she screamed at him. "This instant do you hear me?"

"I certainly hear you Madame. I dare say all of Calais has heard you." He laughed. "Stop squirming and I'll release you."

Lenora stopped immediately.

"Will you behave yourself like a good little girl?"

She nodded obediently.

"Now, that's much better, isn't it?"

She nodded again.

He turned her around in his arms so that she faced away from him, but did not release her. But in fact, held her tighter with one arm as he slowly reached to cup her right breast with his right hand. She watched his hands progression torn between worry for her ruined gown and curiosity at his roving hand.

Practicality won the day.

"Will you release me?"

"No."

She frowned. "But you said if I stilled you would."

"I lied." His hand covered her breast.

"You beast!"

He chuckled behind her.

She attempted to pull away from him and felt him throw his body backward. Suddenly the water washed over her head as he pulled her down with him. The moment he released her she scrambled forward. The receding water making it difficult to stand. She lost the fight, falling on her rump.

Chesterfield's laughter made her aware that he had risen from the waves and was in fact making an effortless exit from the water.

She coughed up a mouthful of seawater. Managing to crawl to shore on her hands and knees.

"The gown is ruined!"

Michael chuckled looking down at her. She was truly heartbroken over the silly gown. He knelt down holding a hand out to her. She looked at him, truly distressed, but did not take his proffered hand.

"Lenora, *mon cœur*, the gown is nothing. I can buy you more."

"But that is not the point. It's wasteful to ruin it." She touched the wet silk and felt nearly on the verge of tears. It was silly she knew it. And as he said he could buy her ten more. But it was the first lovely dress she had ever worn. And to her such things did not come easily or often.

Michael stared at her, not quite understanding what she felt, but suspecting that as always it reflected poorly on him. "You are of course correct. It was foolish of me to ruin your gown. Especially when I knew it was a concern to you."

She looked up at him, silently assessing. She finally nodded.

"What may I do in atonement?"

She gave him a furtive look just before her gaze shifted away nervously.

She had thought of something—he was certain of it. She was simply too frightened to say.

"Tell me Lenora."

She turned to him again, as she took a seat on the damp

sand. Her features were a little more set, while her eyes held a trace of uncertainty.

"A reprieve."

"A reprieve?" he repeated in confusion.

"A three-day reprieve."

He stared at her and like a slow dawn her words began to make sense.

"A reprieve from my bedding you?"

She nodded. "Yes."

He was silent a long time. He looked at her, and then his gaze turned to the seemingly endless ocean. She wanted a reprieve from his touch. From his making love to her. If he had thought she was growing use to his touch, maybe even relishing it, it was disheartening to discovery that he was unequivocally wrong.

Finally, he gave a curt nod. "A reprieve."

She finally took hold of the hand he offered, and he aided her to his feet.

"We should remove your gown."

"Remove it?" She appeared incensed at the suggestion.

"We would not want you to fall ill."

"But your clothes are also soddened." She had no sooner said the words when she immediately regretted their utterance.

He smiled mischievously. "You're quite right as always. Therefore, I have no other alternative but to bow to your superior judgment." With those words he began to remove his clothing.

Lenora turned away, a brief eye scanning the distance. What if he were seen? The prospect was of course scandalous! Thankfully there appeared not to be a single soul in sight. Of course there was no guarantee the situation would remain this way.

"Do you need any help with the gown?" He offered playfully.

Though she had already begun to shiver he knew she would not release the gown easily.

"No, I'm quite fine, thank you," she answered so primly one would think they were at tea in a proper salon rather than drenched by seawater at the ocean. He had only left his drawers on not wishing to scandalize her more than was absolutely necessary.

Goodness, they had made love more times than he remembered in the last few days and yet he worried over her tender sensibilities!

"I'm certain the gown will dry soon enough. In any case, it's not so uncomfortable."

"Don't be ridiculous woman," he approached, and she stepped away from him.

"I assure you I am quite fine."

A slow smile blossomed on his face, and he took another step toward her. She once again took a step back her eyes widening like saucers.

"What are you doing?" She asked shakily, afraid he had happened upon a new game.

"I am going to take your gown off," he answered with the utmost confidence.

"No, you are not!" She held out a staying hand to him. "I forbid it," she threw in for good measure. He smiled.

Suddenly she lifted her skirt and fled. Michael watched her for almost an entire minute in abject shock. And then he heard it. Laughter! Her laughter roused him from his trance, and he took off after her.

She squealed when she heard his steps nearing and attempted to increase her speed. Her heart was pounding in her chest. It "n a long time since she had exerted so much energy.

Her flight was hopelessly doomed to failure of course. She was laden with a sodden gown while he was nearly bare. She squealed again when she felt his arms reach around her waist and lift her from the ground. They both tumbled to the sand. She landing on top of him.

She rolled off of him laughing with an abandon she could not recall having even as a child. She and her gown were soon covered in sand. The poor gown never had a chance.

They both laughed on their backs until their mirth died a gentle death. Lenora turned to him then, her vision nearly blurred by tears. The look he gave her in return suddenly arrested her. She looked away frightened by what she had seen.

"Come, let us swim," he finally spoke filling in the silence.

"But the water is so cold," she turned back to him, thankful that he once again looked his arrogant carefree self.

"It's only cold if one stands still." Michael looked down at the sand that clung stubbornly to his body. A quick soak would be just the thing.

Why not? Lenora answered him in thought. When would she ever indulge in such frivolity again?

"Very well." She slowly rose to her feet. He mirrored her action. "I suppose I will have to remove the dress after all," she said with obvious resignation.

"I promise I shall get you ten more. Far prettier than this one."

"You needn't."

"I wish to."

She did not argue further. There was no purpose. He would do as he wished. It was his money after all. It was not as though she would keep the dresses. Where would she ever wear them again?

"The buttons are in the back." She turned her back to him and he wordlessly set upon the tiny row of buttons.

It was actually a relief to finally step out of the sodden ruins of the sea-soaked silk. It was a true shame.

"We shall hang it to dry." He spied a few pieces of driftwood.

Erecting a makeshift rack, he draped both of their clothes to dry as best they could.

"Come." He held out a hand to her and was pleased that she took hold of it. With a smile he led her into the waves realizing he had not been this happy in a very long time.

LENORA SIGHED deep within the cocoon of her blanket. She looked to Michael making good work of their cold chicken, cheese, bread and wine. Her own belly was full. Swimming in the cold water had sent her appetite soaring to unimaginable heights.

She licked the traces of grease and chicken off her own fingers, then reached for her wine.

"Did you come here often as a child?"

He looked up at her. His hair a tangled mass of curls. His hazel-green eyes brilliant as if he held the sun within them.

"A few times. Perhaps five or six occasions." He reached for a piece of cheese and stopped. "I always cherished this place. It was a haven of sorts."

She studied him a moment. "Your haven from where?"

"From life. From home."

"Was your home so very unpleasant then?"

He looked at her. Perhaps weighing the prudence of revealing too much. But when had he, Michael Chesterfield, ever been prudent?

"My home was very unpleasant." He stopped speaking and she thought he would say no more. But then he spoke again.

"My mother married my father after the late Earl died. To hear my brother speak, his father was a tyrant. But he "n rich and powerful and therefore well respected. The entire family was quite shocked by my parent's marriage. You see, my father was an African merchant. So, he had no wealth or title, and he was of course African. And had they both lived, I'm certain they would have shielded me from the worst of our family's bigotry. But they both died when I was eight. A few days apart from fever. After that the rest of the family made sure to remind me at every turn that I was unwelcome. They drove a wedge between my brother and me. Using the excuse that he was the new earl and therefore there were certain things he had to do or have that I could not. Everyone except my grandmother treated me as a burden. My mother's mother. She was the only kind one in the bunch..."

"I'm sorry. I did not know."

"How could you?"

"The current earl is not cruel to his children."

"No, I would imagine Adrian is a far better father to his children than his was to him." His attention turned to the waves. Sizeable gray clouds had rolled in, turning the afternoon cooler. Casting a melancholy pallor on their afternoon of frolicking. "I do not envy him. Children can be a burden."

"And yet you have two."

He raised his eyes briefly to hers, then turned away. "Yes. But that is different."

"How is it different?"

He did not know if he liked having this conversation with her. But upon further thought he concluded there was no one else with whom to have this conversation. And perhaps there were words that needed to be said.

"Bastard children are not expected to be loved and cared for as children begotten from one's wife. Therefore, the two children I have are no true burden to me. I daresay I've only had brief glimpses of them."

She shook her head. "Tis a shame, for all children are precious gifts. They are to be loved and cherished."

He looked at her with an odd smile. "The ton is not expected to love and cherish their illegitimate children, Miss MacLeod."

"I think the judge of a man's character is not if he merely

does what is expected of him, but if his actions far exceed what is required."

"With each breath you impugn my character." He gave a sad chuckle. "Perhaps I am no better than the devil."

Her gaze shifted uncomfortably from him. He was not the devil. He was perhaps a spoiled aristocrat who had suffered a lonely childhood. But he was not cruel, he was not evil.

"You should make an effort to see your children. They deserve at least a small portion of you. And as you say, you know well what it is to feel unwanted as a child. You could be a comfort to them." She pulled the blanket closer around her body. "Doubtless they will love you despite your worst faults. Children are very much like that. Their love is unconditional."

He did not answer her for what seemed a lifetime. He was perhaps considering her words, she did not know. In any case she doubted he would alter the course of his life even a little because of what she had said. And somewhere in the world two young souls would grow to be men and women always sensing that a large piece of them was missing. How easily he could solve it by giving them even the smallest drop of love. They would blossom on even the meagerest scrap of affection if he would but allow it.

"You are right of course. As always," he finally answered with a sad smile.

They fell into a silence again. And this time both seemed rather reluctant to break it. Their eyes drifted to the open sea. A sea that held no censure or comfort. They remained lost in their thoughts both wondering how the remainder of their time together would be.

Twenty-five more days... an eternity.

CHAPTER 8

"*D*o you play?"

Lenora looked up from her book of old English poetry. It was a heavy tome with a worn brown leather cover giving evidence to many handlings. It had certainly been someone's favorite.

Michael stood beside the pianoforte in the small library, whose shelves fair overflowed with worn books. The room was intimate and lived in. Small windows gave just enough light to see, but not so much to age the books.

Michael's fingers lightly caressed the polished wood. He had not looked at her when he had spoken his question.

"A little." She closed her book of poems in anticipation of what he would ask next. And in this case, he did not disappoint.

"Indulge me then." This time he did look at her. His face placid. She could not read his current mood.

Lenora rose from her seat, the soft silk of her rich pink gown gliding smoothly as she walked to the instrument. As he had promised, Michael had indeed ordered ten more gowns to replace the blue silk that at this very moment lay abandoned at the bottom of the rubbish heap. The pink silk was the first of the gowns to be delivered. To her dismay it appeared this gown was even lovelier than the one it was meant to replace.

Michael watched her now as he had for the past three days—reserved, a little irritated.

She sat down ignoring him. He had already placed music for her to play. Lenora squinted at the piece. She was a little familiar with it, a Hungarian Sonata. It was quite a difficult piece to play. She wondered if he knew this.

She was right—she played only a little. For some odd reason, Micheal found the discovery irritating. It should not have, after all she was human. There could not be an expectation of perfection. If anything, it served to make her seem just a little more mortal. And perhaps it was a good thing. He did grow rather weary of Lenora being perfect in every way.

She struck a wrong note, and her fingers hesitated. He watched her as she started again only to fumble.

"You're not very good," he commented dryly.

"No, I'm not, am I?" she smiled up at him and he frowned in response.

"Move," he commanded, taking a seat beside her when she shifted over on the bench. She made to rise and abdicate completely, but a hand on her arm told her he wanted her to remain there beside him. She gave him another one of her pitying smiles. He grumbled beneath his breath.

Lenora almost laughed, rather enjoying his misery. It "n a freeing existence these past three days without the constant threat of a bedding looming over her like a dark storm cloud. He had even refrained from kissing her, though she had not expected that. She did not mind his kisses after all.

Still, the result of her reprieve was remarkable. She felt so much more at ease with him now. And the continued sun, had even allowed her to take two walks through the surrounding country. The countryside was pleasant, teaming with life and greenery. There was nothing comparable to the joys of spring.

She had to admit—it was rather nice to have a room of her own. This reprieve had allowed her to enjoy the salon, dining room and even led to the discovery of this library.

It was true Chesterfield hadn't been the best company, but she still enjoyed him—at least when he forgot his deprivation. He was quite tolerable then and at times more than a little pleasant.

Lenora's mind suddenly stilled as the music finally seeped through her thoughts. It was beautiful. She turned to Michael as he gazed down at his fingers, he did not even glance at the music sheet.

He must have sensed her staring, for he turned to her, his fingers never pausing. They moved deftly over the keys, coaxing music from them like a tentative lover. She stared at his hands— strong, graceful, long-fingered.

Those were the hands that stroked her when they made love. Those very fingers caressed her skin, delved into secret places that unlocked mystifying sensations...

"Do you sing?" He asked with a voice that seemed far away.

She shook her head. "At least not as well as I play." A thought struck her. "Do you?"

"A little."

He seemed to consider her a moment. Then his gaze turned to the fire. She waited, and he did not disappoint. But more apparent was the fact that he sang more than a little. He sang beautifully. As beautiful as he looked.

She did not recognize the song though she had heard many in her time at the earl's home. The earl was fond of entertaining and apparently had many friends in connection to the theatre. But she had never heard this song.

She stared at Michael, letting the words seep into her brain. He looked like an angel just then. Beautiful and tempting. A fallen angel perhaps.

His beauty frightened her, she realized—because he tempted

her. Despite all she knew of him. Regardless that he was a rake, a libertine. Despite even knowing that he bought women for pleasure. Despite all of this and more, his attractiveness tempted her.

Michael finally sang the last of his song and moments later his fingers stilled. She remained beside him, gazing at him with undisguised awe.

A sudden look of confusion crossed her face and Lenora turned away. Michael reached for her chin, turning her face back to him. She allowed him, meeting his gaze with one less open than she had held moments before.

"What is it, Lenora?" His words were soft and beguiling. Michael sensed a sudden distress in her.

She shook her head, a slight movement.

He continued to stare at her. The moment painfully stretching until she could no longer bare it. Something needed to fill the silence. Some movement. Some word.

Lenora opened her mouth to speak.

"Madame? Mousier?"

They both turned in unison to Madame Louparet.

"Your dinner is ready, Monsieur, Madame." she announced with a generous smile. She was so very pleased that le monsieur had found himself such a good wife. She had worried for the boy throughout the years. He was a tender soul in such great need of love and affection. And it was so evident that he loved his young wife.

It was true that la Madame seemed a little serious at times. But perhaps in the end that was what he needed. She was no foolish girl taken to flights of fancy. No, she was intelligent and well grounded. Those facts were obvious. And how Madame Louparet rejoiced at her employer's good fortune.

. . .

DINNER WAS SERVED in the charming dining room Lenora had taken her first meal in. They were attended by Lorette and the madame herself. And Lenora enjoyed the casual atmosphere they created. It would have been lovely had this truly been her wedding trip. She liked the staff, and it saddened her that she should never see them again after this month.

"The cook has outdone herself again. A succulent roast duck and herb roasted potatoes."

Lenora smiled at the madame's announcement.

"I am certain it will be as delicious as everything else she has made thus far."

"Very smart Madame. I will tell her this exactly and you will be even more pleased on the morrow!" Madame Louparet beamed as she left the room.

Lenora looked to Michael to find him watching her.

"I think you have won yourself her eternal affections," he said with a raised brow.

"Yes, but I think her affections are easily won."

"I assure you they are not."

Lenora paused to study him. It was difficult to discern whether he jested or not.

"Is that to say she would not have treated any "wife" you brought home as kindly as she has treated me?"

Home? Had he brought her home? A small part of him tightened at the prospect. In truth this was a place close to his heart.

"She would have been kind. Respectful," he said with consideration. Madame Louparet had always been kind and respectful. The staff at his grandmother's cottage had in the very least been those two things. But... "She likes you."

"The feeling is mutual, I assure you." She hesitated before saying more. "Perhaps she senses that I am a kindred spirit. A woman more of her station."

"And what station is that?" he asked as he sliced into the tender meat with his knife.

"At heart, I'm a servant, sir."

"Sir? Really? This grows tiring." He huffed in frustration laying down his fork and knife. She mirrored his actions and waited for him to say more.

"Can you truly not say Michael? You're a clever woman, Lenora, and yet…"

"I sometimes forget," she answered quietly.

"Somehow I can't give credence to what you're saying."

She stared at him as he considered her, yet she did not speak.

She called him sir on purpose, he knew it. It was her way of distancing herself from him. He did not like it, and it would end. And just like that, he knew exactly what would end it.

"Then it's settled." He picked up his utensils again and sliced into his meal with relish.

"What is settled?" She asked with a worrisome grimace.

He chewed with enjoyment, savoring the roasted duck. It really was superb. He took time to swallow before speaking. "Your punishment."

"Punishment? Surely, you're joking." She shot him a sharp look. "Because I call you sir on occasion? That's hardly a punishable crime!"

"Crime? Perhaps not. One would have to be heartless if not foolish to consider your persistent blunder a crime. Yet you must be punished for being so obstinate. A man of my station can't accept such mulish attributes from a mistress."

"Mulish?" Her eyes opened wide as saucers. He was almost tempted to laugh.

"Therefore, each and every time you call me sir I will kiss you, Lenora. I will kiss you soundly and senselessly. I will kiss you until your mind is fair swimming with the feel of my tongue in your mouth. I will feast upon your mouth until you're near to swooning."

She did not know whether to scream or laugh and so she settled on staring at him as he enjoyed his dinner.

Until she swooned. How ridiculous. She had never swooned a day in her life—imagine!

She bit her lip, finally turning away from him. It was fortunate he could not see her body's response to his words. Her body desired him, reacted to him. Wanted him after such a brief introduction to passion.

"Utterly ridiculous," she muttered, picked up her knife and fork. The man would have his way. She would never call him sir again. Most certainly not!

She had expected him to assail her, besetting on her defenses by first light on the day after her reprieve. He however did not. And Lenora was curious to discover a little part of her was... hurt by his disregard. Still, she was mostly pleased for she had hardly slept a wink expecting an early morning tumble.

Michael had left her to sleep. With Lorette's help Lenora washed and dressed before heading to the dining room for breakfast.

"I believe Monsieur has gone for a ride Madame," came Madame Louparet's frank answer when Lenora questioned her. She did not appear too concerned and so Lenora took her meal alone.

It felt very odd to be alone. Sitting in the silent room, attended only by Louparet. Lenora felt almost lonely. She could not talk to the staff as she might have done at home. Though in truth, she did not speak to the staff there either. It came part in parcel with the position of governess. She was accustomed to existing in that twilight between stations. She was no stranger to being alone. So why did it bother her that Michael had gone riding without telling her? He was master of his own movements. He need not disclose to her where or when he was going. And yet...

Lenora was seated at the escritoire in the library languishing over a letter she was attempting without success to write to her mother when a sudden commotion in the front rooms alerted her to Michael's return.

Her stomach clenched at the sound of his approaching footsteps. She heard Madame Louparet speak in the hallway and heard his response followed by a robust laugh.

She did not get up, choosing instead to remain where she was. Though it distressed her more than she cared to admit that a mere instant of joy seized her at the notion of his return.

In moments he crossed the threshold. Michael scanned the room, immediately spotting Lenora at the escritoire. She looked up at him with her usual equanimity. And here he stood windblown and disheveled. No matter.

"Come, put on your cloak or whatever you have," he commanded with a brilliant smile.

"What for?" Lenora calmly put down her pen and turned her body toward him.

"I'm taking you into the village." He ran a hand through his already untamed curls.

Lenora did her best to control her breathing. He looked so glorious, so alive. She felt like a moth too close to the flame.

"I must finish this letter," she stammered turning back toward the desk. "I promised my mother I would write, and I've been remised."

She jumped when she felt his hand suddenly on her shoulder. She did not want to look at him. She knew somehow if she did something terrible would happen.

He reached for her chin turning her face to him. "Leave the letter until later, Lenora. The day is radiant. There will be time for writing letters later." His eyes were tender in their vibrancy. He smiled. "Come with me. I ask as your friend."

She could not let this happen, and yet she nodded to him despite herself. His smile widened in response and her stomach tightened. This could not happen. She would not fall in love with him. She would not!

THE DAY WAS INDEED AS radiant as he proclaimed. The sun shone brilliantly in the sky with not a hint of diminishing. The air was almost warm enough to go without her pelisse. Though the cloak did give her a sense of protection as she sat beside Chesterfield in the curricle.

He was in a good mood. He talked all the way to the village, of this and that. Things that caught his attention. The history of the area. It passed the time pleasantly.

The village center was prototypically French with its cobblestone streets, a square, a church, shops and three large inns. That is to say, it was quaint and picturesque.

Michael handed her down from the curricle at the Copthorne Coquelles Inn.

"Have you eaten already?"

"Yes," she nodded looking over the wooden structure. Little red flowers blossomed from flower boxes at each window. It was charming.

"Well, I myself am famished. You do not mind, do you?"

"No, of course not, sir–Michael." She took his proffered arm, and they entered the Inn.

The common room was bustling with activity, and though the genial innkeeper offered them a private salon, Michael told him they preferred to remain where it was livelier.

They were ushered to a table and the innkeeper's wife hurried forward with bread, cheese and dried fruit. It was apparent the proprietors knew whom they were serving, for no other patron seemed to get as much attention. Surprisingly Michael did not notice the disparity, but Lenora did. And she was grateful, for it allowed her to hold some resentment against him. She watched him as the innkeeper returned time and again to the table, bowing very genially. Michael sat back enjoying his meal and receiving their deference as if it were his due.

True, he did so without malice. But she could ill afford to be fair. She needed to hold on to her previous notions of him. She needed to fortify her defenses against him.

"What is it?" he gave her a questioning look before biting into warm fresh bread.

She shook her head, a little embarrassed to be caught in that particular train of thought. What could she say? I was merely thinking of how better to shield myself against your wiles.

Indeed not!

"The food here is really quite good. Though I would not have you repeating this to Cook."

"Heavens no. We would be relegated to porridge and dry bread for the rest of our stay."

"I wager you're quite correct." He chuckled, his eyes sparkling with vitality. Her spirits sank just a little lower.

After their meal they walked toward the shoemaker's shop. Michael wanted to see about getting a new pair of riding boots. Though she could not see why. The boots he had on were in better shape than her own.

"You need not come in with me. If you like there's a lady's shop just two doors down."

Lenora hesitated, looking in the direction he pointed. "Very well," she finally said, but he was already entering the shoe shop. She watched him disappear behind the door and waited a moment longer before heading to the lady's shop.

For a moment she considered waiting outside for him, but then she thought it foolish to not enter the store. After all, what was so frightening about the lady's shop?

The shop was pretty and rather small. Bobbles, lotions and perfumes lined the shelves. Fragrant soaps filled the shop with the scent of roses and jasmine. A plump woman in her middle years came from behind the counter with a brilliant smile.

"Madame, *bienvenue*."

"Oh, no, I'm just looking."

"You are English Madame," this said with a genial smile. "Then I have something *tres* special for you."

The woman beckoned to a front counter where she retrieved a black box.

"Really I am not looking to purchase…" Lenora's voice deserted her when she laid eyes on the necklace nestled beguilingly among rich green silk. It was a simple gold necklace with a diamond and ruby pendant, cleverly fashioned into a heart. It was charming.

"Please try it on, Madame. You will look so beautiful. It will sparkle against your lovely skin."

"Oh, I couldn't, really."

"Try it on, Lenora." She turned to the sound of Michael's voice. He strode into the shop carrying a package beneath his arm.

"I couldn't really."

"Don't be ridiculous." He turned to the shopkeeper. "She will try it on." The woman beamed with pleasure. Michael put down his package and lifted the necklace from its box. "Undo your cloak."

Though she hesitated, Lenora obeyed. Michael easily slipped the chain around her neck and fastened it.

"It is beautiful Madame!" The shop lady brought forth a handheld mirror and held it before Lenora.

It was divine. Lenora fingered the necklace tentatively. She had never owned a piece of jewelry in her life and the necklace looked like it was made for her.

"You do look beautiful."

She turned to Michael, a sense of uneasiness washing over her. Their eyes locked and she did not like what she saw.

"I can't afford it, sir."

"Consider it a gift."

"No, I can't accept any more from you," she shook her head in distress. "It would be too much."

"You already have my heart, Lenora. It is only fair that you wear it." He turned to the shopkeeper "We shall take it, for I think it suits my wife perfectly, do you not?"

"Oh yes, Monsieur. You are a most generous husband." The woman clapped her hands giving further evidence to her pleasure and approval.

Michael chuckled at the compliment. He paid the lady and Lenora inwardly groaned when she heard the woman's price.

"Is there anything else you desire from this lady's fine establishment, *mon cœur*?"

Michael placed a hand on her waist. Lenora merely shook her head. "Come, let's go home."

She remained silent, though her thoughts churned, as they retrieved the curricle. And even more surprising Michael did not press her to speak, but he remained quiet, though a devilish light shone in his eye.

She was considering the way he had looked at her when he told her she was beautiful. She was not, of course. She was hardly passably pretty. But he had appeared so earnest when he spoke. Perhaps it was the practiced art of a seducer at work. She was an idiot for wanting to believe him. And for a moment—she had. But she knew better. Reason won out.

She was lost in her thoughts when their curricle slowed, then stopped. Lenora looked around and they were as they say, "Miles from nowhere."

"Why have we stopped?"

"For two reasons really. First to give you this." He reached for the package he had picked up at the shoemakers and placed it on her lap. "Open it."

"But…"

"Open it," he commanded.

This time she obeyed without question. She untied the

leather string that held the brown package together and the paper fell away revealing two shining riding boots.

"For you."

She stared up at him, feeling as though her chest were being squeezed by invisible fingers.

"Michael, this is too much."

"A simple thank you would do, Lenora."

She stared at him, feeling a little contrite. Yes, she should simply thank him. She did not ask for any of the things he gave her. She should not feel guilty nor unworthy. But years of deprivation had trained her to believe herself undeserving. It was now a conviction nearly impossible to escape.

"Thank you," she whispered staring down at the boots on her lap.

"You're most welcomed," he answered with a gentle smile. Understanding at least a little of the discomfort she felt. She was not accustomed to receiving so many gifts, he was certain. And despite everything he gave her, it was still less than he was accustomed to giving his mistresses. Of course, their tastes tended to run toward the extravagant. A pair of boots and a simple necklace would have been entirely inadequate to any of his past lovers. But to Lenora they appeared to mean the world.

"And now to dole out your first punishment."

"Punishment? For what?" she looked at him in shock.

"'Punishment for what?' she says." He stared down at her in satisfaction. "You were never to call me sir and you, Lenora, you naughty girl, did just that."

"I did not call you sir. And this one does not count because I have to say the word sir to say I did not call you sir."

He looked at her in confusion before shaking his head. "No matter. You're to be punished for calling me sir when we were in the shop." He leaned forward, but she held up her hands against his chest in time to stop his movement.

"I did not call you sir in the shop."

"Yes, you did," he answered smugly.

"I did not!"

He smiled at her indulgently. "I shall replay for you the precise instance. First, I called you beautiful. To which you replied…" he cleared his throat. "'I can't afford it, sir.'"

Lenora nearly smiled at his falsetto voice.

"To which I then said, 'consider it a gift.'" He grinned in triumph as a look of uncertainly settled on Lenora's face. "So, you see…"

"Perhaps it is as you say."

"I assure you it is."

She considered him a moment. "But are we to do it here?"

"Kiss? Yes. I see no reason why not. No better time than the present and all that."

"But people might see us."

"Let them. A little scandal never hurt anyone."

"But…"

"Now, no more of this being contrary. Or I shall kiss you twice."

"No, once is enough."

"You'll find my kisses are never enough, love."

She gave a wry smile. "You think much of yourself, don't you?"

He matched her smile. "And it's high time you did too."

He leaned in and kissed her before she returned with a clever answer. Lenora no longer delayed but accepted her punishment valiantly.

In truth it took little valor to be kissed by Michael Chesterfield. Though she had never been kissed before, still she knew that the man held much skill in this arena. And his lips were soft, and his touch expert.

One hand cradled her head guiding her in the kiss. The other cupped one breast. His tongue dipped into her mouth, and it felt as if he were feasting on her. And there was little more she could do but surrender.

It seemed a lifetime before he released her. She blinked up at him forgetting for a moment where they were. She stared at him, and he gazed back at her.

"That was very lovely... sir," she blinked up with a slow smile.

"You little minx," Michael chuckled just before his lips fell back on hers once more.

She had never known what it was to be kissed senseless—until now.

CHAPTER 9

"*O*nce more."

"No, I can't. Please…" Lenora closed her eyes. She could feel the pounding of his heartbeat against her back. She felt too weak to even rise from the floor. And though the blaze of the fireplace should have kept her body warm, the fine sheen of perspiration which covered both their bodies made her shiver.

"I'm so tired."

He slowly moved behind her, rising to his knees. "What you do to me Lenora. You must be fae." He pulled her by the waist onto her knees and entered her from behind. Lenora released a soft moan.

She was slick and wet from their previous four rounds of lovemaking, allowing him to move effortlessly within her.

Her arms quivered as she braced herself against the force of his thrusts.

"You've enchanted me, my love." He leaned over her, gently kissing her shoulder. He held her to him, cupping one breast. He then moved slowly within her until all other sensations faded into oblivion.

His hand moved down to her curls and Lenora whimpered. She knew what would come and she was powerless to stop him. He easily found her center. The core that unleashed such unbridled wonder.

"No, please." The sensation was too much. She had already climaxed three times. Her body felt weak and boneless.

"Come for me, Lenora," he whispered. "My beautiful Lenora."

It was all too much and yet… and yet…

Lenora cried out her orgasm collapsing to the floor. She vaguely heard him cry out as he withdrew, spilling onto her buttocks. He then collapsed beside her.

She felt the heavy pull of sleep and prayed he would not rally again. As it was, she would be sore come morning.

LENORA OPENED her eyes to the sensation of a solitary finger tracing her features. Michael lay staring at her. A tender look on his face. He gave her a tired smiled. She attempted to return it but could only manage a slight shift of her lips.

"Lenora," he sighed. "What are you to do with me?"

She did not answer him. She was far too weak to even speak a word. Her eyes fluttered shut.

Michael shifted onto his back, turning his face away from her. Their bargain of a month 'n pure folly. It was just enough time for him to fall in love with her. All be damned, he should have insisted on a year. He could have gotten her out of his system in a year. It would have given him time to grow tired of her… perhaps.

He turned back to Lenora's lax form. Sleep had easily overtaken her. Her face was unguarded in repose. Lovely and innocent. And for a month she was his. He knew himself well enough to know he would not want to let her go at the end of their bargain.

Perhaps there was a way.

Michael rose, his body protesting against its abuse. He smiled benevolently. There were things worth a little discomfort. One of them lay serenely before the fireplace.

He entered the small bathing room and took a cloth from the cabinet. He turned on the water waiting for it to grow warmer. He passed the cloth under the spout until it was soaked. He then wrung out the excess liquid.

Lenora's eyes opened to the sensation of the warm cloth against her buttocks. She gave a protesting moan.

"Still yourself, woman," she heard him chide.

"Not again," she grumbled.

Michael chuckled at her protestation. "As odd as it may seem, there are some who rather enjoy my touch," he stated matter-of-factly. "There have been more than a few who have actually sought out my attentions." He gave her buttocks a soft slap when he was done cleaning her.

"Oh." Lenora turned to him. With his hair ruffled and his lids heavy, he made a lovely picture of a seducer. "I daresay none have received your charms quite so frequently as I." She punctuated her words with a yawn.

"You are most probably correct." Michael reached out a hand and pushed a stray curl from her face. "Does my touch please you, Lenora?"

He looked at her then and she nearly drowned under the weight of his gaze. Was it guile or truth that made such a simple look affect her so? Was he truly so practiced and clever that his current appearance of honesty was but a mask to hide nefarious intentions?

Lenora knew in that moment that she did not trust Michael Chesterfield. She knew he would hurt her. It was after all part and parcel with his station in life. Members of the upper class were always pandered to and therefore knew little else than taking.

No, she did not trust him.

"Your touch is pleasing," she finally answered. "But then I have no point of comparison."

Michael sighed. He had thought for a moment she would simply compliment him. But of course, this was Lenora. Yet, for some reason still a mystery to him, he sought her approval. Why should her esteem mean anything to him when he had little cared for anyone else's?

"Stay with me Lenora."

She blinked up at him, her ever-present frown once again reminding him of the governess. He chuckled.

"Stay with me past this month."

Her head shook even before she spoke. "No," she whispered.

"Think of it. I can offer you far more than my brother can. As my mistress I shall place you in your own townhouse. On a fashionable street."

"No."

"Think of the gowns, the parties—the admiration in every eye when you enter the room." God, he did not want to plead. "I'll treat you like a queen. Like a goddess on high."

"I will not be your whore." She turned away from him. Was he mad?

"Not my whore, Lenora. My mistress."

"They are one and the same."

"How can you say that? You know that is not so."

"It'll be over between us at the end of one month," she turned back to him. "It can't be more than it is."

"What if I were to offer you more money. Two thousand pounds. One more month." He saw her eyes waver. Perhaps. "Think what could be done with two thousand. You have brothers and sisters do you not? Think of their comforts. Think of all you could do for them."

Her frown deepened as she digested his words. *Two thousand pounds. One more month. Two thousand pounds. One more month*. Like a devilish incantation it whirled around in her head.

But no. She could not do it. Could she?

Such a sum was no laughing matter. Surely thirty more days would pass quickly. Had not the months of her life flown quickly thus far? Yet this month was taking an eternity already. Could she repeat it? For two thousand?

What of Suzie, and Mama. Mama 'n so sick with worry. They could buy a lovely cottage away in the country. With roses, pink and red. Edward could go to a proper school.

One more month on her back. A servant of the lowest order to a man of wealth and means. To be his plaything to discard when he grew weary of her.

No, she could not do it. Not even for Mama, Suzie and Edward. She couldn't risk anymore for her family. She was not strong enough to withstand him. Another month and she would be lost to him entirely.

"I don't want your money."

"You won't even consider another month."

She shook her head. "I can't."

"You can't or won't?" He frowned down at her.

"It does not matter," she whispered.

Michael stared at her. Anger building in his gut. He finally stood and walked away. "Damn you," he whispered fiercely. "Damn you!"

Lenora jumped at the sound of his fist impacting the wall. She reached for her gown, which lay crumpled on the floor. She raised her head to hear his mad laughter.

"I'm a fool." Michael laughed again cradling his hand. The skin had peeled back from his knuckles revealing raw flesh. It bled only a little, but it stung to high heaven.

Lenora watched him tentatively as he dressed. Once dressed Michael headed for the door. He stopped a moment to look at her.

"I shall be in the library if you need me. I would suggest you sleep," he added. "Lord knows I will be making good use of you. Our time together is limited after all."

He gave a wry smile, but beneath it his pain glowed raw. Lenora watched as he exited the room, closing the door quietly behind him.

She had to breathe, she told herself. Though each lung-full came out tremulously. The man was indeed mad. There could be no mistaking it. Such a reaction at her simple refusal to remain his lover!

Lenora rose, her fear giving her energy. She dressed in her nightgown and went to the bathroom to clean herself.

He had told her to rest. No doubt he planned to abuse her body more in retaliation for her snub. She gave a long-suffering sigh. This was the price of twelve hundred pounds.

Eighteen more nights and she was free. God help her until then.

Breathe.

Such a small act was nearly impossible. He had begged her, hadn't he? Idiot and fool that he was. And she had spurned him. The cold-blooded chit!

Michael poured out another glass of bourbon with trembling hands. Bloody hell, he had made a fool of himself! Think what his friends would have said if they had witnessed his defeat. Bile rose in his belly, and he wanted to vomit.

He had begged his brother's governess to be his mistress—like a common street urchin pleading for a coin. And she had thrown his plea back in his face like rotting garbage.

He had seen her face as he spoke, revulsion apparent in every line. Her cold dark eyes, hard as onyx. The set of her lips firm and unmoving. He had offered himself to her as he had never offered another woman, and she had spurned his vulnerable affections.

He had offered to pay for her to suffer his attentions. Two thousand pounds. A fortune for a girl such as she!

Michael stared into the fire, his eyes burning with agony.

In her lifetime she could never hope to earn two thousand pounds. And yet she refused him. She refused him!

He took a healthy swallow of his bourbon, relishing the warm path it traveled down to his belly. He planned to get good and drunk. Drunk enough to forget his folly.

He had offered himself to her and she had not wanted him. Michael groaned in misery. She had found him lacking, just as his mother's family had. And Miss MacLeod was a superior woman of expert understanding. If she found him lacking it was because he was so.

If she had found him wanting it was because she saw what he had tried all his life to deny. The Honorable Michael Chesterfield, half-brother to the Earl of Walpole was a man unclaimed, too dark for polite society and too fair for his brethren. Behind the money and comely appearance, he was a man unwanted. Belonging nowhere. Having no true value to the ton other than to fulfill a curiosity. And Lenora knew it. Damn her, but she knew it!

CHAPTER 10

*D*elicate clouds drifted softly against a sea of blue. The day was warm, and the air smelled of sweet spring.

Lenora made her way along the wooded path that led from the cottage's garden to a secluded lake on the property. Michael had gone into town not more than an hour ago and had not extended an invitation to her.

She had not expected him to. And she did not mind, truly she did not. After all, his absences always gave her time to reflect and to rest. She had at first planned to write that letter to her mother, a task she'd shamefully delayed since her arrival. Instead, she had gone for walk, the woods calling to her.

It was quiet in the countryside. The cottage was situated on a large property with no other homes in close proximity. It gave one a feeling of poetic loneliness.

To her surprise, she missed the children and the staff. Though her employment was trying, it gave her a sense of purpose. A thing being Chesterfield's mistress would never do. She did not understand how a woman could relegate herself to being no more than a man's lustful diversion. Certainly, the gowns, dresses and parties were nice. Each of the last ten gowns

Michael had ordered to replace her ruined one "n lovelier than the previous.

But to always be in wait. To always be vigilant for the brief few moments that a man might pay attention to you. Lenora shook her head. It was no life for her even if she could stomach it.

Lenora frowned. She had hurt Michael—she knew this now. Whatever fragile friendship they had developed had melted under the heat of her rejection. It surprised her to realize that she missed that friendship.

In the past few days, they had hardly spoken to each other. And the few times they made love it "n mostly in silence.

Lenora shouldn't have minded his inattention. If anything, she should have been grateful for the distance. But like the foolish woman she was, she instead felt she was failing miserably in her current role of courtesan.

She should make it right between her and Michael. It was clear she had the power to do so. She let out a heavy sigh. Yes— she would make it right.

The well-worn path bordered by high grass and wild geraniums dressed in pinks and purples finally opened to the lake. Lenora stood for a moment to catch her breath. Just beyond the lake a path winded through the trees leading out to the main road.

A flock of birds rose, did a pirouette and alighted once again in a distant oak. Lenora smiled. She took in a deep breath of clean warm air and closed her eyes. A person had so few opportunities in life to be truly still. To merely exist.

In this silence, this stillness of mind and body she could sense even the smallest part of nature at play. The hum of a dragonfly as it glided on the water. The feel of the barely perceptible breeze. The sound of a horse galloping in the distance.

Lenora blinked her eyes open and raised a hand to shield her eyes from the sun.

Movement on the road beyond caught her attention. It was Michael. He was returning from town on horseback. Lenora raised her arm to beckon him when a carriage rattled into view behind him. Michael turned to the carriage's driver signaling for the man to follow. He then led his mount onto the path toward the cottage.

Lenora lowered her extended arm, watching the procession with caution. They had visitors. She frowned at the prospect, biting her lower lip in worry. *Who could know they were here? Were they his friends? Neighbors perhaps?*

With a heavy spirit Lenora turned her steps back toward the cottage. Whoever they were, Lenora was certain these visitors would not be a pleasant addition to their already precarious situation.

LADY ISABELLA FOLLOWED Lord Frederick Warrick out of their hired carriage with a petulant frown. Chesterfield was already at the carriage door ready to hand the lady out. She smiled at him, that calculating smile that revealed nothing.

"You are a wicked, wicked boy, Misha," she pouted prettily, her blue eyes piercing into him. "To think you went into hiding, leaving Freddie and me to suffer those London bores."

"And yet you found me, Bella." He leaned in and kissed her hand.

She gave the cottage a once over that lasted all of a second, and her disapproval was clear. "It is not as though you are terribly clever dearest."

Michael smiled at that cutting remark, hiding as he always did the pain that such familiar disparagements caused him.

"As you say, I am not clever. I could never hide for long."

"But you are pretty," Isabella smiled indulgently. Chesterfield tilted his head, having long accepted his role as the ton's comely distraction.

"I say Misha, why this ghastly place," Lord Freddie raised a monocle to the cottage. "You're not turning introspective on us are you, old boy?"

"Of course not!" Isabella answered for him. "Imagine Misha thinking too deeply on a subject." The two of them laughed at him. And normally he would have joined him. But he hadn't been himself of late. So, he let them enjoy their joke on their own. They would hardly notice his silence.

"Come you two, I'll get you settled."

Perhaps it was a good thing that Bella and Freddie had come down, Michael thought to himself. He was growing quite weary of not being himself. Lenora was not gay company, and he was in a dearth of happiness of late.

"And drinking," Freddie suggested helpfully.

"Yes. And drinking."

Isabella took Michael's arm with a smile. "I've missed you, Misha. London is quite tiresome without you."

It was good to have his friends here, he thought as he led them into the cottage. Phillip had already taken hold of some of the bags and was currently bringing them inside.

Michael felt an immediate sense of normalcy. Perhaps they would stay for the remaining two weeks he had left with Lenora. And then he would ship her home and be rid of her forever.

LENORA ENTERED the little salon and immediately felt the invasion. A woman whose loveliness was breathtaking sat on the settee laughing at something Michael said. A portly blond-haired man with red cheeks held a bottle of claret in one hand and an empty glass in another.

"I say, Misha have Bella tell you of her most recent

conquest," the man with the claret spoke, his words already a little slurred.

"Pah, he doesn't want to hear about him."

"Don't be missish. A certain Major Colly. A military man!"

"A Major, Bella?" Michael gave her a teasing grin. "I never knew you had an affinity for the military."

"Oh, the man is tiring," the beauty spat out in distaste.

"Yes, he's a terrible bore. Consider this, the man has made his way in life entirely on his merit," the drinking man laughed.

"Too high in the instep for him are you, Bella?" Michael smiled at the woman indulgently.

Lenora frowned at this exchange. Imagine disparaging a man because he earned his successes rather than was born to them.

"Had I known you wished to follow the drum I would have bought a commission," Michael stated as he took a seat beside the raven-haired beauty. Lenora felt a tightness in her chest at the sight of the two of them together. They were fitting. A lovely pair.

She had perhaps made a subtle movement for the beauty's carnivorous attention was suddenly upon her. Her blue eyes fierce and assessing. The two women stared at each other for a long breath before Michael stood and came forward.

His smile was broad, but she knew him well enough to see the discomfort that roiled beneath.

"Lenora, there you are." He gazed down at her gown almost as if to check if she were presentable. He gave a barely perceptible nod and turned his attention back to their visitors. "Lady Isabella, Lord Fredrick, I'd like to present Miss Lenora MacLeod."

Lenora curtsied more out of habit than anything else. The others merely nodded.

Lady Isabella smiled cryptically as she took in the woman's appearance. She was plain. Quite mousy with easily forgettable features. The gown was of good quality though a tad uninspired. Her boots were muddy and her hair unadorned.

"Lenora MacLeod?" Isabella smiled in amusement. She cast a questioning look to Michael. Was he truly serious? This was the bit he was keeping secret.

"Yes." Michael stared back at her, daring her to say more.

Isabella's eyes widened. He was being a protective little bastard, wasn't he?

"Come here dear," Isabella held out her hand to the woman. "Come sit beside me. I want to learn all about you."

"Bella," Michael gave the simple warning.

Isabella blinked with huge eyes. "What?" She turned her attention to Lenora who had not move from her spot. "Come, sit." Isabella commanded.

Lenora gave Michael a look before complying. He gave no warning, and she did not wish to anger his friends. In any case, Lady Isabella did not seem a woman one easily dismissed.

The settee was small, forcing both women close together. Seeing them beside each other Michael immediately noticed Isabella's beauty easily eclipsed Lenora's. And perhaps that was precisely Isabella's purpose.

Michael reluctantly took a seat across from the women, not trusting his friends to behave. Freddie also looked at both women with interest. He no doubt understood Isabella was jealous of the plainer Lenora and there would be hell to pay for it. Freddie smiled in glee.

Though these two were his friends—in fact, his closest friends—seeing them now made Michael realize how very shallow and cruel they were. And what did that say of him? Was he not like them in many ways? Always seeking pleasure without regard to anything or anyone?

Michael turned his gaze to Freddie. His closest partner in mischief. Freddie was the son of Viscount Ruskin. A man who by all accounts, intended to live forever. He and Freddie "n good friends at Eton. Mainly because Freddie "n disliked by the other boys. Freddie had gravitated to him out of a lack of options and thus became a willing foil to all of Chesterfield's plans. Though he was unattractive and given to overindulgence in food and drink, he was easy natured and loved floating from one pleasure to the next. No doubt it was his dissolution that made his father too afraid to die and leave his only son his fortune.

Isabella was another story all together. She "n lovely since she was a child and had made a brilliant match at the tender age of seventeen to the second son of a duke.

She had thrived too. Despite her growing self-importance and too high opinion of herself she was invited to all the best ton parties. She and her husband appeared the toast of the town. The ultimate couple. But then the poor man had the temerity to die at the hands of her lover.

Though they thrived upon it, the ton did not forgive such scandals easily.

And so, Isabella was currently a bit of a pariah. Invited only to parties given by the *demi monde*. But as she often reminded Michael, those were the only truly enjoyable parties anyway.

"And how is it that you happened to meet our dear Misha, Miss MacLeod?"

Lenora looked to Michael.

"I'm afraid the circumstances surrounding our meeting will have to remain secret, Bella," Michael answered breezily.

"Secret," Freddie chuckled in the background.

Isabella wasn't fooled. Not for one moment. She glanced at Michael then turned to Freddie who was most assiduously getting foxed. "I always love a secret," she said to no one in particular.

Isabella turned to the silent woman beside her. "Do you not, Miss MacLeod?"

"I think all of us have our secrets." Lenora steadied her gaze on Isabella. The other woman shifted a little. "And are all vulnerable to discovery. But perhaps the answers we seek are far less interesting than those we wish to keep hidden."

Michael chuckled when Isabella's eyes widened. "Well said Lenora. As always."

"Well said," Freddie echoed with his own chuckle. He had blissfully slipped into that twilight of inebriation when all he could contribute to a conversation was an occasionally well-placed echo.

Isabella gave a chastising frown to Michael before turning a cheerful face back to Lenora.

"Miss MacLeod, I do believe you are a woman who merits further acquaintance. Fortunately, I plan to stay here as long as it takes to truly say I know you."

Lenora recognized a threat when she heard one. And she was not surprised. It was easy to take Lady Isabella's measure. She was a frightened young woman who believed little in herself. One became rather like an expert on the characters of the upper class when one served them. She was harmless Lenora believed. Unless she discovered Lenora's true identity. Then the lady could become a most bothersome plague.

CHAPTER 11

"*W*ho is she really?"

Though Isabella tried to infuse a sense of boredom into her question, Michael was not fooled. He was prepared for this.

"If I were to tell you such a delicate piece of information it would very likely find its way to her husband."

"Ah," Isabella smiled in triumph. Persistence was key when it came to the gentler sex. "A married woman." She rolled the words around in her tongue as if they were a succulent fruit. "That is dangerous business, Misha."

"I am well aware." Michael leaned against the mantel of the fireplace. His gaze resting on the hungry flames that wrapped tightly around the dried logs. The evening had turned cool, as it was wont to do even this late in spring. He wondered where Lenora was. Most likely in her bedroom. Dinner was not for another hour yet.

"I speak from experience of course." Isabella's words jolted him from his thoughts.

"Yes."

She was enjoying this and in some odd way it pleased him to give her this delight. Nothing made Isabella more content with her life than to see others head down the same destructive path she had traveled. Perhaps it made her feel less foolish.

"You cannot mean anything with this woman, Misha." Isabella had come up behind him. She wrapped her arms around his chest and laid her head on his back. Her touch did not bestow the comfort one would expect from such an embrace.

"She's so dreadfully plain—and dark." She gave a demonstrative shiver to emphasize her words.

Something tightened in him. His first instinct was to push her away. Instead, he did nothing. He would not let her know what Lenora meant to him. Isabella would only use the knowledge to destroy and pollute the tentative relationship he had with his mistress.

Mistress. If only it were that simple.

"What she lacks in beauty," he said in a familiar voice that at the moment sounded foreign to him, "she more than makes up in other... ways."

It tore at him to say something so foolish. Lenora deserved more than this. But what he did he did to protect her. Isabella's knowing chuckle did nothing to alleviate his guilt.

"I would not have expected it. She reminds me of a governess, or parson's daughter. But I know appearances can be deceiving."

Michael did not give an answer to this.

"Am I to assume that you are off limits for our visit?"

"I think that would be best." He moved away leaving Isabella to stand alone by the dancing fire.

She stared after him ignoring the beauty of the flames. Something had changed in him. A part of her panicked. Michael Chesterfield had become very much a part of her life. His beauty, charm and easy nature had served as a salve to her battered soul. True she had fallen from grace but what ton wife did not envy her friendship with Chesterfield?

She put on a smile and followed him to the seat he had taken.

"I've an idea, why do we not make an outing to Lille. It isn't so far from here, is it?"

"Perhaps a few hours."

"Yes, it would be lovely." She had barely placed down her bags and already Isabella was running off to the next amusement.

"Let's spend a night or two at that inn Sir Robert told us about—remember the one with the twins?"

Michael chuckled recalling Sir Robert's story. "A pair of amorous twin maids, so the story began."

"And a friendly Inn-wife, as I recall. One who liked to partake in opiates."

Michael frowned at this. *What would Lenora make of such a place? She would no doubt disapprove.* He already felt chastised, and she had yet to hear of this plan. A part of him wanted to slay the idea. A larger part of him than he wanted to admit.

"Let's go tomorrow, Misha. I'm, ripe for a distraction."

"Why not," he conceded. He would simply deal with Lenora on his own. In any case, it was time he started acting like the old Michael. In two weeks' time he would be bidding Lenora a fond adieu and would once again have to take up his old life. "Why bloody not!"

Isabella smiled and clapped her hands. She looked breathtaking then. The two of them stared at each other. Isabella's smile grew just a little. Perhaps the possibility of an assignation was not quite out of the question after all.

. . .

A MASS DEMONIC possession could have explained much of what Lenora was made to suffer that evening at supper. She stared out with cold eyes at the three fools before her. They laughed and jested with reckless abandon. Most of their jests centering on the meticulous aspersions of their acquaintances' characters.

They were not funny. But she could hardly tell them so. For one, they would not believe her and two, they would more than likely turn their venom on her.

Lenora was not one to suffer fools lightly. And lord in heaven did they cause her to suffer!

The main target for this evening's ribald remarks was a certain Major Colly whom from all accounts suffered from only one flaw and that was his unfortunate taste to fall in love with Lady Isabella.

Lenora's jaw tightened. *Had she thought Michael to be vain? He was nearly a saint compared to Lady Isabella.*

"The man is such a bore. What do I care that he was decorated for such and such battle. Truly, he disgusts me!"

"I find you quite charming my lady." Isabella let out a peal of laughter at Freddie's apparent impression of the Major. He spoke with a pronounced lisp which Lenora was not quite certain was part of the impression since Lord Fredrick was already quite drunk. "Perhaps I may call upon you?" He continued the impression.

"Oh, dear me Major," Isabella answered batting her eyelashes. "I would like nothing better than to be escorted about London by a penniless nobody. Perhaps I shall pray about it at church."

"You did not tell him you would pray!" This coming from Michael whom Lenora blamed the most for this farce.

"She did by Jove!" Freddie laughed until he coughed.

"Well done, Freddie!" Isabella mocked her choking friend. It seemed they weren't even safe from each other.

Freddie smiled sheepishly. "Nothing that a bit of wine will

not cure." He motioned to his glass and Phillip rushed forward to fill it yet again.

With added guests poor Phillip was thrust into the position of footman. After filling the man's glass, the boy went back to his position by the door. Shoulders back. Standing proudly like a sentry guarding the battalions.

All this for such a two who would never appreciate just how admirably he was performing his new task. Lenora turned her attention back to their guests when Lord Fredrick once again let out a chortle that was undoubtedly inappropriately timed.

A drunkard and a Jezebel. These were his friends.

He would not meet her gaze. Her disapproval was a palpable thing. Like a cold damp haze wrapping its tendrils around the room. There was no need to verify her irritation by looking at her. Michael gave a laugh at something Isabella said.

These were his friends—God help him, best of the bunch.

"We must not stay up too late if we're to make an early start on the morrow."

The little queen's words roused Lenora from her thoughts.

"We are to make a sojourn to Lille. I think it will be just the thing," Isabella explained in good humor.

"Just the thing." This from Freddie.

Damn but the man was already drunk! Michael sighed, his charismatic smile never dimming. "I think it will do us all a world of good. I for one look forward to making an escape however brief from this house."

"Poor, Misha. To have been trapped in the country without suitable company."

Michael's spirits plummeted. "What can you mean, Bella? I've had superior company." He hazarded a glance at Lenora. Her stare was as cold as ever. He raised his wine glass to her.

Well dash it all! It was not like he had insulted her.

"What do you presume Miss MacLeod thinks of your plan?

Do you think she approves of it?" Isabella's mouth turned down in a playful pout. Her eyes glittered in excitement.

She could well tell what Miss MacLeod thought of his plans? And by the way, when did the damnable plan become his?

"Lenora?" Michael turned to her. His smile as brilliant and practiced as it "n since his guests' first arrival.

"Will I be expected to join you?"

He blinked at her. "Yes." This one word spoken with no allowances for refusal.

Isabella eyed the two with greater interest. "Then my opinion is meritless. I shall do as expected."

Michael almost groaned aloud. Her words were precisely the wrong ones to have spoken.

"Do as expected?" Isabella looked from him to the silent Lenora. "What is she, your servant?"

Something like it, Lenora wanted to answer, but already she regretted her response to Michael. No sooner had the words sprung from her lips and she saw the ensuing glee in Lady Isabella's eyes then she realized her mistake. It was bad form for her to reveal even a small part of what lay between her and Michael. The woman would no doubt dig deeper and more relentlessly to uncover their true relationship.

Bad show, Lenora chastised herself.

"Your servant," Freddie repeated, seemingly to prolong her punishment.

"What is it between the two of you?" Isabella raised her wine glass to her lips, her eyes resting on Lenora then on Michael. "You are different with her," came her conclusion.

"Different?"

Isabella would not be fooled by his casual manner. After all she was not stupid. There was indeed something different between him and this MacLeod woman. They did not behave in the easy manner of lovers. Even now she noticed the little lines etched on the corners of his smile. Lines signifying unease. This was not Michael who sat before her.

Isabella turned back to the woman who was the undoubted cause of Michael's discomfort. She was as plain as before even with a new navy velvet gown. Her hair "n repaired by an expert hand, but still the woman was a little ugly if truth be told—and this was not jealousy speaking. Everyone knew Isabella was not a jealous woman.

This was not Michael's usual sort of woman. He preferred them a little plump and always gay. Certainly not ones so serious and unsmiling. What was it then with this one? Did she have a hold over him? Was it blackmail? Did she truly have a husband? Was her husband the key to all this madness? Or had Michael simply taken leave of his senses?

She turned back to Michael. A little annoyed that he was hiding something from her.

"Yes, different. And do not lie, Misha. I abhor liars."

No one mentioned that she herself was a liar.

"Yes, everything is different. You are different. She is different." Isabella turned to Lenora. "You are not his usual sort I must confess. He prefers his women pretty."

"Isabella!"

She had not expected to see such anger in his eyes. But it was good to see where he stood.

"Come now, Michael. I speak the truth do I not?"

Freddie stared from one to the other trying very hard to make heads or tails of the conversation.

"Enough Bella. No more from you this evening." Michael rose with a thunderous look. Isabella's heart quickened. Michael was beautiful true, but angry he was glorious!

"Lenora?" he extended his hand to his plain lover and the woman rose.

"Michael, sit down. Really." Isabella frowned. Did he truly intend on quitting them for the evening? What diversions could she hope to find now? Freddie mumbled something about roses to her right. "Can you not take a little teasing?"

"We shall see you in the morning." With that he quitted the dining room on Miss MacLeod's heels.

Isabella stared after them open mouthed. *What had happened? She had merely spoken her mind, and he had turned livid. And for what? A married blue stocking!*

"Had I but known we would have stayed in London."

"Then again marigolds have their advantages."

Isabella turned to Freddie in fatigue, "Lord Frederick, I suspect sanity is trying to catch you. But you appear to be outrunning her."

Freddie returned her tired look with a blissfully ignorant one of his own and Isabella's shoulders immediately fell at the impotence of her clever set down.

MICHAEL GAVE Lenora a furtive glance as he unbuttoned his vest. He had dressed well for dinner, but never before had he felt so... repulsive. And she had yet to say a word.

"Do you need help with the buttons?" He offered when he saw her struggle with her gown.

"Yes, please."

Like an eager child he was happy of be of service. Lord, did he feel terrible.

"Isabella is a vain woman," he offered in contrition.

"She is your friend."

The statement stung like an accusation.

"Yes, she is." Michael unfastened the remaining buttons of the velvet gown in silence. He stepped away when he was done to signal the completion of the task.

Lenora continued to undress, though her face was not quite as rigid as before. He was not fooled, however. He knew she was still very displeased with him.

"We need not go to Lille if that is your wish. Truth be told I hardly know why I agreed." He removed his cravat.

"I do not mind going."

He stared at her. She was slipping out of her chemise. Michael licked his parched lips as he watched her skin come into view. His heart raced just a little.

Sensing his gaze Lenora stopped in her movements and turned to him. He wanted her. Even with such a beauty in the house he wanted her. She did not understand why the realization should please her, but it did.

She let her chemise fall to the ground and stood waiting in her drawers and stockings. He came to her wordlessly, still dressed in his shirt and snug breeches.

There was so much he wanted to say. But he was not the most eloquent of men. There was one language in which he felt quite confident. Michael leaned in to kiss her. Lenora raised her face to accept his kiss.

The touch of their lips was at once familiar and surprising. It seemed almost as though a lifetime had passed since the last time he had touched her.

His hands caressed the soft skin of her shoulders. She made a small noise, and he found himself kissing her with more force. He needed more. He had to taste more of her!

His hands moved to her back then down to her buttocks where he lifted her. Lenora wrapped her arms around his neck and her legs about his waist. Their kiss deepened impossibly more.

This kiss was slow and meticulous. His tongue delving deep into her mouth.

She lost all sense of time. They had perhaps kissed for mere minutes or maybe lifetimes. It was difficult to tell. But suddenly he laid her gently onto her back.

"Lenora," he whispered her name.

He set a path of kisses down to her breasts. There he

lovingly worshiped them, suckling and kissing until her nipples were thrumming with energy.

His thumbs caught on the edges of her drawers, and he pulled. She raised her hips to aid him in their removal. In moments she lay only in her stockings. Lenora made a move to remove them.

"No," he stayed her hand. "Let them stay."

Lenora nodded then watched as he laid kisses down her belly. Her body could barely contain the energy flowing through it. Like electric heat it resonated within her.

Her back arched when his mouth finally found her center. Her mind warred between the wickedness of the act and the sheer pleasure of it. His mouth upon her nearly robbed her of coherent thought. Her body reacted on instinct lifting her hips to his hungry lips. He feasted on her, his tongue exploring every inch of her.

"Michael," she moaned his name, asking for more. Asking for completion. But somehow, she had lost the words. Her eyes flew open when he fell upon her bud. She moaned—a sound caught somewhere between pain and pleasure.

The sensation was at once overwhelming—yet not nearly enough.

"Yes," she panted. She felt the edges of her orgasm coming like the brilliant sunrise. "Yes," she encouraged him. Her hands cradled his head to her. His curls were so thick, so soft.

And then it struck. She cried out as the sensation burst through in one brilliant shocking moment. She felt as if she would tear through her skin and shatter into a million pieces. Her body froze as another wave crashed over her. She whimpered as starburst after starburst exploded behind her tightly shut lids.

Her body was shaken to its core.

It was long minutes before she settled back into herself. And then she was suddenly so tired. Her flesh felt like melted butter, boneless.

Michael lay beside her, his head resting on her shoulder and hand caressing her belly. She gave a little shiver at his touch and then sighed contently as he pulled her into his arms.

A moment like this should last forever, were her last words before sleep lulled her from consciousness. But had she merely thought them, or had she said them? That she could not remember nor had she the energy to try.

CHAPTER 12

*L*enora had never been in love with a man before. Unless one counted the fickle fancies of a six-year-old as love. Even now she could not remember the boy's face or name. All she recalled was that he had had the loveliest flaxen hair. And perhaps that alone had caused her to love him.

She had never minded her loveless state. Quite the opposite. She often felt grateful for it. She had seen and heard far too many sad tales of women falling to ruin over love. She had always counted her blessings to not be included in their number. And yet a fear now grew within her like a carefully cultivated flower, a fear that she was falling in love with Michael Chesterfield.

LENORA SHIFTED in her seat to get a better view of the passing countryside. She gazed out the carriage window in an effort to prevent her mind from thinking of him.

Little sheep blossomed like white flowers in the endless green meadows. They grazed peacefully never questioning the rightness of the world. To them the world was just as it should be, filled with never-ending meadows of green grass.

Lenora let fall a heavy sigh as the others chattered of things and people she did not know and probably never would. They laughed and made jokes that she did not understand. She felt like a being from another world that neither spoke the language nor understood human rituals.

The only anchor she had to this new world was him. And she could not tie herself to Chesterfield. If she dared to cling to him, she knew she would grow to love him and that was an imprudence that did not bear thinking. No, she would not cling to him. And if this caused her to drift aimlessly in a sea of strangeness, then so be it. She had always lived her life surrounded by unfriendly faces. How much more difficult would it be to deal with his friends?

Lenora had a sinking feeling it would prove difficult indeed.

THE TOWN of Lille was very much like Calais save perhaps in its size. It was larger by half and did not lie on the coast but instead bordered Belgium. It was also far more bustling and fashionable than Calais, Lenora realized as she blinked out at the passing Churches, buildings and shops. Her seat faced the rear and Michael sat to her side. Isabella had refused the seat for she suffered travel sickness most horribly when she faced backwards.

Lenora discovered that she also suffered travel sickness, but no one had asked her opinion on the matter and so she suffered in silence.

The carriage passed down the narrow cobblestone streets of Rue Neuve, flanked with an endless string of fashionable shops selling all manners of items from dishes to jewelry, to clothing, to furnishings for the home. It was all rather startling and very interesting. Their journey then led them down the even more gregarious Rue de Bethune.

There they stopped at a very fashionable inn. It was large in size and appeared very friendly. Michael ran in to inquire after rooms. He soon returned with a frown on his face.

"We shall try another inn," he simply stated as he re-entered the carriage.

"What other inn?" Isabella had protested. "This is precisely the inn Sir Robert spoke of."

"Precisely the inn," Freddie chimed in.

Michael gave him only the slightest of glances. "There's no room."

"Bloody hell there's no room. Let me out this instant!" Isabella made for the door and Michael grabbed her arm. She stared up at him in shock.

"I said there is no room. We shall move on." He tapped the roof, and the carriage lumbered on.

Isabella sat back in her seat—her eyes hooded. Lenora watched between the woman and Michael. What exactly had gone on? The inn was large. It had not appeared to be so overly full of patrons. And yet he had told them there was no room. It was evident Lady Isabella had set her sights on this precise inn.

The two remained silent. Isabella staring at Michael, and Michael staring at nothing.

The next inn was certainly not quite so fashionable, but Lenora liked it none the less. It was pretty, made all in dark wood with blooming flower boxes of reds and yellows at every window.

Isabella did not speak as a footman carried her bags to her room. The room was small, and very neat. But when one was in the mood for large and gay one did not appreciate small and neat.

"I hate it here," she stepped into Michael's room without preamble.

Michael had already removed his coat and vest. Isabella eyed his fine figure but refused to be distracted. She had come to say her piece and would not be veered from her goal. To think of him bringing them here when this was not the plan at all!

"Why don't we go back to the other inn," she came forward with her most beguiling smile. "It's far too quiet here—and besides, there's more fun to be had in the center of town."

A movement to her right drew Isabella's attention. It was the woman. A sudden thought came to her mind.

"Why not ask Lenora?" Isabella faced the girl. "Is this place not a horrid bore? I hear that the other inn promises the merriest of times."

Since Lenora 'n staring out the window at a blooming Oleander just moments before and thinking this place was very much like heaven, she could not share in Lady Isabella's desire to quit this inn.

"I find it rather lovely," she answered quietly and returned her attention out the window. Two little girls in matching blue frocks had run into the garden below. Their blond curls bouncing and gleaming in the sunlight. They sang what she assumed to be a nursery rhyme in French. Lenora smiled down at them. As if sensing her presence, the older child turned to the window. Seeing Lenora she waved, a brilliant smile on her face. Lenora waved back.

"What has happened to you?" She overheard Isabella continue. Since she had rendered an unpopular opinion and was now clearly to be ignored. Lenora did not mind.

"Nothing," came Michael's answer. Lenora wondered if Lady Isabella could hear the strain in his voice just as she could. She further wondered if Isabella could cajole him away from here. Could a bat of her lashes or a placement of her hand on his arm cause him to pack them all up and return to the other inn? Deep in her heart she prayed that the Lady could not. She hoped that Isabella did not possess such powers over Michael.

"Then why have you exiled us to this place?"

"Isabella, you are being ridiculous."

Michael continued to unpack as though she were an insignificant gnat. Isabella had half a mind to remove from this place, but what would be the use? The only one who would accompany her was Freddie.

Why was Michael behaving this way? Did he understand that her flight from London "n one taken with great urgency? She had flown to him for secour. And now it was clear he was determined to give her none.

Where were the gay times his presence always promised? Where was the surcease from worries that his friendship always brought? Had they departed with the introduction of that woman?

Isabella looked to Michael's lover. Lenora should have sensed her gaze, but she did not. Lenora instead continued to look out the window, a smile now on her face. This thing was Michael's lover? Michael Chesterfield, perhaps the most beautiful man she had ever laid eyes upon, was bedding this brown mouse. It made absolutely no sense.

Isabella would get to the bottom of this.

"Very well. Have it as you wish it Misha." Isabella took hold of her skirts and walked out of the room.

Michael watched after her, his unease increasing. Why had he not stopped at the first inn? There was nothing overtly offensive that he had seen. Save for the twins. He had taken one look at the two smiling serving girls and every detail of Sir Robert's bawdy tale came back to mind.

No, he would not destroy his two remaining weeks with Lenora just to please Isabella. He would make it up to the woman when they returned to London. But this time was sacred. He would protect it like a fragile treasure.

"Why does she call you Misha?"

Michael turned to Lenora. She had moved from the window and now stood on the other side of the bed.

"What was that?"

"Why does Lady Isabella call you Misha? She hardly ever calls you Michael." Lenora fingered the embroidered edges of the bed's ivory linen.

Michael watched her for a moment before answering. "My mother was half Russian. She always called me Misha when I was a boy. Misha is a pet name for Michael."

"Oh."

Michael smiled at her. It made him happy to share this information with her. She usually never asked him to share anything about his life.

"Do you prefer to be called Misha?" Lenora looked up at him with questioning eyes.

Michael froze for a moment considering what she was offering. Did he want her to call him Misha? Very few people did. Isabella only knew of the name because he had told her after one of their earlier times together. The combination of drinking and sexual release had made him positively chatty.

She had taken to the name because no one but the Earl of Walpole still called him that, not because she thought it particularly endearing.

"I think I would like that very much."

"Misha," she practiced the word, feeling out the sensation.

His breath had caught at that singular word. She spoke it with the very same softness his mother had. As if that one word was a delicate jewel.

He gazed at Lenora and tried to evoke all the gratitude he felt into his eyes.

Lenora bit her lower lip. Was she being jealous? She did not need to be she told herself. Michael's friendship with Lady Isabella was hardly her affair. After all, he had known her long before this month. And he would undoubtedly know her well after their time together had faded to a distant memory.

Then why did she suddenly feel that Michael was hers and that Isabella was the interloper? This was so very unlike her. Lenora had never been jealous of anyone. She had always been content with her life and possessions.

It was madness to wish to compete for Michael's affections. She frowned recalling each time Isabella had uttered his name. "Misha." Each one a slap to her face.

Lenora shook her head with a sigh. *This was ridiculous.*

"What is it?"

"Nothing," she answered quietly once again shaking her head.

"Don't allow Isabella to penetrate your defenses, Lenora," Michael spoke his words with gentle encouragement.

Lenora looked up at him. Isabella "n correct in her assessment, he was different.

"I'll try."

"And you'll succeed. I know you, Lenora. My little fortress."

She should have told him she was no fortress. The furthest thing from it, in fact. But she would try to bear up against Lady Isabella. What other choice did she have?

IT WAS STILL early afternoon when they had arrived in Lille. After getting settled they took a light refreshment in the common room where a few other of the Inn's patrons had gathered.

Lenora had expected Lady Isabella to pout for the remainder of the day, but the woman was instead gay and smiling. She chattered on with Michael as though they "n and would always be the very best of friends.

They had to take a drive to the ruins this afternoon. They simply must! This uttered with as much passion as all of her other proclamations. It was becoming increasingly difficult to discern just what precisely must be done and what could be gotten to if one had sufficient time.

The chatter went on incessantly through their brief meal. Lenora was fatigued by the woman's vociferousness. Yet, if she were to be truthful, she envied Lady Isabella's vitality. It grated her that she was being led to question her serious nature. It had served her well after all. But to laugh and smile with Michael with such unabashed ease would be pleasant. Their time together would benefit from this effortless rapport that the Lady seemed able to conjure up with everyone. Everyone save Lenora.

Their repast ended abruptly when Isabella complained—most becomingly of course—of the late hour. She bade them to hurry for their afternoon trip. And like good little soldiers they all obeyed.

"Well, it seems that Isabella has recovered her spirits. That is always a good sign."

Lenora did not answer Michael's assessment as he escorted her down to their waiting carriage. If he did not find it odd for a woman to go from misery one moment to the picture of gayety the next, who was she to complain?

THE RUINS of *l'Abbaye de les Anges*, Abby of the Angels, revealed themselves to be far more expansive than Lenora had assumed they would be. Yet in all other ways that mattered the monastery was very much as medieval ruins should be. Substantial enough to be of interest and yet in enough decline to invoke a sense of wistful romance.

The ruins had captured these feelings perfectly. And Lenora stood completely in its thrall.

A portion of a covered portico with carved stone pillars led to what was perhaps once a garden. It now stood wild and uncared for. A few other visitors dotted the monastery's ruins. Everyone spoke quietly as if hushed tones were expected for the fallen edifice.

L'Abbaye de les Anges or what was once the monastery stood on a bit of a rise, allowing visitors a mostly unobstructed view of the country.

They were surrounded by a hundred shades of green. From the deep pines full of ancient secrets to the bright almost yellow buds of new spring leaves.

The air was sufficiently cool and the unhindered sun sufficiently hot to declare the afternoon utterly perfect!

The four of them, Michael, Lenora, Isabella and Freddie had reached the highest portion of the ruins when Freddie complaining of side pains elegantly plopped his plump posterior on a bit of crumbling stair. The impact caused the stairs to disintegrate just a little more. This only added to the ruin's beauty.

"Go on without me," Freddie waved cheerfully though it was evident to all he was painfully out of breath. And not wishing to cause him further consternation, the trio indeed went on without him.

By chance or perhaps design Michael ended up sandwiched between the two women. Isabella to his right, bright and smiling. Lenora to his left quiet and reserved.

"I think ruins are just the thing, don't you?"

Lenora once again marveled at how Isabella was able to infuse just the proper amount of awe and reverence in such meaningless words. "Can you just imagine what it must have been?"

"Quite spectacular I would wager," Michael nodded. His eyes strayed to a well-dressed couple just ahead of them. The woman pointed to something in the distance. From the side view she looked rather pretty. The mustached man beside her chuckled. They seemed happy, he mused somewhat taken aback by the wistful tone of his thoughts. When had he ever looked at a couple with longing? Never was the answer.

"It's so lovely here," Isabella spoke gently as she looked to Michael. The tone of her voice called Lenora's attention to the woman. And for a moment Lenora thought she had a glimpse of the more serious woman beneath all that glamour. Isabella's eyes strayed to hers revealing something unguarded, something pained. But that moment was fleeting, for the lady suddenly frowned. Isabella appeared ruffled and quickly turned her attention to the surrounding country.

Isabella was quiet for a long moment and Lenora felt a little contrite about her earlier uncharitable thoughts toward the woman. Plain and simple she was behaving like a jealous lover. But as if sensing Lenora's charity and wishing to end it Lady Isabella spoke on.

"I daresay it's a lovely spot for a grand house. Seems a shame really to simply leave it as it is." She looked around her, eyes calculating. "Something on the order of Waverly would suite wonderfully." She turned to Lenora and Michael with a brilliant smile. "One would have to imagine these silly crumbling rocks gone, of course. But I do believe—"

"Oh, really!" Lenora huffed and deserted the two. *How much was a person supposed to take of such foolishness?*

"Lenora!" She heard Michael call, but she did not turn or slow her steps. His friends were as shallow and unfeeling as he was! No surprise there. Imagine looking at such beauty and thinking to ruin it with a "grand house".

"Lenora!" Damn it all to hell and back. Michael ran off after her.

Isabella watched with open mouth as Michael deserted her to chase after that woman. She looked around, making certain no one else had witnessed his desertion. She was positively livid, though good breeding prohibited her from revealing it in public.

She smoothed out her gown and pulled her back just a little straighter. The last order of business was a smile. Not too brilliant. No, just so. She continued on her walk. Alone.

If Isabella had ever been a person to closely examine her own feelings, she would have realized that what she felt most at the moment was relief. Lenora had come far too close to seeing what lay beneath her carefully constructed veneer. It would not have done to let her any closer.

"Lenora," was the only warning he gave her before he grabbed her arm and spun her to face him. "What is the matter with you?"

"I can't bare it. It's inhuman," she spoke, embarrassed to be so near tears.

Michael stared at her as though she had taken leave of her senses. And perhaps she had. But could one blame her?

"What can you not bare? What precisely is inhuman?"

"That woman," Lenora shook her head in indignation. "She just… she…"

"Shhhh, Lenora. Calm down," Michael pulled her into his arms chuckling. She tried to pull away from him. She did not find anything funny about this situation.

"Don't laugh at me!"

"I'm not laughing at you," his chuckle gainsaid his words.

She allowed him to hug her only because she did not wish to appear any more crazed than she already did.

"I don't like her Michael."

"I can see that. Your feelings are, as they say, as evident as the elephant in the room."

Their embrace had pushed her straw hat askew, and Michael carefully removed it. She gave only the minutest of protest but settled back in his arms.

"Do you wish me to send them home?" He offered—a little surprised that the thought did not lack some appeal.

"But she will know it's because of me." Why in heavens did that matter, Lenora could not say.

"I need not tell her."

Michael stroked his lover's back. He had not expected Lenora to stay so long in his embrace, most especially since they were out of doors and well within the sight of the other visitors.

This moment was pleasant in its simplicity. He was just a man giving comfort to the woman he cared for. And he tried to enjoy its sweetness. Truly he did. Despite a certain degree of trepidation of the inevitable rejection that always came in his dealings with Lenora.

"You won't have to tell her. She's a woman, she will know."

Michael chuckled again. This time Lenora looked up at him with a frown.

"What's so funny?"

"I had begun to wonder if anything on this earth could ruffle your well-placed feathers. I would never have guessed such a silly woman as Isabella could bring down the mighty Lenora."

"So, you admit she is silly," Lenora looked at him in triumph. With all he had said, this was her response.

Michael nodded with a sigh. "Yes, I admit she is silly... at times."

"And Lord Fredrick?" Lenora pulled away, watching him closely.

"Freddie, my dear, is a drunk."

"Yes, well... it's good you can admit this."

"I quite agree," he answered carefully. Michael shook his head and smiled.

Lenora stared at him uncertain.

"I never thought I would see the day. Isabella has you truly beaten."

"What!" Lenora stepped further away from him. Her beaten? By that vain creature!

"Admit it. Isabella has you running for the hills," his laughter had her seeing red. Michael sighed inwardly. She always looked her most beautiful when she was angry.

Lenora crossed her arms before her.

"She does not have me running for the hills," Lenora informed him in a most governess-like manner. "The thought is ridiculous."

Michael grinned.

"She has not bested me!"

"Perhaps a little," Michael chuckled. "Isabella is a formidable opponent I assure you. Your defeat was inevitable."

Michael smiled down at her unaware that the sun had taken that very moment to filter through the surrounding trees and drench him in golden light. He was breathtaking—like a fallen angel. Lenora froze, unable to speak. Unable to give any reply at all.

He was a beautiful creature, and it unnerved her. It had always irritated her in the past. But at least then she had cause to dislike him. He 'n arrogant and selfish. Now his beauty only made her feel that she should not be at his side, bargain or no. Someone lovelier should be here in her stead. Someone more fitting. Someone very much like Lady Isabella.

"You're teasing me now, I know it," she finally spoke quietly.

"Am I?" he batted his eyelashes. "Am I teasing you Lenora?"

Lenora smiled despite herself. "Yes, I believe you are teasing me." She took in a deep breath as she considered her course of action. She would be brave—after all, she was the one at his side, not Isabella. She would not be overwhelmed by the lady. "I am not beaten I assure you."

"No one would blame you for raising your white flag," Michael persisted despite her assurances.

"I am not beaten... Misha."

Michael's smile faded to a ghost of itself.

For a moment Lenora thought she had perhaps said something wrong. She was therefore surprised when he held out his hand to her and said, "You know I rather like it when you call me that."

Lenora nodded. She placed her own smaller hand into his waiting one.

They looked at each other as they so often seemed to do. What a very odd situation they found themselves in. They were lovers and strangers. Bound to each other by nothing greater than a bargain. In another time or place perhaps, they could have been more. But as with so many things in life, they would never know.

AT DINNER that evening the foursome were joined in the private dining room by a charming young American couple from Boston. They were very rich and thus had gained Isabella's immediate attention.

Angela Bennett was a pretty petite brunette with small features and soft heavy lidded doe eyes. She was in her early twenties, only two years younger than Lenora, though to the elder the distance between their ages felt as wide as the English Channel. She kept casting shy glances at Michael throughout the entire meal and one could hardly blame her. Poor dear.

Arthur Bennett was suitably in his early thirties. He was of average height. Handsome in that ordinary way that made him a little forgettable if one saw him only once or twice. He had a thick mustache and the loveliest brown eyes.

Dinner with the Bennetts proved to be a more than pleasant affair. The couple was very likeable, and Angela in particular "n groomed especially to please. She was the consummate hostess, never allowing the conversation to lag or become the least bit uncomfortable.

She had a surprising sense of humor which her husband appeared to adore. Lenora liked her immensely. They could have been friends in another lifetime she thought as the dessert was finally brought out.

"I think French food will be my downfall," Angela smiled as she brought a spoonful of the crème brûlée to her mouth. "But what a way to succumb!"

"I find the French are excellent chefs," Michael chimed in. "That is why I have a French cook at both my town home in London and country home."

"You have French chefs?" Angela directed her question at the most ignorant person at the table, clearly mistaking Lenora to be a fellow married woman.

Lenora gave a brief look to Michael before answering. If he said he had French chefs, he must.

"Yes." She brought a spoonful of the sweet dessert to her mouth but had trouble swallowing.

Angela beamed at Lenora. "I've told Arthur that we must get a French chef. Haven't I dear?"

"Constantly," her husband answered with an indulgent smile.

"Now he sees exactly what I've been talking about. He said so just this morning. Didn't you say so this morning?"

"I did. Just this very morning." Arthur winked at Lenora, and she found herself smiling.

"So, you see we should get one. Even Mr. Chesterfield thinks so, don't you Michael?"

"Yes, I do." Michael gave her a conspiratorial smile. Angela blushed most becomingly.

"I for one prefer Italian dishes far better," Isabella chimed in.

"Far better," Freddie echoed.

Good heavens he's drunk, Lenora and Michael thought in unison though they did not know it. Freddie, in fact, had gotten very drunk over the course of the evening.

"I find their dishes to be bolder and more filled with

passion," the sensual look in Isabella's eyes was enough to give everyone pause. "There is much to be said about passion. When it comes to cooking that is."

Angela looked at Isabella blinking. "I do like Italian too, I suppose." Ah the consummate hostess. "They make such delicious food," Angela added with a believable smile.

"My grandfather was Italian," Isabella continued a wicked light in her eye. "He was a nobleman from Florence."

"Really?" Angela's eyes brightened at this.

"Yes." Isabella gave a slow creeping smile. "He was found in bed shot by his much younger lover."

Angela stared at her. Michael frowned.

"That is hardly a tale to tell our new friends, Bella," Michael chided good-naturedly. Lenora could immediately sense the tension that radiated from him in waves like a crashing ocean.

Angela simply stared with large eyes at the smiling Isabella.

"And why not?" Isabella swirled her wine. It was rich burgundy close to the color of the gown Lenora now wore. "As I said, Italians are very passionate. I for one find grandpapa's colorful life quite inspirational."

"Inspirational," Freddie repeated. "I'd say."

"Freddie," Isabella cautioned too late.

"Her own husband found her in bed with her lover," he said by way of explanation. Michael shook his head. "As they say, apples and trees... falling and such..." Freddie mumbled a few more incoherent words before drifting off into silence.

The Bennetts sat frozen. No doubt shocked by this scandalous piece of information. Lenora felt an overwhelming sense of pity for Isabella. She made the mistake of allowing it to show when she turned to the lady. Isabella met her look of pity with one of rage.

"I think perhaps we had better—" Michael began when Isabella suddenly stood.

"Oh, shut up, Michael! Really!" She glared at Freddie who

was too incoherent to have the decency to look contrite. "Look at you."

Freddie, unable to follow even this simple instruction, looked at her instead. "Is dinner over? I say..."

"I think perhaps I should take Freddie to his room," she spat out through gritted teeth. She then took hold of him roughly by the arm, causing Lenora to feel concern for his safety. She looked to Michael, who was at the moment focused on Lady Isabella.

"Isabella," Michael said in warning.

"I say," Freddie repeated but allowed himself to be brought to his feet.

"If you're going to say anything it's best you say goodnight," Isabella warned.

"What say you to a little port later," he addressed Michael.

"I think you've had quite enough for the evening." Michael had never before felt such embarrassment at Freddie's behavior.

"Poppycock," Freddie smiled.

"Come along Freddie," Isabella pulled him behind her. "And we've had a truly lovely evening." She gave a saccharine smile to their hostess then gave brief glances first to Michael then Lenora.

Lenora leaned in toward Michael's ear to ask, "Is he going to be all right?" Michael shook his head as if to tell her she needn't worry about them. It did little to allay her fears.

"Well," Arthur finally spoke after the two had closed the door behind them.

Angela looked to her husband in obvious befuddlement.

"We still have two guests left dearest," he reminded her gently.

"Perhaps we too should be going," Michael offered elegantly.

"No," Angela seemed suddenly to break out of her daze. "Please do stay. Please." The look she gave them was so endearing that they obliged her by staying, though Isabella had achieved her end and poisoned the remainder of the evening. Dinner lasted only a half hour more. All topics of conversation paling in comparison to Isabella and Freddie's performances. Their acquaintanceship with the Bennetts was too new and far too shallow to sustain such a social debacle.

Michael finally excused himself and Lenora and the two headed for their room.

"THIS OR SOMETHING close to it was what I had hoped to avoid during our little holiday," Michael spoke as he tugged at his cravat. In his inattention he further knotted the silk causing him to struggle a little more.

"Here, let me help." Lenora approached him and aided with the cravat's removal.

He smiled to himself. They were behaving like a long-married couple. It disturbed him to realize he did not find the idea distasteful.

"What had you hoped to avoid?" Lenora gave him only the briefest glance as she devoted her attention to his cravat. How had he made such a mess of it?

"Whatever mischief Isabella was capable of brewing."

"It really was not so terrible." *It could have been much worse,* she thought to herself.

"I intend for us to leave tomorrow." Michael let out a deep frustrated breath. "If you do not mind, of course."

Lenora shook her head. From this proximity she could smell the sweetness of the wine on his breath. "You foolishly thought a more deserted inn would safeguard you from her mischief making?"

He chuckled. "You're quite right. What on earth could I be thinking? Isabella could find trouble in paradise."

Lenora made a move to step away when he took hold of her hands.

"I am sorry."

"What for?" Though she did not look up at him as she spoke, he could still discern a small frown on her face.

"For everything."

Lenora finally looked into his face. A face that for all the world was full of beauty and charm, but at that very moment showed much of his sadness. Melancholy seemed so very out of place on him.

"You have nothing to be sorry for, Misha," she said by way of comfort. "You've done nothing wrong."

Michael took in a deep breath, releasing it as he released her. "I should have let you go home that first day. Before I even took you."

She looked at him unable to keep the astonishment from her face. Whatever she had expected him to say it was not that.

"You could not have. We had a bargain."

"Bargain be dammed!" Michael turned away from her as he raked his hands through his hair. "I took advantage of you. Of your situation."

Lenora stared at him as if he had grown another head. *Where had all of this come from?* Their evening had not turned out as well as they had hoped, but the blame lay squarely on Isabella's shoulders. No one else's.

"How can you possibly think you took advantage of me when it was I who came to you?"

"I could have helped you. Without all of this," he answered honestly.

"And I would not have taken your charity. My pride would never have allowed it."

"So, you sold yourself to me," he turned to her, his confusion burning in his eyes. "Why me?"

She could not answer. She did not know what to tell him.

"Why me, Lenora?" His gaze unswerving as he posed the

question again. Lenora was forced to look down at her hands to escape those luminous eyes.

"I don't know," she whispered.

"Somehow I don't believe you."

They were silent for a long time. The emptiness between them filling up the room until it was nearly bursting with all the words unsaid.

"I…" she opened her mouth at last—not certain what to say next. He stared at her patiently almost as though he were willing to wait until the sun stopped burning in the heavens and the world and all its memory of life faded away. He would have stood there waiting for her to explain what she could not. What she did not wish to explain.

"Let me help you," he finally said with a pained grin. "You had a low opinion of me. Have, I should say. You thought that I would accept your bargain with the least amount of hesitancy."

She looked into his eyes and answered just a singular "Yes."

There was more she should have said. Something to qualify her answer. This she knew. Had she been merciful, she could have taken some of the sting from that one answer. Yet, despite her intentions, despite what she knew was fair and right, her mouth would not move to form even the simplest of words.

Michael smiled at her. A smile without mirth. He nodded. "You were right to have such a low opinion of me. Look at my set. If you needed a clearer assessment of my character, you need only look at the company I keep."

"Is that what this is all about?" She gave him a steady gaze. "Isabella's behavior has no reflection on you."

He chuckled again. "No reflection she says." He then gave her a steady gaze. "I'm not a fool Lenora. Isabella and Freddie are direct images of me. I could not look in a mirror and see a more accurate reflection of myself than when I gaze at those two."

Michael waited for her to say something. Preferably to

vehemently deny his statement. But Lenora did not. She merely clasped her hands before her and looked to the ground. This irritated him to no end.

"What? Nothing to say?"

"What do you wish me to say?"

"Where are all the judgments and aspersions I have grown accustomed to?"

She looked up at him. "I thought we were seeking to be friends."

"Friends?" He threw his hands in the air. "We can never be friends. You made that claim yourself." He approached her then and she took a step in retreat.

What did she think he intended? he wondered.

"What friends do you have Lenora? Tell me of them?" Michael knew he should not have asked such a vicious question. He knew she was a woman who kept to herself. There was no harm in that was there?

And yet, even as she stared at him like a beaten animal afraid of the next blow, he felt compelled to deal another.

"I grow weary of your judgments—of always fearing I won't say just the right thing. For all their faults Isabella and Freddie are my friends. They accept me as I am. You don't. You never have and most probably never will. When we return to Calais I'll send you home. Consider your debt paid."

She stared at him with such naked distress that he felt as large as a gnat. *This is what a man must feel like when he's beaten a puppy*, he thought.

"Why are you doing this?" finally came her words.

He turned away from her, not wanting to see the hurt he had caused. Why was he doing this indeed? Michael blew out a breath.

"It is what you want is it not? To go home?" he turned to her again, waiting for her response.

It took her long while to answer but when she finally

nodded his shoulders slumped. He knew at that moment that with all of his being he had wanted her to say no.

Of course, it would have made not the least bit of sense for her to wish to stay. Lenora was a good woman. Their situation was most certainly a grief to her. Try as he might, he could not fool himself into believing that she cared for him or that she even liked him. She tolerated him. Nothing more.

He groaned. He was so tired. Tired of this delicate dance that they performed together of hurt feelings and chilling judgments.

"Let us go to bed. I no longer have the patience to talk."

Lenora watched silently as Michael finished undressing. He did not so much as look at her, not even when he finally entered the bed.

He lay quietly under the covers before she herself began to undress. Some of the buttons of her gown were difficult to reach, but Lenora did not dare disturb him. She still reeled from the shock of the evening.

He was sending her home. Just like that. But what did she feel about this development? She was relieved certainly. She had served only a little more than half of her sentence. But if she were to say that relief was her only feeling she would be lying.

She felt hurt and a little rejected. Michael had rather part with his money than be forced to continue bedding her. It was because she was a cold unfeeling woman, unlike Isabella who had beauty, charm and passion. It was that last, she was certain, that was her greatest failing.

He had spoken his words without thought. She knew him well enough by now to know this. Did he regret them now as he lay there? Planned or unplanned, the words "n spoken, nevertheless.

It took far longer than ordinary to undress, but Lenora was relieved to finally get under the covers. The night had turned unseasonably cold. Or perhaps it was only their little room.

Somewhere in the distance, a feminine laugh rang out. It was rich and smoky. The sort of laugh that promised sensual pleasure. She would never laugh that way.

Lenora pressed her lips together. She would not cry. Not from self-pity, not from humiliation. She caught her breath refusing to give in. And yet the tears still streamed down unabated. She had never felt more miserable than she did at that very moment.

He was sending her home.

CHAPTER 13

*T*he next morning Lenora awoke alone in her bed and discovered nature had granted her a second of reprieve. And it was the first time in her life that Lenora had considered a womanly burden as a boon. The coming of her monthlies was both evidence that Michael had not given her a child and was a good excuse for them to refrain from future beddings. Especially when they were not in the best of circumstances.

MICHAEL STARED at the paper before him, not seeing a single word. Once again, he discovered himself to be an idiot. Always an idiot!

He could not believe he told her he would send her away. And why? Because in one moment of frustration and self-pity he had lashed out at her. Now she would be going the moment they returned to Calais.

Michael gritted his teeth. Why had he done that? Why? He took a deep breath, running his hand over his face.

The Innkeeper came to his table with a genial smile. He

offered breakfast and tea. Michael accepted both. He then sat in silence waiting until Isabella made her appearance. He did not wait long. She appeared a quarter of an hour later with dark circles rimming her normally bright eyes. She made her way to his table and sat without invitation.

"Up late again, Bella?"

"Go to hell, dearest." She gave a faint smile when the Innkeeper scurried forward to offer her breakfast. She took dry toast and very strong tea.

Michael waited for the man to move away before attempting further conversation.

"I've made arrangements to leave within the hour. I hope you're amiable to this plan."

"What does it matter?" This spoken with a Gaelic shrug.

Michael frowned in concern. This was not like her. He stared at her for the first time noticing the lines that creased her eyes and mouth. Isabella was still quite young and a very beautiful woman. But in that moment, she appeared worn and wasted.

"You look like the very devil. What happened to you?"

"I hope the tea is strong," Isabella stated instead of answering his question. "If there's anything I detest is weak tea in the morning."

Michael made no answer to this. He was not even certain a response was expected. Thus, the two sat silently until the Innkeeper returned with his breakfast and her tea and toast.

"How is it?" Michael finally asked after Isabella had taken the first sip of the hot brew.

"Excellent," Isabella sighed as she sank into her seat. "I feel at least partly human again."

Isabella looked up to see Michael staring at her. It was not an uncommon experience, though he usually wore that secret smile she liked. The smile that said all the world were fools save for the two of them. No, this morning his look was cold. Assessing. She found it unsettling and told him so.

"I won't lie to you Misha. I don't like this change in you. Not in the slightest."

"Change?" he raised his brow as though in complete ignorance of what she referred to.

"You know precisely what I mean. You're not that daft."

"That is to say that I am somewhat daft?"

"What on earth is the matter with you?" She stared at him in annoyance. "Is it that woman? Is she the one making you so... prickly?"

He smiled as he repeated the word. "Prickly?"

"If not prickly, then what?" Isabella challenged. "You're certainly not yourself. I've been saying so since we arrived."

"I'm quite aware of that and I'll thank you to stop."

Isabella sipped her tea, staring at him over the rim. They never battled before. Michael had always been so affable—a good sporting sort of fellow, they often said. But this... this stranger before her was not Michael.

"She's not married," Isabella made the statement as a fact not a question. "She does not act like a married woman. No, this woman is quite unattached."

Michael turned away and sighed. Isabella continued with a smile.

"I've thought upon it. Your relationship with her." She placed down her teacup and leaned back into her chair. "And it did not make the least bit of sense. Even after devoting hours to your situation... as any good friend should."

"I appreciate the effort, I assure you."

"And well you should." Isabella narrowed her eyes. "She has something over you. Some sort of sordid secret. Honestly Michael, if that is the case you are a bigger fool than I. For the woman seems hardly one to blackmail. But if she is, blackmailing you that is, you must tell me."

"What sort of sordid secret would I keep Bella? Everything sordid regarding me has been lain out for the entire world to see." He leaned back in his chair, almost in challenge. Daring her to unravel his secret.

Her frown deepened. A part of her was a little afraid she was losing him.

"I only mean to help. You needn't bite at me."

"I do not need your help. But if I should find myself in need of it in the future, I will be sure to ask for it."

"Why are you behaving this way?" her breath hitched, and she turned away in embarrassment.

Michael's gaze narrowed. *What game was she playing now? Isabella cried for no one.* She certainly would not cry for him.

"What are you at Bella?" He sighed leaning his chin on his hand. "Why this sudden show of emotion? You're also behaving very unlike yourself."

"Then we are a fine pair, the two of us."

Michael nodded not wishing to answer. He did not want to be like her he realized. It did not make him proud to think that until very recently he was.

"He asked me to marry him."

Michael's eyes narrowed. "Who?"

"Major Colley," she waved her hand impatiently. "Who else have I been speaking of?"

Michael frowned. He had never realized before just how irritating her condescension could be. Far more aggravating than Lenora's he concluded. *Why was that?* he wondered.

"Then marry the man. What do I care?"

"What do you care?!" She stared at him. "Really you are merciless this morning."

"Bella, I've met Colley. He's a good sort. Most women find him quite attractive. His only flaw is that he has earned his way in life. If you had any sense, you would see that he may just be your last and only hope of salvation."

"Do you not think I know that!" she spat back at him. "I am reduced to relying on a commoner for any semblance of respectability," she cried out in obvious distress. "But I cannot marry him!"

"Then don't marry him. Continue your life as you are." Somehow his words did not bolster her spirits but did quite the opposite. Michael continued. He was unaware of the disastrous effect his words were having. "You're still beautiful, Bella. In time there may be other offers."

She gave a bitter laugh. "Are you consoling me, Michael?"

He did not answer her.

"A fine pair we are indeed." She sighed, staring at her half-finished cup of tea. "Should I accept Colley's offer, Michael?"

He looked at her prepared to tell her just what she wanted to hear. But then he thought better and spoke the truth.

"Yes, you should."

She made no response for what seemed an eternity. She merely nodded in silence. "And you?" she finally asked looking up at him. "Are you in love with this woman?"

It surprised him to no end that Isabella would ask that question. He for all the world did not want to think of the answer.

"You are in love with her," Isabella stared at him amused. Michael shifted uncomfortably in his seat. "How very common."

"Perhaps I am more common than you and I both realized," he said with very little feeling.

"If that is a reference to the color of your skin…"

"I did not say so."

"I never had a problem with your… heritage."

Michael smiled. How kind of her. Isabella frowned at his response.

"I blame her for this."

"Who? Lenora?"

"I came to you for help Michael." Isabella leaned forward a

gleam suddenly in her eye. "You were to talk sense to me—not fall head over heels like some simpering schoolboy."

"Me? Talk sense to you?"

"Yes!" She rolled her eyes in irritation. "For heaven's sake, I hardly expected you to be pining in the country after some brown mouse."

"Have a care," he warned.

"I mean brown as in her essence! Her dullness. Michael in love. Hah!"

"I think this *tête a tête* has reached its end," he said with some measure of irritation.

Isabella looked frantic for a moment. "No, I am sorry." She rose and approached his side of the table. "I am so very sorry." Michael watched as she knelt placing her head against his arm.

"Perhaps we could marry. Is that not a thought?" She gave a little desperate laugh.

"That is a thought. We would kill each other within the month."

She frowned at his joke. "We would get along far better than that. I've always thought so."

"You can't be serious, Bella?" Michael looked at her. She was serious! "Bella," he chided reaching for her. She pulled away rising.

"You're probably correct. It was folly to think of marrying you. Imagine us as man and wife."

Michael knew he had hurt her feelings though he had not meant to. But really the thought of them marrying was ridiculous. Two vain peacocks in one house were two too many.

Add to that the fact that he would never trust her. He had seen how she behaved with men. He was certain she had deep contempt for them. She had already proven herself to be faithless. Could he fool himself into thinking that she would be any truer to him than she "n to her husband?

"Not folly, Bella. Simply impossible."

Isabella rose to her feet and returned to her seat. In those few seconds she had once again donned the carefree air she wore just as comfortably as Lenora wore her reserve.

"Do you plan on offering for your Lenora?"

"She will not have me."

"She has some sense. She knows you are too good for her."

"No. Quite the opposite. She is too good for me."

Isabella frowned. *Imagine that mouse too good for him! She most likely had told him so. And Michael like a fool believed her!*

"Be ready to depart within the hour," Michael suddenly rose to his feet.

Isabella opened her mouth to say something but appeared to think better of it. In the end she sent him on his way with a frosty, "Do tell Miss MacLeod I said congratulations."

"For what exactly?"

"For besting me, of course."

Michael did not know how he knew but with a sudden clarity that occurs so rarely in one's life he knew that his friendship with Isabella had come to its inevitable end. He was sorry for it. But as with all things in life, that which has a beginning must also have an end.

"I shall."

Isabella did not watch him leave the dining room. She was too miserable to care.

*How had it come to this? They 'n such a good trio she Michael and Freddie. Now Freddie was constantly foxed. Michael was in love with a plain mouse—*and she? Isabella spat out a curse. *And she was to marry a one Major Colley.*

CHESTERFIELD ENTERED their room to find Lenora diligently preparing for their departure. He smiled to himself as he watched his constant and always efficient Miss MacLeod.

She turned to him with a tentative, "Good morning."

"Good morning," he returned and gently added, "I hope you slept well."

"Yes, thank you."

They remained quiet for a moment as she continued gathering her things.

"Lenora," he began then did not seem to know where to go from there.

She stopped moving and turned to him expectantly.

"I must apologize for my abominable behavior last night. I had no right to speak to you as I did."

Her silence didn't make it any easier for him to continue. But he knew he must.

"You're of course free of our bargain. Consider your debt paid," he said when she threatened to speak. "There is nothing left to account for between us. Is that clear?"

She nodded slowly.

"Good." Michael cleared his throat. Now came the difficult part. "I ask only for one thing if I may."

"You may ask," she spoke cautiously.

"I had somehow hoped that our last time together would be memorable... for the both of us that is."

She waited for him to say more. He appeared hesitant but did not disappoint.

"I would ask that you grant me one last time."

"But I can't..."

"Oh..."

"I mean to say... it's only that my... monthlies..." Her words drifted away, and she could no longer meet his eyes.

"Oh, of course. We can certainly wait..." He hurried forward to assure her.

"Then am I to stay until... I am ready?"

"If you're willing," he gave a cautious smile. "I hardly think I could get you to come back if I tried." Then his smile disappeared just as quickly as it had appeared. "I know I ask much of you. I've no right after all the things I've said. But you know I am a selfish man and so I ask for one last time together before you go."

She thought over what he asked. She did not mind staying to grant him one last time. In fact, it seemed only right. But this meant she had five more days left. That would bring her time with Michael to just over three weeks.

"Very well," she answered. "I'll stay a little longer."

"Thank you, Lenora."

She nodded, surprised at the relief she suddenly felt.

CHAPTER 14

*E*ndless countryside.

Fields, huts, villages, cows, sheep, then fields again. Like a colloquial miasma that would never end, France's countryside stretched out in all directions. Surrounding them with its quintessential charm. She was sick of it!

The carriage rolled onward, and Isabella's mood became blacker with every mile they covered.

Freddie released a snore as his head fell once again to her shoulder. She carelessly shoved him away. He came awake for a moment when his head clanked against the side of the carriage.

"Bella!" Michael gave her a dark look.

Freddie looked around in confusion. "Are we there yet old boy?"

"Not quite," Michael answered with a frown. He was looking at her as he spoke. Isabella returned his look with one even angrier. He was first to look away.

She smiled in triumph though she did not know why. Because her life was an utter misery.

She reflected on the evening before. It "n a disaster, almost from the very beginning. It was good that she and Freddie had left dinner early, she thought as she stared blindly out the carriage window. Freddie and she had talked in her room and drank wine until the early morning hours.

To both their surprises Freddie had suddenly leaned in and kissed her. Stammering out some drunken declaration of eternal admiration. For one moment—less than a moment really—Isabella had considered marrying Freddie.

But that "n only momentary insanity and with a gentle push she had seen him out her door. He had forgotten the incident in all likelihood. Which was really for the best.

It was not that she did not care for Freddie in her own way; it was that she did not respect him. And knowing herself, she would quickly grow to resent him and in the end she would be cruel. And Isabella did not want to be cruel to a man who "n her friend when others had not.

In any case, Freddie was a hopeless drunk. And if a woman had any hopes of wedded happiness, the last thing she needed was to marry a drunk!

More countryside. More sheep. How was it possible? One would think there was only a finite amount of such things in the world.

Her eyes turned to the graying skies above. At least it had not rained. There was hope yet the storm would hold off until Calais.

Isabella thought about her coming life. She would marry the Major, certainly. After all he had respectability and lord in heaven was she tired of being so unrespectable. She had suffered enough, had she not?

She turned to Lenora for the first time since first entering the carriage. The woman stared silently out of the window, as she had for the last hour. Isabella knew this despite never turning an eye toward her.

She was not pretty, not even by the farthest stretch of the imagination. She had forgettable features. And yet she entranced Michael.

She was also cold and spoke very little. *How had Michael come to be with this woman? How had he taken such leave of his senses?* Could she let him make a fool of himself with this mouse?

Freddie's head plopped once again on her shoulder. Perhaps it was the thoughts that plagued her or the terrible headache she had developed. She would never know what led to the terrible string of incidents that culminated in the most dreadful day of her life.

It began when she pushed Freddie away... again.

"Damn it Freddie, you blasted drunkard!"

"Bella," Michael chided again.

It really was too much! Couldn't he see what a nuisance Freddie was making of himself?

"Do not speak to me. Speak to him. He is the one who got bloody drunk last night." She stared at Freddie as he blinked at them in confusion. "Look at you, you are repulsive!"

"Bella, what the hell is the matter with you?" Michael growled in annoyance.

"The matter with me? Nothing is the matter with me." Isabella realized that Lenora was now staring at her with that bloody awful judgmental look. "I am as I've always been. It is you and Freddie who are different."

"Me?" Freddie looked at her and belched.

"Freddie," Michael frowned at his friend.

"Always with a bottle in his hand this one." Isabella pointed to Lord Frederick. "What once was slightly amusing has long turned insufferable."

Michael could not answer to this. It was true; Freddie had long passed the line of what was acceptable drunkenness even for the demi monde.

"And you..." Isabella turned her eyes on him.

"Have a care," came Michael's warning.

"I mean look at her!" Isabella turned to Lenora. "Have you lost your wits? She is ugly, Misha. Plain and—" Her words were cut short as the left side of her face exploded in pain. She raised her hands to her lips, a look at her fingertips showed she was bleeding.

Lenora looked from Michael to Isabella in horror. She had never seen Michael cause physical harm to anyone before. And for him to have struck a woman was beyond belief. She had it in mind to tell him so until Isabella laughed at the look on her face.

"It will not change what she is," Isabella continued. "She is rubbish. Less than nothing."

"Isabella, damned you, shut that mouth of yours!" Michael was well and truly angry which only seemed to feed Isabella's fervor.

"I'll not shut my mouth!" Isabella screeched. "I'll not shut my mouth!"

The mad woman suddenly spat at Lenora, and Michael was powerless to stop it.

"Have you lost your senses?"

Then in one moment two things happened. Michael pounded on the carriage's roof and Lenora launched herself at Lady Isabella. The women screamed and slapped at each other even after the carriage had rolled to a stop. Though Michael called for Freddie to help him separate the two, Freddie could do little more than look on in bewilderment.

The driver was called upon to help him disengage the women, though Lenora seemed singularly focused on retaining a hold of Isabella's hair. In the end Lenora was forced to release the lady though she did come away with quite a sizeable chunk of rich auburn hair.

Isabella was immediately put out of the carriage as she was considered the more volatile of the two. Though Michael considered briefly that Lenora had proven to have perhaps more than a bit of fire in her as well. In the end he decided to deal with Isabella first.

Michael walked her a distance away from the carriage as the two argued.

Lenora could not hear most of what was said but she did see that Michael had to prevent Isabella more than once from laying a blow on him.

She looked down at her dress. Another one ruined. The lace trimming around the collar had come undone. A blood stain decorated her right breast. The gown was completely wrinkled, and she was certain her hair was an utter mess.

She felt wonderful!

Lenora had never fought another person in her life. And until that very moment she would never have condoned such savage behavior. But she could not regret what she had done, at least not when the feeling was so exhilarating! She was even now quite tempted to exit the carriage and resume the battle. She hadn't realized just how badly she wanted to thrash Lady Isabella until the woman spat at her. All rational thought had evaporated in that very second and a primal rage had replaced it.

Lord Freddie let out a loud snore from across the carriage. The man had fallen asleep, his head thrown back and his mouth wide open. He would wake with a dunce of a sore neck. She considered changing his position, but she did not want to risk waking him. She preferred him asleep just then.

Lenora looked out the window once again. The two were no longer yelling. *A shame.* She would have liked nothing better than to go defend Michael's honor. But she realized she could not, Michael had set their driver to guard the door. Lenora was a little proud that he felt the need to do so.

"What has come over you? Have you taken leave of your senses?" He seemed to be asking for the hundredth time.

"I do not like her!"

"It does not matter what your feelings are concerning Lenora. I've told you before. She is my concern, not yours."

Michael stared down at her relieved that Isabella had lost a good part of her rage.

"Perhaps if we could talk, just the two of us," Isabella was now pleading. "You would see sense. For you have clearly lost yours. Of that I am convinced Misha. It's the only thing I can credit this foolish affair to."

"No, Bella. The time for talking is past."

"What are you saying Misha?" Her eyes searched his.

"Our friendship, it is over."

"Misha," she stared at him in shock. "You can't mean this. You can't mean to let this come between us?"

Her eyes were suddenly glassy, and he saw her heartbreak at losing him. But she had not loved him, of this he was certain. Then why all this?

"Bella don't cry over me," he frowned, irritated that she should feel such emotion. Irritated that it truly hurt him to see her thus wounded. "I am not worth even a moment of sorrow. You can't possibly care for me so much. You can't love me."

"But I could, I know I could if I but tried."

He watched in heartache as a tear streamed down her cheek. She looked remarkably young just then. So fragile and so afraid.

"I don't want you to try to love me." Michael took her into his arms. Her body began shaking in earnest. How could he have guessed Isabella would take their parting this way? "You must forget me, Bella."

"But perhaps it could be…"

"No, Bella," he said as he pulled away from her. He looked down at her stricken face determined to make her see, to make her understand. He spoke sternly when he spoke again, like a grown-up trying to show sense to a stubborn child. "There was nothing deep between us. There was never love. We were friends. The only thing we shared was our common selfishness."

"If we but tried, Misha. I can change…"

"No, Bella. No."

"You bastard," she spat out, eyes brimming with rage—or pain, he could not tell. She pushed him away from her. "This is ridiculous," she said as she brusquely wiped the tears from her cheeks.

"I am sorry," he offered though he knew she was in no mood to hear it.

"I'm sick of looking at you. Sick of being here. I wish to go home," she turned on her heels with the intention of returning to the carriage.

Michael quickly grabbed her by the arm. "Then you must promise to behave yourself or you'll be put from the carriage and left to your own devices."

"You would not!" The haughty look she gave him was proof that Isabella was regaining control of herself.

Michael suddenly felt very tired. "I would."

She stared at him, and he swore he had never seen such pure hate from a woman. Yes, he had seen anger. He seemed lately quite adept at causing anger in women, but the look on Isabella's face just then truly saddened him. Whatever his desires he had not wanted their friendship to end this way. Not with her hating him. But she did.

"You needn't worry. Freddie and I will not even stay the night. We'll find lodging at a village inn."

He wanted to say that there was no need, but he thought it was most likely for the best if Isabella did not stay. Even if it were for only one night.

"We will only stop at the cottage long enough to gather the remainder of our bags," she informed him.

He nodded in reply.

"I am sorry we could not end this better," he told her as they headed back for the carriage. She did not answer so he continued. "I wish you only the best Bella. Truly I do."

"And I for one pray she breaks your heart."

It was Michael's turn not to answer. Isabella could not know that her prayers had already been answered.

He refused to believe the evidence in front of him and so he tried the lever again. It would not budge.

Michael knocked on the carriage window with some irritation.

"Lenora, open the door please."

No answer. Michael glanced at Isabella who wore a satisfied expression much like a child who knew their sibling was on the verge of suffering grave consequences.

Michael gave the window another tap.

"Lenora?"

This time her face did appear in the window, she looked like a wild woman, her hat long gone, and her hair sticking out at odd angles. She had a scratch on her cheek. For a brief moment his anger flared up. Isabella had hurt her. If he were not already getting rid of the woman, he would certainly have made her account for hurting Lenora.

"Perhaps we had better walk home," Isabella offered with a wry smile.

"Shut up, Bella," he said it so calmly one would think they heard him incorrectly.

Isabella blinked up at him, malice apparent on her face. She had not heard him incorrectly.

He turned his attention back to Lenora who stared down at them from the window.

"Lenora, please unlock the carriage door."

"No." Lenora felt no shame regarding her refusal. Only peace.

As for Michael, her answer startled him. For a moment he

did not know what to say. Isabella's sudden laughter called him from his shock.

"What do you mean 'no'?" Was this his sensible, always practical Lenora?

"I'll not ride in this carriage with that woman," Lenora offered up her simple explanation. Michael was baffled. On the one hand, he felt very much like cheering her on. Bravo Lenora, he wanted to say. It was good that she showed some spirit. But on the other hand, this left him in a rather awkward position. How would they get home? The trip had not turned out even close to what he had hoped for, and he was beyond ready to see it come to its conclusion. He would simply have to appeal to her better senses.

"What would you have me do, Lenora, let her walk home?"

"Yes, I think I rather like that idea."

So much for her better senses.

"Dash it all, you know I can't do that!" Michael raked his hand over his curls.

Lenora sat back in her seat, feeling rather calm despite this afternoon's bout of fisty cuffs. She made up her mind; she would no longer suffer Lady Isabella's insolence nor her presence. In fact, she would like nothing better than to see the lady walk home.

With that she wiggled her rump in order to get good and comfortable. They were likely going to be here a while.

Michael panicked when her face disappeared from the window. "Lenora, please. Lenora?"

Lenora frowned inside the carriage. She did not like being a bother to Michael. It was only that she would go mad if forced to ride in the carriage with that woman.

Michael waited for some sign of good sense to come from Lenora. Heaven knew he could expect nothing from Isabella.

"We can't stand here all day," Isabella spat out with some irritation.

Michael gave her a black look that appeared to do the trick. Isabella turned her back to him and continued to fume in silence. If he could, he would have switched the women and plucked Lenora from the carriage and replace her with Isabella.

The idea had merit. The only question remaining was would Lenora go along with it?

"Lenora, can you hear me?"

A muffled, "yes." Answered his call.

"What say you open the door–?"

"No."

Michael gritted his teeth. "You have not heard the rest of it, *mon cœure*." He took a deep calming breath. "What say you open the door and come out? Then Lady Isabella may enter, and I'll send the carriage ahead without us."

Michael noticed that Isabella had turned to stare at him.

"The driver can send a carriage to fetch us when they stop at the very next village."

"You can't be serious, Michael?" Isabella placed both hands on her hips.

"I am very serious, Bella."

"You would let her get the best of you?"

"Shut up, Bella."

"She certainly has a hold of you by your—"

"Please, shut up, Bella!"

Isabella's mouth snapped shut at his angry tone. She crossed her arms before her and stared at him with a mulish look.

The latch to the lock clicked and the carriage door swung open. Michael was pleased that Lenora's stubbornness had not persisted. He did not know what he would have done had she refused to open the door.

"Are you certain you wish to do this?" Lenora looked at him apprehensively.

"I think it a rather fine idea."

She stared at him a moment longer. "You needn't stay behind with me."

His eyes widened. "Don't be ridiculous! I would never have you stay alone. You never know who roams these roads. And I would never forgive myself if anything happened to you."

Lenora gave a fleeting look to Isabella and for a moment he feared the exchange would not go well. But as proud as a queen Lenora nodded and descended from the carriage with his help.

Isabella did not give him so much as a glance, nor would she take his hand when he offered it but struggled into the carriage on her own. She took her seat on the rear facing side since Freddie was now sprawled quite inelegantly on his side.

"Will you not even say goodbye, Bella?"

She did not turn to answer him but spoke facing the carriages interior. "I'll never say goodbye to you. Never."

What could he answer to this? And so, he closed the carriage door without another word and secured the steps.

He gave brief instructions to the driver to send back a carriage with all due speed. The skies gave an ominous rumble as Michael watched two of his dearest friends disappear from his life, perhaps forever.

Oh, they would meet again in London. This was inevitable. But they would never again be as they were. Too much had changed for them now. And he was no longer the man he "n just a few short weeks ago.

He turned to Lenora who stood looking at him expectantly. He then scanned the horizon. They would need to find a place to sit. The wait could be long depending upon whether a carriage was found or not.

"I took the blanket," Lenora volunteered if a little sheepishly.

Michael turned back to Lenora and chuckled. "Practical as ever."

"Not so practical." She lifted her chin as she said "I'm not the least bit sorry for striking her. That woman was dreadful, Michael."

He smiled at her. "You needn't be sorry. You were quite provoked. We both were."

Lenora nodded in agreement. "But I am sorry to cause you so much trouble."

"You have not caused me any trouble, Lenora."

"Oh, but I have. Though you are kind to say otherwise." She looked up at him, her eyes expressing her regret. "I am not normally so obstinate. And now you are forced to suffer for my behavior."

"Lenora, it is no suffering to be here with you. But if it's forgiveness you seek, you have it." He took hold of her chin and forced her to look into his eyes. He wanted to be certain she understood him clearly. "I believe you are repentant, and you are of course forgiven. Do you feel better?"

Lenora nodded. He was glad to see that she did in fact feel better. It touched him that his forgiveness meant something to her.

Michael smiled down at her. "Come, give me the blanket and let us find a spot to sit and wait."

Lenora smiled back at him in relief. She gladly gave him the blanket—grateful he hadn't railed at her for her foolish behavior. She would have deserved it of course. And though she was not sorry for fighting with Lady Isabella, she truly did regret forcing him into this current situation.

"I am sorry for one other thing," she admitted as they began walking.

"That you did not come away with a larger patch of Isabella's hair," he asked with a raised brow.

"Well, perhaps I'm sorry for two things then." She smiled up at him, her eyes twinkling with mischief.

Michael marveled at her. He had never before seen such range of emotion in her. It did his heart good.

"I was going to say," she continued, interrupting his train of thought. "That I am also sorry that our trip to Lille was not as pleasant as it perhaps should have been. I know I do not always make the best company."

"Your company is fine Lenora. I quite enjoy it most of the time." He directed her to a shady spot where they had clear view of the road. "Why else would I have asked you to extend our arrangement beyond this month?"

"Hmm," was her only answer.

He gave her a brief look. With her hair ruffled, a gleam in her eyes and that nasty scratch on her cheek, she looked rather wild. He liked it. And he suspected this bout with Isabella was just the thing Lenora needed to rouse her from her icy fortress.

"Give me a hand, will you?" He held up the blanket to indicate he wished to lay it on the ground.

She obediently helped him in spreading their blanket. She then took a dainty seat, and he nearly laughed out loud. *Would she be so prim and proper if she could but see herself?* He smiled.

Lenora turned to catch that smile. Her cheeks immediately felt flushed. She looked away in embarrassment.

Michael did laugh out loud just then. "Admit it. You are more than not sorry. You loved that fight with Bella."

"I'll admit to no such thing," she turned her nose up at him. But nothing could hide that gleam in her eyes.

"It is nothing to be ashamed of Lenora," he teased. "You were quite glorious."

Michael watched as a small smile played on her lips.

"There is no glory in brutality, Michael."

"But tell me, did it feel good?"

She stared him, wondering if she dared. "It felt wonderful!"

Michael let out a hardy laugh as he pulled her into his arms. Lenora had no choice but to join him in his laughter.

Their mirth was such that no sooner did they quiet down

they needed only to look at each other and they fell into another fit of laughter.

Michael was soon groaning, holding his side. "I haven't laughed so heartily in ages," he finally spoke as he released her and lay on his back. His body relaxed with unfamiliar sense of ease. He had finally stopped running. From what—or to what—he could not say.

"I haven't laughed so heartily... ever." There was a sudden sadness in her eyes, though her smile remained firmly on her lips. It had felt good to laugh. She felt lightheaded and so happy. Lenora had never had such a feeling before. There "n nothing in her life to cause true happiness.

"Has your life been so bleak, Lenora?"

She looked at Michael where he lay. His eyes so soft and kind. Their cool, soothing hazel-green reflecting the bright grass. She wanted to tell him every blessed thing about her life. To pour out her sorrows and murdered hopes and have him sooth away every last one of them. But it was difficult at this advanced age to learn to release one's pains.

"Not so very bleak, I think. Not like others I've known." She frowned in thought.

"Your mother and father, are they alive?"

"My mother is." She hesitated a moment. "My father has passed."

She seemed hesitant in speaking of her life. But he was so curious about her. And their time together would soon be drawing to an end. Perhaps it was selfish of him to push for more when she was so evidently uncomfortable.

"Do you miss him terribly, your father?"

Lenora had not expected this delicately probing question from Micheal. She had to stop and think. Did she miss Papa? She supposed she did. But she did not grieve his loss. "I think in my own way I do."

"In your own way?" He raised a brow at this obtuse answer. "Why? Was he a cruel man?"

"Oh, no! Not cruel. He was quite kind. He simply was... well, let us just say he had his vices." She nervously smoothed out her skirts though Michael could have told her the gown lay immaculately. If he were merciful, he would have abandoned the conversation and allowed her solitude of thought. But clearly, he was neither selfless nor merciful.

"Is that why you needed the money? To pay for his vices?"

She heaved a heavy sigh. Lenora considered confessing all.

"My father was an extremely proud and serious man," Michael volunteered to help her unease. Lenora was obviously one who did not overly share her feelings. If truth be told, neither was he. "Though I don't remember him much. I do recall holding him in high esteem and wanting always to please him."

"So, you miss him?"

"Yes, terribly. I think I would have come to know my African side had he lived. Visiting Senegal many times by now. As it stands, I've never set foot on the continent. I was made to feel ashamed of my heritage. I know without a doubt, had my father lived, he would have sheltered me from the harsher cruelties of my mother's family."

"What did they do? Your mother's family?" Lenora asked this hesitantly. Michael wavered, causing Lenora to immediately regret her probing question. "I'm sorry. I should not have asked."

"No, it's quite all right."

It was clear that whatever pain "n inflicted upon him was still felt quite acutely.

"I lived with my mother's older brother for a time, before I was sent away to school. He was a brute who was not easily pleased, and I suffered greatly at his hands. His wife was no better. Though her preferred weapon was her tongue. She often called me a "wicked monkey" or "a dull beast". I was by no means an angel and as I grew older, I began to fight back. Thus, I was sent away to school. And school was no better. Despite my best efforts, trouble always found me... for obvious reasons."

Lenora nodded. He was no doubt the only brown skinned boy at his fancy school. It would have made him an easy target.

"In time I learned how to survive in the world I found myself in. I became a jolly gay fellow. And soon I realized that my comely appearance was another tool to use to ward off the bigots. And so, I used it."

"And now, are you happy in your life, as it is?"

Michael took a deep breath as he considered the question. "Happy? I can't say. I never sought to be happy," he confessed. "Only to survive and get along in a world that always saw me as an outsider."

Lenora found herself entranced with Michael's story. "What of your mother?"

"She was a good mother. Quite beautiful as I recall. A clever woman. But clearly naïve to think she could love and marry any man she wanted."

"She must have loved your father very much."

"Yes. And she paid for it with her life."

Lenora's brows furrowed in question.

"They died of fever, as I said, while visiting Senegal. I suspect her manner and location of death was also a little to blame for some of the abuses I suffered at the hands of her family. They saw me... the African part... as the reason she was taken from them."

"Tsk." Lenora shook her head in disapproval. *Poor child. Poor Michael.*

"My sentiments exactly," Michael smiled up at her. It was odd talking to Lenora like this. Laying out his childhood before her like a feast for her consumption. He never would have told Bella or his previous mistresses any of these things.

It was nice to share at least a small part of himself with someone. He immediately felt lighter and freer for having done so.

Michael reached a hand to brush back a stray strand of hair from Lenora's crown. She stared down at him and they exchanged one of their familiar silences. These were moments he was growing rather fond of. Moments that allowed each to examine the other. To digest just how very intimate their relationship had become. And it had become far more intimate than either would have expected he wagered.

There were worlds that existed between things unsaid, he suddenly realized. In those brief quiet moments that came and went like the wind there were emotions unexpressed and dreams unrealized. If only one or the other was brave enough to fill in those barren silences...

"My grandmother died when I was away at school. My mother's mother. It is her cottage we are staying at."

Lenora's eyes widened at this bit of news.

"In any case she left me a generous bequeathment and I began my moral degradation that summer."

"Poor Michael."

"Hardly. I had money, social connections and a bit of looks."

A bit of looks, he says. Lenora shook her head as the picture of his adolescence came into her mind. *No parents to guide him. A brother with his hands full in running their many estates. A near bottomless well of funds. Dear heavens! It's a miracle he's still alive.*

"I remember when you first came to work for my brother," Michael threw out seemingly out of nowhere.

Lenora turned to him at the abrupt turn in subject.

"I watched your interview with Mrs. Hennings." Michael surprised himself. He had never before realized how badly he had wanted to share this memory with her. To let Lenora know she had not been alone during that dreadful interview.

"From behind the screen," he added when he saw the

confusion on her face. "I sat with my brother. To give my opinion of course."

He 'n there! Lenora moistened her dry lips with her tongue. She remembered that afternoon. How could she ever forget it! She 'n frightened out of her wits. All that day she wondered if that battle-ax of a housekeeper could smell the desperation that clung to her like perfume.

She had never needed employment more desperately and yet was never more certain she would not be hired on as governess. And then she realized in that moment she likely had Michael to thank for being hired on that day. The earl having a half African brother was undoubtablly the reason he had even been open to hiring her. Was life not odd? One would almost think it 'n preplanned down to the smallest detail.

"I was struck by how very impregnable you seemed. I'm certain I made a wager as to how long it would take to bed you."

She frowned down at him.

"I merely thought much of myself," he hurried on. "I was certain I could have you. And I was wrong."

"Not so wrong after all," she answered quietly.

"In the way that I assumed yes. Had you not been in dire need of funds you would never have allowed me in your bed."

She did not answer him, which forced him to stare at her silent profile.

"Have you never been in love, Lenora?"

Her heart stopped for a mere moment. It took a few seconds for her body to relearn how to breathe. Why was he forever pushing beyond her boundaries? She was so frustrated that she put the question to him.

"Why must you always ask such provoking questions?" She frowned at him.

"How can such an innocent question be provoking?" He argued back.

"Asking if a woman has ever been in love is not provoking?"

"No," he answered seriously. "I think it a fair question. We have become lovers after–"

"We are not lovers–"

"We are, Lenora." He was suddenly angry. "No matter what you think or what you say, that's what we are."

Why in God's name must she always provoke him when things were going so well? Michael stared at her in frustration.

She suddenly surprised him. "No," she shook her head as she looked into the distance. "I believe I've never been in love." She turned back to him. "I did fancy a little boy once."

"Has a man ever kissed you before me?" He asked with some curiosity.

She looked away again for only a moment, then turned back to him, "Once."

"Was it so terrible?"

"I did not care for it." She linked her fingers together so tightly before her. "He was a much older man and my employer." She could not believe she was telling him of Mr. Grace-Martin. Of course, she did not tell him that it had taken six months to build to that terrible kiss. Six months of avoidance and dread. But the man always managed to catch her alone.

"How old were you?"

"Twelve, I think. The same age my sister Suzie is now."

"A man kissed you when you were just a child?"

"Yes, and he was married besides."

Michael stared at her doing his best to keep the sudden rage that had ignited at the pit of his belly from showing on his face. He did not want to frighten her, which would prevent her from revealing the rest to him.

"Who did you tell?" He asked with far more calm than he felt.

"I told no one. I did not wish to lose my position. But it did not matter. His wife suspected something I think, and I was sent away without my last week's pay."

Michael took in his breath and slowly released it. He was tempted to ask for the bastard's name so that he would have the honor of shooting the man himself. No doubt he would probably save some young girl from a worse fate than Lenora had suffered.

"What that man did to you was perverse, Lenora. It's only good he did not do worse." Something tightened in his belly when Lenora made no response. "Did he do worse, Lenora? Did this man do other things to you?"

She nodded—though she did not speak immediately. Michael clenched his fist, the rage building within him.

"What else did he do?" It took all his strength to speak quietly. To not frighten her.

"He would come to me at night," her voice had grown quieter still. "He would touch me. And ask me to touch him. Though I would not."

"That man is a monster." Michael reached to touch her hand. Lenora looked at him and nodded in agreement. Mr. Grace-Martin was a monster. She had known it even then. Though she had made no complaint. Her family 'n in need of money and so she sacrificed herself then as she was doing now. What are a few morals when money is needed to feed one's family?

"I was glad to be gone from his employment. His name was Mr. Grace-Martin. He was a banker in Luton."

Did she know she had just sealed the man's fate? Michael nodded to her in silence. As soon as he returned to London, he would make a trip out to Luton. How difficult could it be to find the banker in such a small town?

Lenora suddenly released her breath. "I've never told anyone any of this before."

"I'm glad you told me Lenora," he sat up so they would be

face-to-face. "If ever any man hurts you again, please come to me and know I'll do all within my power to protect you."

She nodded even though she did not quite know what he meant by "protect her". After this coming week she would be out of his life for good and they would only see each other on the rare times he made visits to his brother. Surely, she would have no need for protection while under the earl's employment. When would she ever have need of Michael again?

"Take down your hair," he suddenly commanded.

She blinked at him.

"It's an utter mess." He smiled tenderly.

"Oh," her hands flew to her head. She had quite forgotten about her appearance. "I must look a fright."

"Not quite so ghastly," he chuckled. "Here let me help."

"No, no. It's quite all right." She pulled away instinctively. No one ever touched her hair. Not anymore. Not since she was a child.

"Please," he asked simply.

Lenora pursed her lips. She really did not want to. And yet, she thought, they 'n so intimate in other ways. It seemed silly to not let him touch her hair. Finally, she gave a small nod. Michael smiled. She sat still as he removed the pins from her hair with an expert hand.

"You do this rather well. You should have been a lady's maid."

"I've had much practice," he chuckled at her rare jest.

Her heart constricted as she thought of the many women he had done this with. She was being ridiculous of course.

"I believe it started with my mother," Michael continued.

"You dressed your mother's hair?" Lenora asked in some surprise.

"I became quite proficient. She especially liked it when I would brush her hair. I'll do it for you tonight when we arrive home."

Home.

That one word evoked a sudden pang of loneliness. The home he spoke of—the home they shared—was only a temporary one. In a very short time that warm and inviting cottage would no longer be home. Instead, it would be a memory. A lovely tormenting memory.

Lenora was silent when he began to run his fingers through her tangled coils. She could feel him examining their texture between his fingers. She suddenly could not remain silent any longer.

"Do you dress the hair of your other mistresses?"

Oh dear. She did sound jealous, didn't she? But she had to know.

"Not even one," he finally answered. And Lenora smiled.

IT HAD NOT BEEN RAINING for very long when their carriage finally appeared. The carriage driver looked at them suspiciously when Michael waved him down. He 'n promised forty sous to get them to Calais. A nice price any day. And they seemed harmless enough.

Lenora huddled close to Michael within the confines of their carriage. The vehicle had seen better days. Today was not one of them. The two laughed as they bounced at another rut in the road.

"I don't know why I'm laughing, I should be utterly miserable," Michael shook his head with a smile.

Lenora looked at him in silence, her eyes bright and shining. Yes, she should have been miserable, wet from the rain in this shabby poorly sprung carriage. But she was not. She was content.

"Perhaps it is the company. Do you think that might be the case, Lenora?" He looked down at her cuddled within the crook of his arm. A thought came to him then that this was how it should be. What "it" might be he did not know. But had it been Bella in her place, he was certain the two of them would have complained and been miserable.

How funny it was that life seemed not a dreadful inconvenience, but in fact a pleasant adventure with Lenora at his side.

"I think the company is very fine, Misha." She looked up at him and her heart constricted at his smile. Her eyes turned away immediately. She would not allow it. She would not allow herself to fall in love. Not when their time together was nearing an end.

CHAPTER 15

$\mathscr{H}$e did brush her hair that night as promised after she had bathed and changed into her nightgown. The two of them sat before the fireplace in her bedroom, he on a chair and she on a cushion on the floor between his legs. Lenora closed her eyes drinking in each stroke of the brush. *Was there anything more divine,* she thought, *than to have a man lavish such attention on a woman?*

She 'n certain he would have forgotten. After all, it 'n an eventful day. After more than two hours riding in the borrowed carriage, they had arrived home wet and miserable. Only Madame Louparet's gentle admonishments and motherly caretaking eased Lenora's mood.

Michael had ordered whatever warm food that could be prepared quickly to be brought to the room. A fresh loaf of bread, cheese and beef stew had answered their call and the two set to their meal like savages. Both had laughed when Madame Louparet clucked her tongue in disapproval.

"You will swallow your tongues if you keep eating so fast!" She had shaken her head in disapproval.

After dinner and a bath, Madame had administered a nice

salve to that nasty scratch on Lenora's cheek and proclaimed her patient would make a full recovery.

Lenora let fall a slow sigh as the brush traveled through her hair and pulled it back, away from her face.

"I take this as a sign of approval," Michael chuckled behind her. She felt the gentle shake of his body as he sat at her back. Should a thing feel so comfortable? The touch of a man. The feel of his strong thighs encasing her.

Lenora gave a little frown. She should not allow herself to think such things. She should not allow herself to feel so comfortable, cradled against his body. What would she do when he was no longer there—when emptiness lived where Michael once had?

"Perhaps not approval then."

She turned to look at him. "Yes. Approval." They stared at each other. It was so odd the two of them together like this. Both knowing the end was imminent. Lenora turned back to the front. For a moment he did not resume brushing.

"I think we should go into the village tomorrow."

"If you wish," she answered quietly.

Michael heaved a sigh. Lenora did not turn this time. He once again took up the brush and slowly ran the bristles through her hair.

Had he once thought her hair ordinary? He did not know why. It was quite thick and so soft to the touch. It now fanned out like a halo. *Would their children have this hair,* he wondered.

Michael shook his head of the image like a dog shaking from a soak. *Tread carefully old boy,* he told himself. There was little time left, and he could not spend it imagining things that could never be.

Lenora gave an unabashed yawn.

"Do you wish me to stop?" He asked cautiously.

"No, please continue." She turned to him with a careful smile. "Please continue, Misha."

He answered her smile with a gentle one of his own. "As my lady wishes."

LENORA HAD ALWAYS trod a narrow path through the world. All the days of her life had summed up to one word—constancy. There "n little deviation of any kind at all. Never did she consider, perhaps I should go left just this once, or maybe today I shall try right. She always did what she was told and had always behaved as expected.

MICHAEL STARED out at the passing carriages from where he stood at the shop window. The cobble-lined streets were painfully narrow in this old section of the village. It was quite charming when one took the time to admire it sufficiently.

He could hear Lenora and the shopkeeper behind him discussing various lotions and perfumes the shopkeeper wished to sell. The woman was in good cheer, perhaps remembering the necklace she had sold them a week ago.

Had it only been a week? Why then did it feel like a lifetime ago?

Lenora was as usual being her cautious self though he had told her she was free to indulge. She had stared at him as if he had suddenly broken into tongues. She would not waste his money she told him. Not when she would more than likely never use such frivolous things as scented lotions.

She was by far the most miserly mistress he'd ever had, Michael thought to himself. He would have loved nothing better than to have had sufficient time to break her of that habit. But time was one thing they did not have.

She could not decide between one item and another. He let her look over each item knowing that he would more than likely get her both. What did it matter? Money was no object to him, after all.

"I do like the rose scent," he heard her say. A smile came to his face.

"But then the gardenia is quite lovely too? What do you think, Michael?"

He turned to look at them.

The shopkeeper held up both bottles patiently. Lenora tapped a finger on her lips. She looked remarkably young just then. Michael raised a brow. He had never seen her do that particular gesture before. Of course, she had had relatively few things to decide during their time together.

"I say you choose the rose and the gardenia," he approached, placing his hands on her shoulder. From this proximity he caught a strong scent of the mingled lotions. She smelled like a country garden.

He told her so on their way home.

"I smell like a garden?" she looked up at him from under the brim of her straw hat. Another purchase he had made for her. A cheerful periwinkle ribbon matching her gown waved from the crown.

Michael smiled down at her. She looked very charming— nothing like the cold Miss MacLeod of before.

"Yes, like the gardens of Vauxhall in spring."

She turned to him with an odd smile.

"What?" he looked at her.

"That was almost poetic."

"I'm a man of many talents."

"Yes," she answered, turning away. *Of too many talents,* she thought to herself. But aloud she said, "Will you play the pianoforte tonight?"

"If you wish."

"Yes, I wish it."

It was like this between them, all politeness and accommodation. It was almost unnerving to pass the days this way. But neither seemed inclined to show strong emotion.

Neither wanted to be the one responsible for ruining their last days together.

And so, their days were filled with pleases and thank yous. They took several walks around the property. Michael played the pianoforte each evening.

Both waiting patiently for their last day together. And just as dawn followed night, the day came at last.

CHAPTER 16

$\mathcal{L}$enora woke on that cloudy morning to immediately discover two things. One, her monthlies had ended and two, the cottage was completely deserted. The first she was not surprised of being quite constant even in this aspect of her life. She had told Michael two evenings before to expect her services again that morning. Therefore, all the arrangements were made for her departure on the morrow.

What did surprise her was that the cottage was deserted of even a single soul. Lorette did not answer when Lenora summoned her. Which forced her to dress on her own—a thing she did not mind and rather thought she should get accustomed to again.

She put on her periwinkle gown, which was the easiest to slip into. She then braided her hair and headed to the dining room.

Lenora immediately knew something was amiss when she did not hear any activity outside. Usually, Phillip was busy chopping wood for the fires. Madame Louparet or Lorette usually traversed the halls and stairways carrying linens or some other domestic errand.

Although it was considered a small house (though in Lenora's humble estimation it was quite large) and thus had a small staff, there was always activity in the cottage. But just then the house was as silent as a tomb. *Where had everybody gone,* she wondered?

The gentle sound of rain called Lenora's attention to a nearby window. All was silent outside save for the steady rainfall. Lenora scanned the horizon. Beyond the window, the only movement was the gentle sway of the trees surrounding the house. It appeared that even the world "n purged of every living soul and only she remained.

After a brief look into the salon and library—both of which yielded more of the same nothingness—Lenora finally made her way to the kitchen. She stopped in her steps the moment she went through the door.

Michael turned around and gave her a grin. Lenora shook her head at his flour-covered face.

"I thought I would make you breakfast."

She looked at the flour and sugar strewn upon the counter and floor. One solitary egg lay cracked and open on the floor. A forgotten martyr.

Michael's gaze followed hers to the smear of yellow on the gray stone floor. His smile dimmed just a little.

"I thought it a dashed good idea at the time. But now that I have had time to reflect..."

"You find it a terrible idea," Lenora offered carefully.

He gave a shrug, and his smile widened once again. Lenora chuckled.

"At least it's good to discover where one's talents do not lie," he said as he wiped his hands on his vest. A cloud of flour billowed from his once immaculate clothes.

Lenora entered further into the room. "And what precisely is that supposed to be?" She stared at six dark lumps neatly lain on a silver serving platter.

"Scones," he said with pride.

"Scones?" She blinked at him.

"Yes, scones," he answered with a little less certainty.

"Are you quite sure?"

A puzzled look settled on his face. He stared down at his creation as if expecting them to explain themselves.

"Perhaps stones would be a more appropriate description," he confessed after a moment of reflection.

Lenora gave a laugh and Michael smiled. He did not mind if she laughed at his expense. There was a difference between this and what Isabella would have treated him to.

"I suppose you're probably a tad more talented than I in this arena."

"I think I may just be." She nodded with a smile.

"Then I concede to your better… talents."

"And just why is it exactly that we find ourselves in this position?"

Michael watched as she filled a bowl with flour. She easily broke open two eggs that had survived his earlier experiments.

"I've given the staff a holiday."

"A holiday?" She looked at him in question, not even pausing in her preparation.

"Yes." He looked at her face. "I wanted to be alone with you today."

Lenora did pause then. She certainly had not expected him to take such measures. She took in a deep breath. She would take the day as it came. It was her last with him. She must not ruin it.

Michael released his breath when she returned to preparing their breakfast. He had thought of this day since their return to Calais. If truth be told, he had thought of nothing else. This day with her would be his last.

Panic had gripped him as he thought how he would have to force into his memory each moment, each movement she made.

The taste of her skin against his lips, the feel of her breasts under his hands. All of it would have to be carefully catalogued in his brain.

He had never been forced to give up a woman before he was good and ready. Never!

They were barely getting accustomed to each other and already their time together was coming to an end. True he had forced it to end sooner than it should, but would one more week have made their parting easier? For him, he knew it would not.

LENORA'S SCONES were leaps and bounds better than the lumps of coal he had offered. With butter, cream and strong tea, breakfast "n salvaged after all.

They had not bothered to eat in the dining room but instead remained in the kitchen. They sat at the wooden bench and table where the staff usually shared their meals. It was a heavy solid piece with all the nicks and cuts that showed it to be well used. Michael felt surprisingly at home.

"It's odd that I've never been in here," he mused at the intimate setting. "One would think a man would know every last inch of his house."

Lenora gave him a wise smile.

"And yet now I feel as if I've been in here a hundred times. It's odd, isn't it?"

"Not so very odd. There is a sense of comfort here."

"Yes," he nodded in surprise. She felt it too.

"I think this is just the sort of place that makes you feel as though you've been here before. It's a rare thing," she spoke quietly. "A thing to be treasured."

Michael watched her, all the while battling with himself to keep the day light and gay. He did not want to talk to her of deep feelings. He wanted to share mindless pleasure with her and let her go. But his mind would not let him.

"Do you think you will miss… Calais?" he started tentatively. He did not wish to frighten her. Not yet.

She thought about his question for a moment. She wanted to give a truthful answer.

"Yes, I think I will."

Michael stared at her. His eyes going to her lips. Today was a day for every indulgence to be explored. There was no room for reservation.

"I want to kiss you, Lenora. Will you let me kiss you?"

She stared at him with wide eyes. Whatever she had expected, she had not expected him to ask permission.

She nodded, not trusting herself to speak. Her heart suddenly pounding in her chest.

Michael rose from his bench and came over to her side. He sat with his back to the table. She looked up at him, waiting for him to close the distance.

He raised a hand to caress her cheek. He had to memorize the texture so he could recall their softness a month from now.

"You are an utter surprise to me Lenora," he whispered as he drew their faces closer together. "Sweet Lenora." She closed her eyes in expectation of his kiss, but he did not make contact. Not as she had predicted.

Instead, he rubbed his clean-shaven cheek against hers. She released a shaky breath not having been prepared for this intimacy.

"Dear Lenora." His lips grazed her neck. Michael took a deep breath at the soft skin just where her hairline began. She smelled faintly of roses and gardenia. He smiled and for a moment he was afraid he would cry.

"What will I do without you Lenora?"

Lenora bit her lip. She had not expected such tenderness.

She would not last the day like this. She would be frayed and shattered if he continued this way.

To force him to action Lenora turned her face to his and sought his lips. He immediately opened for her, allowing her to lead into this kiss.

Her body relaxed under this familiar action. Sex with Michael, this she understood. This she could guard her heart against. She did not want him to be tender. Lord in heaven knew she would not survive it if he were.

Michael responded to the frantic nature of her kiss and the embrace deepened. This was not how he had planned it. He had wanted the seduction to last all day. He had wanted to take his time with her.

Lenora reached for the buttons of his vest. He tried to stay her hands.

"Slowly, my love."

"Please, Misha."

He pulled away from her to stare down at her agitated face.

"Please." She leaned into him once again closing the distance between them.

He felt as if she would devour him, and he would go to his demise a happy man. He kissed her back with equal fervor now suddenly turning into the aggressor. He was afraid she would pull away, but she did not. She searched for his hand and placed it upon her breast before returning to the buttons of his vest.

Suddenly all thoughts of a slow seduction evaporated like morning mist in the sun.

They both rose from the bench locked in their embrace. They pulled frenetically at each other's clothes, unable to get undressed quickly enough.

He pulled away from her and she whimpered in distress.

"No," he chided gently, turning her away from him.

"Michael please," she whimpered.

"You'll have me soon enough."

He bent her over the table, pulling up her skirts. She turned a frantic look to him over her shoulder and he swore beneath his breath. He would not last like this!

He quickly pulled down the soft linen of her drawers and the fabric ripped under his hand. Lenora's eyes widened and Michael had to take a deep breath. She could not know what her looks were doing to him.

And he would not allow himself to spill before burying his length deep inside her!

Lenora released a moan when his fingers found her. They carefully stroked her entrance searching for that familiar wetness. She caught her breath as a finger pushed inside of her finding that hidden spring which lay just below the surface.

"God you're already wet!" he marveled at the feel of her.

"Yes," she whispered fiercely.

Could this be Lenora? he wondered. *She had never responded like this!*

"Do you want me inside you?"

"Yes, yes, please," she begged him.

He pulled one of her hands and placed it on the hardening length of him. It jumped at her touch and begged to be released from its prison.

"Do you want this inside of you?"

"Misha," she whimpered.

Michael fumbled with the fasteners of his pants and in a spill of flesh he was suddenly free. The length of him strained out as though it knew where her opening lay, and it need only stretch long enough, and it would find her.

She suddenly wrapped a hand around him and Michael bit off a curse. He immediately pulled himself out of her grip. "No sweet lady. Not like this."

He moved her to lean deeper over the table and Lenora was forced to use both hands to brace herself against the wood. And before she could turn her head to beg him for release, she felt him pressing against her entrance.

"Yes." This was what she wanted. Mindless rutting. No thoughts. No feelings.

She moaned as he pushed past her entrance. He felt like a large blunt object, far too big for the opening he was trying to enter!

"Lord save me from you," she heard him whisper as he pushed deeper into her. She was wet and tight and so very hot! It was maddening!

Michael wanted to bury himself to the hilt, but he could not push all of his length into her yet.

He was forced to rock back and force, like the ebb and flow of the tides. But with each retreat Lenora knew the next assault would be deeper.

She let fall little moans that drove him to the brink of insanity. Her body squeezed at him, trying violently to milk him with each stroke. Her wetness made his movements slick and easy, which did little to aid in his attempt to not spill prematurely. With one final push he buried himself all the way in her. There was nowhere now to go but out. He waited a moment, trying to recover his breath, his sanity. But she would show him no mercy. With a move of her hips that was effectual and artless, she drew Michael out and plunged him back into her.

Lenora took in her breath at the result of her movement. Despite their position, she still had some control. She made to move again when he held her hips still.

This time he was the one to pull out. He pushed in again just as she pushed back, and the impact of their bodies caused an erotic slap.

"Do you want me to slow down?"

Lenora shook her head not certain she could speak at that moment. She felt him withdraw and she knew what would come next. He pushed back into her, and she moved back to meet him.

"Yes!" Lenora cried out.

It was hopeless from then on. His mind became focused in just one moment, pushing into her. Her moisture surrounded him, and her little moans filled his brain. The only other sounds were their bodies slapping against each other.

And it was not enough. He wanted to push inside her until he filled the very space in which she lived and breathed. He was certain if he pushed deep enough, he would fall into her.

She cried out gripping the table like her life depended upon it. He worked at her, pumping into her and she felt her orgasm descending upon her. It was wild and ferocious like a caged beast and each time he delved deep into her it taunted her beast.

"Yes, yes, yes…" It became a litany in her brain. "More," she wanted more. It was just out of reach.

"Tell me you love me," Michael panted over her. "Tell me!" he demanded.

Lenora frowned not quite knowing what was happening. Her mind could not make sense of his words. Not when release lay just beyond her grasp.

"Tell me," he demanded with more urgency.

God in heaven, tell him what? Lenora shook her head, not certain what she was answering.

He suddenly stopped his movements; he was still deep inside her. Lenora groaned in frustration.

"Tell me you love me!"

Lenora shook her head violently. "No," she whimpered. *Why was he doing this?*

She suddenly felt him twitch inside her and she took in her breath.

"Please," she writhed her hips against him, urging him to move. She was so close, so very close.

"Only say the words and I'll give you all you want." He leaned over her, his mouth resting by her ears. "Say it, Lenora."

"Do not ask me to, please." She had never felt more miserable. Why would he not give her what she wanted? Why would he not give her release?

As though he could hear her thoughts Michael pulled almost all the way out and slowly pushed in.

"I'll give you all of this. Just say that you love me."

"I can't."

Michael pushed deep into her and Lenora cried out. Yes, this was what she wanted. What her wanton body needed.

He began working into her, pumping into her body all his frustrations. Slowly at first but soon building up speed and force. He was determined to pour it all into her. But she did not complain or spit out that frustration. No, she drank it in like a sweet draft. And she demanded more. Her body singing with pleasure. More she wanted to tell him! But was it physically possible?

"Yes!"

He pumped harder, more mercilessly until she was certain he would come out the other side of her.

And then in one brilliant heart-stealing moment her world crashed down around her. Lenora screamed her orgasm. Her body convulsing around him still embedded deep within her. He pulled out of her almost too late, a part of him wanting to stay. To pump her womb full of his seed, but instead his spilled onto the floor.

Breathe.

She had to force herself to breathe. Lenora blinked her eyes open, forcing them to focus on her surroundings. She lay bent over on the table, her arms stretched out before her. She was very aware of Michael's weight on her back. His head resting at her shoulders. She felt the rise and fall of his chest. He was still breathing heavily.

Lenora suddenly became aware of the wetness between her legs. Her cheeks burned red in embarrassment as she thought of her wanton behavior. Just what had possessed her? Never had she behaved like this in her life.

And what he must think of her. Certainly, no prim and proper governess was she.

Then she thought of his demand. It was as if her mind had tried to protect her from feeling too much all at once. Now it allowed her to understand just what he had asked of her. And even in blind lust she had not given him the response he sought.

But why had he sought that response? They were nothing to each other, nor ever would be. Therefore, why ask her to speak such words?

Michael forced himself to move. He had to raise himself off her body. He had to escape this moment.

Why? Why had he asked her to say those foolish words? He knew she did not love him. Then why demand her to say so? What had he hoped to gain by it? Could he not stop for even a minute in this headlong race to make himself the fool?

He took in a resounding breath and slowly released himself from her body.

Lenora stole a deep breath, which his weight had prevented her from doing before.

"Let me clean you up," he spoke as he finally moved away from her.

"No, I can do it." She stood up and pulled her skirts down, smoothing them around her as if what they had just done had not happened.

"I want to."

"Really, I can." She had already taken hold of a pitcher and was pouring water into a bowl.

"Lenora!"

She froze in her steps.

Michael took in a deep breath. She could not help what she

was. She was his efficient and practical Lenora. Never mind that they had just shared the most earth melting sex he had ever had! Never mind that even now he wanted more of her, though he was certain he could not perform for some time. She stood before him pitcher in hand ready to make everything tidy and orderly—just like her world must be.

"Never mind," he finally said. "I'll go prepare a bath."

She nodded to him. She turned from him taking a clean cloth from a cabinet and dipping it into her bowl of water. Michael waited a moment. Perhaps he should say more. At the very least apologize for his foolish request. But all words escaped him just then. He therefore left with the vision of Lenora bent over the cold stone floor wiping it clean of his seed.

SHE HAD NOT KNOWN if he meant to share a bath with her. They had never done so before. But it was their last day, and she did need to get clean.

Lenora entered her room and the sound of running water told her that the tub was still being filled. She had entered and was suddenly uncertain what to do. It reminded her of her first day at the cottage. This time however she could not just stand in the corner while Michael went about his business.

Michael suddenly exited the bathing room as though merely thinking his name had summoned him. He was shirtless now and Lenora took in a breath at the sight of him.

He stared at her at first in surprise, but a frown followed it immediately. He was angry at her, she was certain. Michael raked a hand through his curls. Lenora bit her lip to keep from smiling. He looked charming and reckless all at once.

"I did not hear you enter the room," he finally spoke, though it was clearly not what he wished to say.

"You could not over the water," she nodded.

They stood facing each other, neither speaking for a time. Then, quite unexpectedly, they both began at once.

"Should I leave you to your bath?" asked Lenora.

"Regarding what I said earlier," said Michael, his voice overlapping hers.

A pause.

"I beg your pardon?" They said in unison.

Michael frowned harder, if such a thing was possible. *He looks positively thunderous,* Lenora thought.

"I wish to apologize for my earlier behavior," he began. "I should not have asked you to say things you do not feel."

Lenora nodded, not daring to speak.

"I hardly know where it came from. Perhaps temporary madness."

She nodded again, smiling gently.

Michael looked at her, then down to the floor. He took a much-needed deep breath before meeting her gaze again. "This is our last day. We should part as friends," he held up his hand to stop her from interrupting. "Though I know you do not think such a thing is possible."

"You are wrong, Misha."

"Am I?" he stared at her intently.

"Yes. I think we are friends... of sorts."

He gave a sad chuckle. Lenora had given him the most truthful answer she could. Their stations in life, their circumstances, and their beliefs prevented them from being more. But more than these, this bargain they had struck between them prevented them from being more than "friends of sorts".

And in Lenora's opinion though Michael was not as heartless as she once thought him, he was still a playboy. He still lacked morals. True. But because of this damnable bargain she was no longer one to judge.

"Come let us take off the gown before the water cools."

She must have given him a questioning look for he added. "Did you think this bath was for me alone?"

"I did not know what to think," she answered honestly.

"Here, let me help you," he approached her.

Lenora allowed him to divest her of her clothes. They exchanged quiet smiles as he unbuttoned her gown and helped her out of her chemise.

He gazed at her body with admiration as he removed the last of her clothes—her stockings. She looked down at him, as he sat on his haunches, rolling down her remaining stocking.

Michael suddenly felt compelled to say something he had wanted to say for a long time.

"Lenora, I have been with many women," he began, rising to his feet. He chuckled at the widening of her eyes. "Don't give me such looks or I shall never be able to finish."

Her expression immediately sobered.

Michael sighed before continuing. "I say this because I wish you to know I speak from experience when I tell you you are beautiful."

She gave a frustrated sigh, and he was certain she would have gainsaid him, but he continued on.

"You are beautiful, and you must believe me," he spoke seriously. He wanted her to believe him. He willed her to believe him.

She turned away in clear annoyance, therefore he was forced to move so that she could not help but see him.

"True, you do not have the overt beauty of women such as Isabelle. Such beauty is, I find, uninteresting in its commonness. No, your beauty is far more intoxicating because of its subtlety."

She looked uncertain and he could see the practical Lenora fighting to dismiss his words. But he could also see the lonely young woman who needed to hear such things.

"When I look at you, I can hardly breathe for the wonder of it."

This she clearly did not believe. She turned away again.

"Your body is the loveliest I've ever known. Do you know how many times each day I must fight to keep from touching you," he gave an ironic laugh. "Even knowing this bargain gave me full reign of your body I still was too vain to allow you to know just how entranced the sight of your naked flesh made me. Makes me even now."

Lenora turned to look at him and indeed he appeared to be entranced as he stared at her breasts, her belly, then further down. His eyes eventually worked their way up to meet hers.

"The thought of no longer being able to touch you is terrifying." His hands reach to stroke her cheek. Lenora's eyes closed of their own volition. Had he wished to, he could not have spoken words more singularly designed to break down her defenses than the words he had spoken.

"You are by far the most beautiful woman I have ever known, Lenora. You must know this."

Lenora once again looked into his eyes, and she believed him. For the first time in her life, she felt beautiful.

A solitary tear escaped her eye, and she turned her head in shame. Why should she cry simply because the Honorable Michael Chesterfield told her she was beautiful?

He forced her to turn back to him by turning her chin.

"I simply wanted you to know this." He leaned down and kissed her lips gently. "In case you ever were to doubt it. You are beautiful Lenora."

She nodded; mostly because he appeared to want some answer, and she desperately needed him stop his gentle assault.

He thought her beautiful. For his sake she would believe him.

"Are we ready for our bath?"

Lenora nodded again, suddenly too tired to do much of anything else.

Perhaps sensing this, Michael bent down and slipped a hand behind her back and knees. "Then to our bath."

He placed her gently in the hot water and Lenora's bones melted immediately. She lay back, lids half closed and watched as he removed his trousers—the only bit of remaining clothing he had left.

He was a beautifully made man—of this she was certain. A woman did not need to see many men to know that Michael Chesterfield was a prime specimen. He was just exactly what a man should be, firm and well formed. All broadness at the shoulders leading to that tantalizing narrow waist.

She watched as he bent over his pants, his tight buttocks well displayed. His well-muscled legs covered in a fine layer of hair a shade or two lighter than the hair on his head.

She told herself she must memorize each element of his body so that at some time in the future she would be able to recall every detail.

"Move forward a little."

Her body obeyed his command and Michael slipped into the water behind her then pulled her against his chest. Yes, this was far better than the cold porcelain, Lenora thought to herself.

Lenora gave into the pull of sleep and closed her eyes. She did not know why she was suddenly so weary. Perhaps it was the vigorous lovemaking, or maybe it was the hot bone melting water.

"I'd have given the world to have had such a lovely governess when I was a child," Michael broke the silence. "Instead, I was burdened with a certain Miss Rothtrend. Perhaps the nastiest piece of womanhood to ever walk this green earth."

Lenora gave a slow smile. "You were probably a wicked little boy deserving to be punished often."

"Not so wicked," he chuckled. "But if I deserved punishment I would have much more preferred receiving it from your hands, Miss MacLeod." He nipped her on the ear causing her to jump.

Lenora shook her head. Thank heavens she had not been his governess! She could only imagine the handful he 'n as a boy. Bertie and Sarah were just the sort of children she preferred, a little precocious, but obedient in the end.

Lenora suddenly felt a soapy washcloth moving over her skin. Did he really intend to wash her? It was scandalous. But she made no move to open her eyes. She would let him do what he wished. At least that was her intention as he soaped her arms, then her breast and belly. When he moved lower her eyes popped open.

She gasped a soft "Oh."

He did not use the cloth now, just his hands. His finger delved between her nether lips and Lenora bit down on her lower lip. Should she tell him to stop?

"Michael?"

"Hmmm." A hand came up to cup one breast, while the other continued in their supposed washing.

"Michael, I think I'm quite clean." She turned her head to see that his eyes were closed.

"Not just yet," he answered with a slow smile. He placed a soft kiss on the side of her head.

"Misha?"

"Yes?" it was a long slow drawn out yes. All warm and sticky like the pulling of warm taffy.

"You are enjoying yourself, aren't you?" She questioned him already knowing the answer.

"Very much so." One eye popped open. "Do you really wish me to stop? Could you be so cruel?"

She thought to say yes. But somehow a "No" fell from her lips. He gave a chuckle behind her. The rumble of his chest making her feel relaxed and tight all at the same time.

"Of course, turnabout is fair play," she warned him.

"I'm hoping so Lenora. I'm hoping so."

She proved to be a woman of her word, lavishing just as much attention on him, as he had on her. She turned around to face him. With no preliminaries she took a hold of him working him through soapy hands.

She had marveled at the softness of his skin; it was by far the softest part of his body.

The consequence, of course, was that she worked him into a right frenzy.

"Enough," he had cried out, once she had gotten him as stiff as a board. He pulled himself out of her eager hands. Her triumphant smile had not lasted long after he rose to his knees in the tub and shown her just what her busy hands had created.

"Oh," 'n her monosyllabic response just before he pulled her into his arms, wrapping her legs around his waist.

He was now far gentler than earlier in the kitchen but even making love to Lenora in a tub was not what he wanted. He wanted to take his time with her. Explore every inch of her body until he was numb. Then he wanted to make love to her. He wanted her to always remember him no matter how many men came after.

But for now, he brought her down onto his straining length. They both sighed as he pushed into her.

"I'll never get enough of you," he said with shaky breath before he lifted her, drawing himself almost completely out of her. Lenora tightened her hold around his neck when he brought her down again. She buried her face in his hair. Only then did they begin the slow mating dance.

I'll never get enough of you either, she told him in her mind, not yet brave enough to speak those words.

AFTER THEIR LOVEMAKING and yet another bath they sat by the fire, Michael once again brushing out her hair. Lenora had said it was entirely unnecessary, but he had wanted to do it and so she let him. It was their last day after all she reminded herself for the hundredth time.

"Does anyone know that you are here?" He asked when her hair was mostly dry. He placed down the brush and leaned back in his chair, the leather creaking with his movements.

While Lenora had placed on her nightgown and robe, he sat only in his trousers.

"Yes, Mama knows I'm here." Lenora turned to face him and realized suddenly that her face was in line with his private parts. She blushed and he smiled at her.

"That is one thing we have yet to do?" he stated with a cryptic smile.

She looked up at him with such innocence that he knew she did not know what he was referring to.

"You've not taken me into that lovely mouth of yours," he explained casually.

Lenora blinked up at him. Since she had not yet moved, she was still very much in line with that part of him. She did her best to ignore it and to meet his eyes.

"I wouldn't know how," she answered quietly.

"I could show you," he returned easily.

She did not answer. Her eyes instead strayed to his male parts, but she immediately looked away. She had thought herself so very bold in their bath when she had taken him in her hands. She had seen his immediate reaction to the petting and stroking of his body. But to take him into her mouth! She could never be so brazen!

Michael leaned forward with a sigh. "It would please me greatly Lenora. But I would never force you."

She stared up at his gentle face. She knew he spoke the truth. He would not force her. But he desired it. It would please him.

Michael watched her as she appeared to give serious

consideration to his request. She bit at her lower lip, a gesture he now found endearing.

"I'll do it," she suddenly said with a decisive nod.

"Just like that?" he smiled. "You've decided you'll do it?"

"If it pleases you, I'll do this once before I leave."

He considered her where she sat before him on the floor.

"It will please me very much." It meant a lot to him that she had agreed to do this. Not all women enjoyed it. But most women who decided to be his mistress performed the act like they did. Yet it would be different with Lenora, just as everything else was different with her.

"You say your mother knows you are here?"

Lenora stared at him for a moment. Not quite realizing he had returned to his original question.

"Yes," she finally answered. "Though she did not know it was to be this house precisely. I was to write her upon my arrival."

"But you did not know what to say," he finished for her.

Lenora shook her head.

"Do you think she's worried?"

"I do not think so. In any case I shall be leaving tomorrow." She said the last word quietly as if to say it any louder would cause the day to rush headlong to its conclusion.

THE RAIN CONTINUED unabated until late afternoon, it stopped just for an hour, long enough to catch its ragged breath, then continued on cheerfully with renewed purpose.

They made a luncheon of bread, cheese and dried figs. They drank wine, getting a little tipsy. The two mainly talked of nonsense. Lenora spoke a little of her family. She told him of her younger brother Aubrey who aided her in supporting her mother and younger siblings. He was a sensitive boy who had enjoyed painting as a child.

"He works as a clerk in London. He's a very clever boy," she told him proudly. Like so many, he deserved a better hand than he was dealt. It was for him also that Lenora had sold herself. So that the poor boy would no longer need to work himself into the ground. He was already too thin for a young man of nineteen, nearly twenty.

Lenora also spoke of her sister Suzie with her endless questions, why is the sky blue, why cannot people fly, where do wishes go once they are wished?

Lastly, she told him of the little ones, Dora, ten, Cecile, eight and William, seven. All far too young to know just how truly poor they were.

"Are you able to see your family often, working for my brother?"

The answer "n no. But it was not said with sadness. "No," Lenora spoke as Miss MacLeod would. "It was impossible to take leave when there was so much to do with Bertie and Sarah."

Michael could have told her that as spoiled as his niece and nephew undoubtedly were, he was certain they could spare her presence for an afternoon here and there.

"Do you enjoy working for my brother?"

"Yes, he's very kind." Her eyes shifted nervously to the side when she answered.

"What are you not saying?" Michael caught the movement, and his curiosity was immediately peaked.

She opened wide eyes at him. "Nothing at'all."

"You are hiding something. I can tell because you can't meet my eyes. What is it?" Michael rose to his elbows on the bed.

"Truly it is nothing," Lenora made her escape to stand beside the French doors. Michael frowned at her response.

"Has he abused you in some way?"

"No, heavens no!" She turned to him in surprise. The earl had never even said a cross word to her. She rarely saw him and when she did, they did not speak for any great length. And then only enough for her to apprise him of the children's progress.

Michael felt his shoulders relax. What would he have done had he discovered Adrian treated her poorly? The answer did not bare thinking.

"It is only that..." how had she gotten herself into this, Lenora wondered.

"Only that?" he said by way of encouragement.

She looked to Michael then looked away. "I saw him once... with one of the upstairs maids. Lizzie."

Michael stared at her.

"She was most willing. Of that I'm certain. She spoke of the earl all the time."

"You caught Adrian in a compromising position with an upstairs maid?" Michael tried to bite back his smile. The old dog! And to think it was the earl himself who had warned him to keep away from his staff.

"It's hardly a laughing matter, Misha. I find such behavior inappropriate for a married man and an employer."

"But you said this Lizzie was willing."

"But he is still married!" she exclaimed in distress.

"Lenora, calm down," he rose from the bed to approach her as he spoke.

"I know that it is to be expected for a man to be unfaithful," Lenora spoke the words for him, "but I could not bear it if I knew my husband lay with another woman." she shook her head fiercely.

Michael stared down at her suddenly realizing what she must feel.

"Lenora," he spoke softly. "Any man you marry will be the picture of moral rectitude."

"You're making fun of me now."

"No. Perhaps a little." He gently took her into his arms, and she let him. "I simply know that your marriage will not be the sort that my brother has with his countess. You dearest have the luxury of marrying for love." He pulled away a little to look down at her. "Unlike he and I who must marry for a myriad of social reasons, none of which involve our hearts."

"But why can you not marry for love? I understand your brother; he after all has a title and must make a prudent match."

"I assure you, I am as equally bound, perhaps more so."

"But why?"

"It is simply expected," he answered in frustration.

"But why?"

"Lenora…" Michael raked his hands through his hair. He did not know why, he just knew that it was. Was that not sufficient explanation for her? He had accepted it long ago.

Lenora stared at him not certain why it mattered that he could not marry for love. It was not as if she ever expected him to marry her. And yet still it grated her that he should attach himself to a woman merely out of duty to his class.

"I did not mean to get angry," Michael said with a sigh.

Lenora was surprised by his words. She had not realized that he had gotten angry.

"I suppose it is possible to marry a woman I love. It's simply that with all the constraints on who I may pursue it seems very unlikely for it to be a love match. Not impossible mind you, but very unlikely."

"Would you not want to have a marriage like the Bennetts," she persisted despite her better judgment.

"I would give my right arm and perhaps bits of my left to have a wife look at me the way Angela looked at Arthur."

Lenora smiled despite herself.

Michael once again placed his arms around her. "What they have is something you will have, Lenora. Of this I'm certain." His lips caressed her forehead as he spoke.

Lenora felt his warm breath on her skin like a soft caress.

"You deserve no less," he continued.

"Neither do you, Misha." She looked up into his face. "And I'll pray every night that your marriage is indeed a love match."

His heart contracted violently at her words and Michael had to force himself to take in a ragged breath. She would pray for him. Looking down at her face he believed her. Perhaps God would answer her prayers. He certainly would never answer his.

"That is more than I could ever ask of you," he confessed trying desperately to keep his voice from wavering.

"You needn't ask," she answered quietly before reaching up to kiss him.

He allowed her to lead in this kiss, still stunned as he was by her words. He looked down at her when she finally pulled away. A small smile played on her lips. He would have sworn it was a seducing smile if he had not known her.

Lenora reached for his hand pulling him back to the bed. Michael followed willingly like a trusting child who knew nothing of heartache or shattered dreams. She led him to the bed and sat him at its edge.

When Lenora kneeled before him Michael had his first clue of what she had planned for him.

"You needn't," he began to say.

"Shh." She placed a finger to her lips. He fell quiet in response watching her breathlessly. "I told you I would."

He let fall a sigh when her nimble fingers reached for the fasteners of his trousers. Already he felt himself go rigid with anticipation.

Moments later he sprung free and eager. He hissed as though her fingers burned when she touched him with tentative hands. She stroked the length of his shaft, as he jumped in her hands like a thing alive.

"Mmmm..."

Lenora looked up at Michael's face fascinated by his reactions to her touch. She stroked him again watching him closely, he released another groan. She traced a finger over the purple veins just beneath his skin.

"Teach me how to do it," she spoke her eyes reluctantly

leaving the part of him in her hand. "Teach me how to please you with my mouth."

Such words to be uttered by her! Michael was almost rendered mindless.

He reached for her hand, not daring to speak. He brought her hand to his mouth choosing one finger he closed his lips over it. Lenora swallowed deeply at the erotic gesture.

He pulled the finger deep into his mouth his tongue simultaneously swirling around it. Michael had never before shown a woman how to please him this way. It was a thing he had always taken for granted that his mistresses simply knew. Never had he stopped to consider just where they had gotten the knowledge. He had merely been content they eagerly demonstrate their well won skills on him.

Lenora watched Michael in fascination, her jaw slack and her eyes wide. Her fingertip felt warm and wet in his mouth. The sensation was odd, while the visual utterly captivating. He suckled hard on her finger pulling it in and out of his mouth in a simulation of their lovemaking.

Michael watched her reaction to his mouth play. Her gaze remained firmly on where his lips met her hand. Her mouth opened wider—ready to take him inside.

Michael finally withdrew her captured finger and waited patiently for her to look at him. He noticed she took in a few deep tremulous breaths before returning his gaze.

Her eyes then went to his body, not quite as rigid as before, yet still as daunting.

Michael watched in fascination as her mouth lowered over him. Her lips closed around him, trapping him in her hot mouth.

Michael bit off a curse, throwing his head back. He did not dare watch her for fear it would be over too quickly. Michael gritted his teeth as she grazed him with her hers, a sensation that sent shivers down his spine.

She slowly pulled him out of her mouth, suckling him all the way. A very apt pupil came the observation along with other thought fragments. Just as soon as she had pulled him completely free, she began her downward journey again.

Merciless!

For what seemed an eternity she worked at him with her mouth moving just as he had shown her. She then suddenly veered off from her curriculum and tried her own movements watching for his reaction. She was immediately rewarded with groans and muttered curses—a sure sign of his pleasure.

Her eyes captured his as she worked him in her mouth, pulling, licking along the veined shaft.

Michael shut his eyes tight, yet the image of Lenora's mouth on him, her heavy-lidded gaze blazed behind his own lids. And with the sensation of sight arrested, his other senses seemed to flare to life. He felt her take him deep in her mouth. Her tongue caressing him.

"Yes," he hissed as the tip of her tongue passed over his most sensitive spot. Testing his reaction, she stroked him there again. He made a move to pull away from her when she once again changed her movements. Still, it was too much!

"Enough." He pulled himself out of her mouth, valiantly fighting to regain his sanity. "Had I but known you would be this skilled I'd have asked for the pleasure of your mouth sooner."

Lenora gazed up at him through her partially closed lids. A slow, knowing smile curved her lips. She was no doubt pleased with herself. Michael smiled pulling her toward him.

"Still, this is what I prefer." In one movement she was suddenly on the bed with him buried deep within her. Lenora took in a surprised breath at the easy invasion.

Michael groaned feeling her wetness swallow him. How could he be expected to release her now? He wanted her too badly.

They easily fell into the familiar dance like old lovers. He knew her body, knew every inch of it as if he had studied her. As if the knowledge of her body ʾn imprinted on his soul prebirth.

He knew how to move within her to make her climax, to make her mad with passion. And he used this knowledge mercilessly. It was now Lenora who bit back curses, who groaned from the misery of sensual pleasure.

"Yes," she begged him, encouraged him as he pumped into her.

She was slick and inviting. So very hot. He was almost mindless with it.

She was first to cry out. And her release brought about his own. But just as he made a move to pull out of her, she wrapped her arms around his neck and her legs tightened around his waist.

Michael knew a moment of panic, which was quickly replaced by selfish desire. Yes, he wanted to spill into her. He wanted to fill her womb with his seed. And with a few purposeful strokes he poured into her as he had never allowed himself to do before. The act seemed more complete. Before, it had always felt unfinished.

He relaxed onto her, his body feeling boneless and satisfied. Fear over what they had done would not nag his brain for a few minutes yet.

Lenora stroked his hair as she hugged him to her. She knew what she did was foolish. But she had not thought in that moment, her body had only reacted, wanting him to climax within her. It ʾn her animal-self thinking.

Her fingers drifted down his back, her nails raking his moist skin. He gave a slight shiver, and her body tightened. She would never hold him again. They will never have this again.

Lenora swallowed against the coming tears. She did not want to feel sorrow at their parting. She wanted to feel relief.

She would be free of him. She would on the morrow return to her old life. To her family, her employment. She need never touch him again. She need never lie beneath him as he filled her with his body. She would be free.

Michael moved to his back, pulling her into his arms as he went. Lenora snuggled against his chest, and he pulled the sheets over their bodies.

The rain had continued outside unabated and with unabashed pride. They watched in silence as the grey wet world subsisted beyond the French doors.

They watched in silence because there was nothing left to say. And so, the last hours of their affair melted away with little fanfare. It was the end of their bargain. The end of a love that never had a chance to flourish because they were creatures from two very different worlds.

It was the end at last.

CHAPTER 17

*T*he rain had ceased sometime before dawn. Lenora knew this because she "n awake then, much as she "n most of the night. It had not been in love making as one would have hoped. He had not touched her in that way again after that last time. It "n because her ceaseless thoughts would not allow her to sleep.

She had lain beside Michael, listening to him breathe, her hand upon his heart. She had stayed awake, her body refusing to give in to sleep. And only when she was certain he was blissfully asleep had she dared to echo his words back to him.

"Tell me you love me," she had whispered to her sleeping lover. But just like her, he had not complied.

Lenora now stood on the balcony that led off the bedroom. The sun had risen, but it was still a grey day. Her mind recalled standing in this very spot weeks ago on the morning after her arrival. Her eyes went to the wrought iron chair Michael "n sitting in. It stood empty as though waiting for his return. She remembered his casual air that morning and her fear thinking perhaps she had not the strength to survive their bargain. But she had survived.

Her eyes raked the countryside, her brain working furiously to remember each and every detail. It was a hopeless pursuit. In time all of this would be an unclear blur. The house, the staff, even Michael as he was now would someday become a haze haunting the recesses of her memory.

Lenora's hand reached for the necklace around her neck, hidden safely beneath her gown. It was the only thing she would bring back with her. The only reminder of him she would allow herself.

She was going to miss him. The thought disturbed her more than a little. For, at the beginning she had not expected to feel this way.

"The carriage is ready Madame."

Lenora turned to where the maid stood holding her old cloak. "Merci, Lorette."

Michael stood by the front door. He was dressed immaculately though she knew he would not leave for two days yet. Lenora was suddenly glad it was not she who had to remain behind. She would have gone mad if it "n so.

He gave a genial smile. Not at all the one she had grown to care for. His hair was rigidly tamed and coifed—no longer endearingly wild and unruly. He wore a smart coat of dark gray wool, matching form-fitting trousers. A green undercoat peaked from beneath a shade or two darker than his eyes.

Standing there as he did made the last few weeks seem almost like a dream.

"I shall walk you to your carriage."

Lenora nodded, not trusting herself to speak.

He led her by the elbow to the carriage that waited outside. They did not speak. Nor did they look at each other.

The sky was cloudy, coloring the scene with a hint more melancholy than it otherwise would possess on its own. But would a sunny day truly have made a difference? Somehow Lenora was not certain it would.

"You didn't take any of the gowns," he finally spoke, a forced cheeriness apparent in his voice. "They are yours after all. I certainly have no use for them."

"I cannot take them," she answered without looking at him. "Where would I wear them?"

"I see your point."

She nodded, though she did not know why.

"I shall miss you," the cheeriness had left his voice. Strange it should be at those words.

Lenora nodded once again, not daring to speak the thousand words she longed to say. She could not allow herself to speak. Heaven only knew what words would pour out.

"Will you not miss me even a little Lenora?" He sounded a little desperate then. Lenora swallowed. She did not want to cry. She didn't wish him to see her cry.

"Can you not even give me a miser's farewell?" Michael stared at her with sad eyes.

She had to look away. She could not bear this. "What more do you want from me that I've not already given?"

"Give me your love."

Her eyes widened at his answer. Lenora shook her head even before she spoke.

"Do not ask it of me." Do not ask me for the thing I fear giving you most, she should have said. She didn't want to love him—but she suspected she already did. But he certainly should not be asking for it. Not when she was at that moment to walk out of his life forever.

She heard him sigh before he spoke, "Farewell, Lenora."

She took a fortifying breath and said, "Farewell."

They did not kiss. They did not embrace. In this their last moments together, she did not even dare meet his eyes.

Michael aided her into the carriage, closing the door and securing the stairs. She was pleased to leave him, of this he had no doubt. All their shared intimacies had amounted to less than nothing. He had offered her his heart and she had found him wanting.

He shook his head as the carriage lumbered forward. She had left everything, wanting no reminder of their time together. When was the last time he "n so completely and irrevocably rejected?

Michael Chesterfield now knew without question that he was a man unworthy of being loved.

LENORA STRAINED her head out of the window watching him stand before the cottage's double red doors. A sob escaped her lips, and she was suddenly powerless to stop the flow of tears. How was it possible for a person to be more miserable leaving a place than she "n coming to it? Why must she be so contrary!

Neither of them waved to each other as true lovers would have. They merely watched as the other faded into a speck in the distance. She watched long after the cottage had disappeared from sight, and she suddenly knew her heart would break into a thousand pieces.

Her body shook with the violence of her grief. She didn't want to leave him! She didn't wish to return to a life without him! The days of her life stretched out like an endless barren landscape. Neither sun nor starlight penetrating the thick clouds which cast a shadow on her future. Was there ever a more miserable woman than she? How was she to survive without him? The simple answer—she wouldn't.

But she could not be his mistress, his whore! She would rather be the dirt beneath his feet, than be his plaything. And this was what he spoke of when he spoke of caring, of loving. He did not speak of a home with children. Of a marriage between equals. He did not speak of respect and fidelity. This he would never offer her, a governess. His brother's employee.

She would rather be nothing to him than to languish at his

side with no more than a hope of stolen moments. To watch him marry well. To read of his exploits in the society pages.

And yet she would miss him. Miss his smiles. His touch. His laughter. She would miss the scent of him. The look of abandoned bliss as he pumped into her body when they made love.

Lenora bit her lip, tasting the coppery tang of blood. The carriage rushed forward swaying with the road. Flying her toward home and tearing her from a happiness she would never know again.

CHAPTER 18

It was raining again. Pedestrians rushed along the streets with their uniform black umbrellas. They looked like little dark mushrooms sprouting along the fashionable streets of Mayfair.

Chesterfield alighted from his carriage and rushed up the steps of his townhouse. The front door opened without preamble as it always did. Langley stood at attention ready to relieve his master of his hat and coat.

"Demandable rain," Chesterfield muttered more to himself than anybody in particular.

"Yes, sir," Langley answered for lack of anything better to say. These past three weeks had not been the easiest to traverse. Wherever his master had gone during his month-long absence the man had returned reserved and brooding.

Not once had he gone hellraising with his set, though Lord Fredrick had called on him twice. Langley had it on good authority that Chesterfield had even gone to visit his two children. Something he had never done before!

"I shall be leaving for Luton tomorrow," Chesterfield informed him in a clipped tone. "Be sure to have my bags ready."

"Shall you be gone long, sir?" Langley had to rush in his question as his master was already ascending the stairs two at a time.

"Not long," was his abrupt answer.

"Sir, there is a lady," Langley rushed on before Chesterfield could make his complete escape. "In the salon."

Michael paused immediately; his ascent arrested by Langley's words. "A lady?"

"Yes, sir. In the salon."

Could it be?

Michael did not wait to hear another word. He doubled back down the stairs, his eyes blind to everything. Had she come back? Was it Lenora?

"Sir? Shall I—"

"Not now," Michael was rushing to the salon's double doors. He once again felt a happiness that had quite deserted him since his return to London. With the kind of eagerness reserved for children at Christmas, he flung open the double doors.

Langley watched his master in complete mystification. Never had he seen him act this way. What had happened to him?

"Michael?"

Chesterfield stopped having just entered the room. He stared at the woman before him.

"Michael, why haven't you come to visit me?"

It wasn't Lenora.

"I am sorry, I've been remiss Victoria." It was the lovely widow, Victoria Dalton. The very woman he "n on his way to see when Lenora came to him not so long ago.

The lady rose from the settee, dressed in a powder blue dress with matching bonnet and pelisse. She lifted her pretty heart shaped face to him. There was a time he had thought her a rare beauty. There was a time he had thought himself a most fortunate man to have garnered her attentions. Today her loveliness was lost on him.

Chesterfield's face darkened and the lady was obviously aware of his sudden mood.

"Have I done something wrong, dearest?" She looked at him imploringly. "I very much expected a visit from you the moment you returned to London. But I daresay it's been weeks and yet you've been remised?"

"I do apologize for my inconsideration, Mrs. Dalton."

"Mrs. Dalton?" The widow's eyes went wide. "Since when have we been on such formal terms? Michael, what's come over you?"

Chesterfield felt an overwhelming frustration. He did not wish to be here having this discussion with his former lover. Though she did not yet know she had that distinction. He raked his hands through his hair looking at the room nervously.

"What is it?" The widow demanded, losing her own patience. "Is it another woman?"

"Victoria please," he sighed in frustration.

She took a few tentative steps toward him and Chesterfield moved out of her reach. "I think it best that you leave. I am sorry."

Victoria Dalton stared at her favorite lover in pity. The man looked a positive wreck. This was not the carefree playboy she had known from before.

"Talk to me Michael. We are friends after all."

Chesterfield shook his head. "There is nothing to tell." He turned his back to her, once again running his hand through his curls. He had to make her leave. He was in no mood to humor her. "Really Victoria, now is not a good time."

"Now is never a good time, is it?" she responded pragmatically. "Let us begin at the beginning. What is her name?" The widow continued undaunted. She was a woman quite accustomed to the tempestuous moods of men. Had she not been married to her dear husband for ten years? The male sex was a subject upon which she was quite well versed. And if she were not mistaken Michael Chesterfield was suffering from love. Then again, perhaps he had merely murdered somebody.

"What is whose name?" Chesterfield stared at the lady suspiciously. Could he be so transparent that Victoria guessed his predicament within minutes of being in his presence? Were his emotions written so clearly on his sleeves?

"The woman who is causing you all this anguish," Victoria encouraged gently. "Michael we can speak frankly. I assure you nothing you tell me will be made known to anyone else."

Chesterfield considered this for a moment. The very fact that he was contemplating her offer spoke to how very desperate he had become. But could he speak of Lenora to his former lover? And if not her, then who? It seemed he had very few options.

"It is a woman as you say," he spoke slowly, not quite believing he was speaking at all. "But the details of our acquaintanceship would not be ones I wished made known."

"Certainly not," Victoria Dalton assured him with a decisive nod. "I would be the last person to wish details of her private life to be made public. Thus, I can assure you I'll be very circumspect with yours."

Chesterfield nodded, torn between relief and fear. He did not want the details of his affair with Lenora known. It would devastate her, and he would not wish her harmed in any way. But since their parting he "n tormented by all the things he should have said but hadn't. He thought endlessly on the possibility that she may yet be with child. His child! Would she contact him? He had not told her to do so. He had not run after the carriage on that day and confessed his undying love to her. He had not asked her to marry him.

"This woman is employed… by a dear friend. And I believe I've fallen in love with her."

Victoria stared at Chesterfield in shock. Did the man just say love? This was serious!

"I've not told her that I love her. Though I've selfishly demanded her love." He shook his head recalling Lenora's face on the morning they parted.

Give me your love.

Do not ask it of me.

"We've parted ways. I don't believe I shall see her again. And even if I do, it will never again be as it once was between us."

Victoria stared at Chesterfield for a good long while. She believed him when he claimed he was in love, though he was the last person she would have suspected of falling prey to that emotion. To be in love was something that could at once be wonderful and a torment. Like a pretty gilded cage that grew tighter around you until you suffocated.

"Perhaps if you told this lady of your feelings," Victoria suggested wanting very much to alleviate Michael's anguish. "Perhaps if she knew of your love for her…"

"What would it signify?" Michael interrupted with some frustration. "She's made her position painfully clear. She wants nothing to do with me."

"Perhaps she doesn't," Victoria said with a Gaelic shrug. "Or perhaps she does. You can't know what is in a woman's heart unless you ask her. And even then, it might still remain a mystery. So, ask her Michael. She may simply be too afraid to love you if she suspects you do not return her affections. Is she a woman who has had many lovers?"

"No. I was her first."

"See, then there you have it!" Victoria spoke with a gentle smile. "It's all quite clear to me."

Chesterfield held his breath, wanting desperately to believe that she had the answer.

"Michael, she is new to love. And if she's given you her body, but suspects you don't love her, she may well be afraid. I certainly would be."

Chesterfield turned to his friend, a sudden ray of hope blooming in an otherwise dreary day.

"Do you think that is all she fears? That I do not return her affections?"

"It may well be," Victoria offered helpfully. "But you will never know if you do not tell her."

Chesterfield smiled. He should have told her. He would tell her. Perhaps that is all she feared. Lenora was a girl of good sense. She would not throw her affections away if they were not returned.

"I think I will tell her."

Victoria clapped her hands in joy. "Good show Michael."

Chesterfield looked at her in earnest. The smile she wore was brilliant, and it was for him. It did his heart good to see it. "I did not believe myself to possess many friends. Thank you, Victoria."

Mrs. Dalton looked at him in surprise. "You have friends, Michael." She approached him, placing a gentle hand on his arm. "Don't ever forget it."

"I won't."

Victoria nodded in response. "Now, I think perhaps I'll take my leave. You've placed me in a rather desperate situation." She wagged a finger in mock reproach. "How I'm to find another lover half as talented as you, I'll never know."

Chesterfield smiled at his friend. "Victoria, you always did know the right thing to say."

"I know dearest. I know."

CHESTERFIELD ARRIVED in Luton on the next afternoon in far better spirits than he "n in for the last few weeks. Though that fact would make no difference to the man he was visiting.

He asked at the posting inn for the address of a certain Mr. Grace-Martin and was pointed to the banker's home without difficulty.

The house his carriage came to was decidedly quaint and would have even been called pretty if his errand "n of a different nature. As it was not, the house appeared rather sinister in his mind.

Chesterfield descended the carriage under the notice of a few neighbors and passersby. He had taken great care in dressing and had chosen his very best carriage to make the trip. He wanted Grace-Martin to know precisely the man he was dealing with.

He made a quick rap on the door with his silver tipped walking stick and waited. It took only a few moments for the door to be opened by a young girl of perhaps ten or eleven. Chesterfield froze for a moment when the girl looked up with questioning eyes. She was a nervous little thing, and her clothes were quite shabby.

"Yes, sir?"

"Who is it?" came a woman's voice behind the girl.

The girl looked at him in fright.

"Mr. Chesterfield," he volunteered as he examined her.

The girl hardly had time to repeat his answer when the rather plump lady of the house approached the door. She froze immediately staring at him in his beautiful suit and coat and polished boots. The woman was suddenly flustered, a smile coming to her face.

"Mr.?"

"Chesterfield. Michael Chesterfield." Chesterfield gave a most becoming bow and smiled charmingly. The woman was immediately a simpering fool.

"Oh, do come in, Mr. Chesterfield," she opened the door wider as she spoke, pushing the young girl out of the way."

Chesterfield wondered if the woman realized she had not

asked him his business yet.

"If you would but take a seat," Mrs. Grace-Martin led Chesterfield to the waiting room.

The house was small, but well decorated, Chesterfield noticed. It did not make sense for their servant to be in such rags. Not when she was expected to greet guests.

"What may I owe this visit to, Mr. Chesterfield," Mrs. Grace-Martin appeared to be making eyes at him. Chesterfield raised a lofty brow. The woman was old enough to be his mother!

"I've come to speak with your husband. You are Mrs. Grace-Martin, I presume?" Chesterfield gave a lofty turn to his nose, which had its desired effect. The woman became even more solicitous.

"Oh certainly, certainly," she bowed as she backed from the room. "Bring the gentleman some tea," she said sternly to the girl who watched them from the entrance of the sitting room. The girl immediately turned and fled.

Chesterfield frowned at the exchange. Had Lenora been forced to live with these people? Had she had to endure this sort of treatment?

The girl returned moments later, struggling with a tray of teapot and dainty cups. She threw covert glances as she made her way to a side table. She placed the tray down with a clatter, nervously looking toward the doorway for an expected chastisement. When none came, she took a relieved breath.

Chesterfield watched as the girl brushed a stray hair from her face before pouring the tea. The task looked as if it required every ounce of her concentration and even then, she did not have the steadiest hands.

"Have you worked for the Grace-Martin's long?" Chesterfield made all effort to sound as unthreatening as possible. Still the girl stared at him with wide eyes.

"It's quite all right. I shan't hurt you child."

She finally shook her head.

"Do you like this position?" he prodded further, not certain she would confide in him. "Do you like working for the Grace-Martins?"

The girl merely looked at him, but did not speak. Nor had she the opportunity when Mr. Grace Martin made his presence know.

"Taking a bit of tea, sir?"

Chesterfield turned to the friendly looking man who entered the room, and his mind fought to reconcile the letch Lenora had spoken of with the smiling man before him. Grace-Martin had a friendly face with rosy cheeks. He like his wife was quite plump. While their servant girl was painfully thin. The man was also balding, and the hair he had remaining had turned quite white. This? This was the man who had touched Lenora?

Chesterfield's frown caused Grace-Martin's smile to waver. Chesterfield turned to the servant girl.

"Perhaps the girl could be sent to wait outside Mr. Grace-Martin?"

Grace Martin's smiled dimmed a little more. "What precisely is this regarding, Mr....?"

"Chesterfield," Michael provided.

"I don't believe I know that name," a little more of the true man was making its way to the surface. Grace-Martin regarded Chesterfield with narrow eyes.

"I am the younger brother to the Earl of Walpole."

Grace-Martin nodded, though he did not know the earl. Still, he could tell that the man sitting in his waiting room was a man of consequence. His fine clothes and the manner with which he carried himself told him as much. And an Earl's younger brother besides. But what could such a man want with him? What could merit a visit to his home?

"You heard the man. Out," he spoke gruffly to the girl.

Chesterfield frowned. "There's no need to speak to those under our employ in such a manner."

At this point Mrs. Grace-Martin made an appearance. The worried look on her face made him certain she had somehow been listening.

"Is everything alright?" She approached her husband with a worried look.

"Quite fine," he said without feeling.

"Why don't you go play outside Eleanor," Mrs. Grace-Martin spoke gently to the girl. She *had* been listening.

Chesterfield's heart contracted. Eleanor. By what twist of fate would her name sound so much like Lenora? He watched as the girl made her careful way to the door, her eyes shifting from him to the Grace-Martins. Chesterfield was certain that was the kindest Mrs. Grace-Martin had ever spoken to the girl.

Once Eleanor was outside, Grace-Martin was first to speak. He wore a deep frown. "Now what is this about, Mr. Chesterfield?"

"I would suggest that your wife excuse herself too. What I wish to speak of is not for the ears of a gentlewoman like yourself madam," Chesterfield spoke casually as he removed his gloves.

The Grace-Martins both looked quite worried.

"Perhaps you had best go," Mr. Grace-Martin told his wife, a frown on his face.

"What is this about? Who is he to dictate what I can hear in my own house?" Mrs. Grace-Martin was shaking her head at her husband. She was no fool. This was not a good visit. But what business could this stranger have with her husband?

"Go woman. Do not make me tell you twice."

The Grace-Martins were locked in a battle of scowls when the woman suddenly surrendered. She ran from the room, though Chesterfield was certain she would be listening.

When the two were finally alone Chesterfield rose from his

seat. Grace-Martin watched as the man proceeded to remove his coat.

"What is this?" The man was beginning to show signs of true fear. "Who are you really?"

"I am a friend of a past acquaintance of yours," Chesterfield spoke easily, though a certain heated undertone colored his words. "She is a lady for whom I have great admiration and respect."

Grace-Martin watched as the younger man began to roll up his shirtsleeves. The man could tell where this was going though he had no idea why. What acquaintance could he have in common with this dandy?

"An acquaintance you say?" Grace-Martin placed a nervous smile on his face. "I can't quite believe it possible sir. I hardly think we run in the same circles."

"Do you remember a certain Lenora MacLeod? She was just a girl when she was in your employment." Chesterfield knew the exact moment when realization struck Grace-Martin. The bastard!

"See, here," the man began. "I don't know what the girl told you, but I assure you nothing happened."

"You assure me?" Chesterfield asked in perverse amusement.

"Yes, yes," Grace-Martin was rapidly nodding his head.

"Somehow, Mr. Grace-Martin, your assurances mean nothing to me. I wonder why?"

"See here, Chesterfield," Grace-Martin made a sudden show of being incensed. "If you want to believe a penniless, chit—"

"Lenora is governess to the Earl of Walpole's children."

Grace-Marin's eyes went wide. "Is she?"

"Yes, she is?" Chesterfield answered with an air of boredom.

"She did well for herself," Grace-Martin said genially. Apparently deciding on a different tactic.

"Yes, she has. A more shining example of womanhood you would be hard pressed to find." Chesterfield had slowly crept closer to Grace-Martin as they spoke. He now stood just a few steps away from the man. "Thus, it pains me to know that some cruelties committed upon her long ago, still haunt her to this day. Lenora is a friend, Mr. Grace-Martin and I don't suffer transgressions against my friends lightly.

"I did not know... I did nothing..." The man began to back away.

"You did not do anything?"

"No, sir. I did not."

"You did not touch her, night after torturous night?" Chesterfield's voice had taken on a dangerous air. The man looked truly afraid and all he could do was shake his head.

"I do not believe you. What I believe is that you take pleasure in touching young girls. That you are a filthy snake, and your life should be taken from you," Chesterfield's words were as cold and deadly as steel.

"Get out of my house, with your lies! That girl was a dirty whore–"

Grace-Martin would have perhaps said more, but he did not get the chance for Chesterfield's fist crashed into the man's face. Grace-Martin tumbled backwards to the floor. Mrs. Grace-Marin immediately ran into the room and to her husband's side.

"What have you done, you monster!" she screamed at Chesterfield as she took her husband into her arms.

Chesterfield shook out the pain in his fist.

"It is your husband who is the monster," he said quite coolly as he rolled down his sleeves. "And if ever I hear that you have touched any girl from this day forward, I will kill you sir. And that is a promise. Good day to you both." With that he retrieved his, gloves, coat and stick and made his way out the door.

Once outside he noticed Eleanor standing near his carriage. She regarded him with wide eyes.

"If you wish for different employment, you may come with

me." He approached her and she stood her ground staring up at him. "Has he ever touched you?"

She did not answer for a long time, but then the girl finally nodded.

Chesterfield cursed under his breath.

"Do you wish to stay?"

"No, sir," the girl finally answered.

"Then come along." With that he made his way to his waiting carriage with Eleanor in tow. He did not know what he would do with the girl. He simply knew he could not in good conscience leave her there.

He tapped the roof of their carriage when the two were settled in. They would first go to her parent's home where he would leave her for now. When he returned to London he would enquire about a position for her. Perhaps Victoria would be of help. Then he would pay his brother a long overdue visit. To see the children of course. And a certain obstinate governess.

Pleased with his plan, Chesterfield leaned against the upholstered chair of the carriage with a smile.

CHAPTER 19

*I*t was now over a month since her return from Calais. And in that month, there were two things Lenora discovered: one, she did not carry Chesterfield's child and two, that summer's arrival could not thaw the coldness that continually surrounded her.

The first bit of news she received with an odd mingle of relief and sorrow. To be pregnant at this point in her life, with a bastard child no less, would have been the worst folly. There would be no talk of pride then. She would have had to return to Chesterfield and beg for his aid. He certainly would not have kept her on as his mistress at that point but instead shuffled her off to some remote cottage in the countryside so that she could have her baby and her shame all to herself.

No, she was glad and heartily relieved not to be carrying his child. But how to account for the unrelenting sadness that descended upon her once relief had run its course? A child with Michael would have connected him to her for the rest of her life. Was that what she wanted? To be forever linked to him? Could she be such a fool as that?

No, she continually told herself, she didn't want a child with him. It was best that she returned to her life and continue on the course she had set for herself. A course that "n carefully planned and mapped out long before their bargain.

Lenora's first few weeks back at her life "n far more difficult than she could ever have predicted. She cried ceaselessly long into the night, sleep only coming after she had worn her body ragged. The sorrow was unending it seemed.

She would often catch herself lost in thought when the children practiced their letters. She found herself often gazing out the window at nothing in particular. She would recall herself only when Sarah or Bertie called her attention back to the lesson at hand.

There was more than one time, she was ashamed to admit, that she'd use some pretense to exit the schoolroom for fear the children would catch her in tears. Those were terrible days those first weeks. Weeks she would have preferred not to live again. And she was certain the household suspected something. But her pretext of taking leave for some family emergency went along well with her current cheerless mood.

She felt particularly ashamed when the children would give her odd looks. Or when Sarah would pat her hand by way of comfort. She felt a veritable ninny at such times.

And because of this, sometime in the beginning of her third week home, she made a decision that she would mourn him no longer—refusing to even think his name. She would build her world of order and sameness again, brick by painful brick. She would devote all her energies to the singular focus of reclaiming the woman she once was.

Gone were the foolish daydreams—useless things that had never led anyone anywhere. Done with the silly tears. Done with pining for a future that could never be.

Thus, she donned her plain, dull gowns every morning like an armor against foolish sensibilities. She was once again Miss MacLeod. Cool, efficient and heartless.

The children were first to notice her return.

"But she is different from before," Bertie told his older sister when they had a moment away from their governess.

"She is not so nice I think," Sarah agreed with her younger sibling. This new Miss MacLeod who came back from her leave had at first been very sad. It 'n confusing to say the least. But nice in that she had not nagged them nearly so much when they did not practice their lessons. But suddenly, as though someone had blown out a candle, a cold governess had taken shape.

"I don't think I like her very much," Bertie complained just before he was shushed by his sister. Miss MacLeod had entered the room, and the children fell silent as they watched her. No, they did not like this new Miss MacLeod one bit.

IT WAS TIRING, she quickly found—erecting her wall every morning. It was draining work to shore oneself against the softer emotions that always threatened to break through. Lenora found herself exhausted every evening from the simple act of existing.

She could tell that the children did not like her very much. But at least they focused more on their lessons she tried to tell herself. But in truth she didn't enjoy the fact that the children disliked her.

Even the other staff trod a little more carefully around her. That, she didn't mind so much. She'd never had true friends among them anyway. It came part and parcel with her position.

Thus, every evening she sat alone in her room, barely touching her tea, trying valiantly not to think too deeply about any one subject.

She sat like this one quiet evening in early summer. The sky outside her window surrendered to the encroaching twilight. She had not yet lit her lamp, and so shadows were quickly devouring the room.

She stared with blind eyes at a letter she held before her. A letter from her brother Aubrey. She had read it twice now, both with an unfocused mind that only allowed her to understand fractured bits of his missive. He was happy she gathered. Now that he no longer sent most of his salary home, he was able to indulge on a few luxuries that boys his age took for granted. There had even been a mention of a girl. A Sophia. But Lenora could not remember much more of what she had read.

A tentative knock at the door roused her from her trance. She looked around at the darkened room and frowned.

The knock sounded again. A little louder this time.

"Come in," Lenora spoke as she rose to light her lamps.

Lizzie entered, a little shyly. She looked around the room suspiciously.

"I've come to take away your tray, miss," the girl spoke with that odd look on her face she often had of late. That many of the maids had. It told Lenora that they considered her an odd bird.

Lizzie made her way to the mainly untouched tray and picked it up. Lenora lit both of the lamps in her room and waited for the girl to leave. Lizzie however did not leave immediately. Something sparkled in her eyes telling Lenora the girl had gossip brimming to tell.

Suddenly another of the maids appeared at her door. It was Meg. Lenora gave a heavy sigh. She wanted nothing more than to be left alone.

Meg giggled as she entered the room. "Hurry, he's in the salon." Meg waved for Lizzie to come with her.

Lenora felt an inexplicable sense of impending doom. "Who is in the salon?"

Lizzie smiled at her, a faraway glow in her eyes. "His Lordship's brother!"

Lenora's heart immediately contracted. Her hand went to her throat where she could feel her necklace beneath her gown.

The silly maids ran off, entirely oblivious to the havoc they had caused.

He was here.

Lenora rushed forward. The maids had left the door open in their eagerness to quit her room. She leaned against the ancient wood door as if any minute he would come barging in like a plundering Viking. She was surprised to notice her hand still resting on the necklace. She pulled it free from the gown and examined it. It sparkled ready to please. Weeks hidden beneath plain gowns had not diminished its beauty or dimmed its scarlet fire.

Lenora carefully replaced it beneath her gown. Stroking the small lump that it formed.

He had come—and she didn't know whether to feel fear or elation. So, she settled on dread.

The next morning the children were more chatty than normal. Their uncle had come to Waverly for a rare visit, and he had visited with them in the nursery for a short while.

"I wish I were a grown-up," came Bertie's complaint. "Then I would have gone with Papa and Uncle this morning."

"Don't be silly, Bertie," Sarah reprimanded in her usual big sisterly way.

Lenora's eyes darted to the window, her hand going subconsciously to her neck. He was out there this moment, riding with the earl. Would he come to the schoolroom? Would she see him during his visit? Surely, she could avoid it if she but tried. And perhaps he had not come to see her after all. Perhaps it was simple vanity that made her think he had come for her.

But why else would he be here? He had seldom come before.

"I think Uncle is very handsome. Do you not think so, Miss MacLeod?"

Lenora turned to the children like she only then realized they were there. Bertie was making a terrible face.

"I think Uncle very handsome," Sarah repeated.

"Yes," Lenora nodded stoically. "He is handsome."

Sarah gave a triumphant look to her brother who seemed very displeased with the turn of conversation. Poor Bertie. Surrounded by women.

"Let us turn to our letters," Lenora began efficiently. She could not allow his presence at the house to distract her from her work. "Sarah, you begin."

The children seemed loath to focus on their lessons. They proved a handful that morning, so full of energy and excitement. Their uncle had come for a visit, and they simply could not concentrate. Then again, neither could she.

THE EARL PUSHED his mount to gallop at top speed—his brother close at his heels. Both men raced headlong into the wind only stopping when they reached the sloping chestnut. The earl had won by a mere fraction of a second.

Both men laughed as they continued toward the house, this time at a slower pace.

"I do believe you cheated, old boy," Chesterfield called out to his brother. The earl laughed hardily in response. "This damnable horse you've given me has one foot in the grave."

"Don't be a sore loser, Misha. It hardly becomes you."

"I'll have you know that despite my handicap, I still nearly beat you."

The earl turned to his brother with a regal raised brow. "You have never beaten me. I am after all the earl."

"Don't be such a cocksure bastard, Adrian. That does not become you."

The earl chuckled at this set down. He took in a clean refreshing breath. The day had risen quite spectacularly. The high clouds were thin and deferential, letting the sun reign supreme in the heavens.

Even Chesterfield turned his face to the burning globe

overhead. "I miss Waverly. I sometimes forget what a perfect piece of paradise this is."

"I thought you hated the country. It being dull and all that," his brother gave him a piercing look. "You never go to your own house. Though I sometimes believe Harewood to be far lovelier than Waverly."

"Yes, I've a mind to visit Harewood more often. I've changed my opinion on the country it seems," Chesterfield answered honestly. "I have changed my opinion on a great many things."

The earl pulled on the reins stopping his horse. He turned to his brother who had done the same. "Why the sudden visit, Michael? What is it?"

Chesterfield turned away from his brother's piercing stare. This man knew him better than anyone else on this earth. It was a little disconcerting to think that his true mission might be found out.

"Can a brother not visit another without raising alarms," Michael gave his most practiced smile.

The earl stared at him a moment longer. He perhaps didn't quite believe him, but he appeared ready to let him pass with this pretense.

"I was thinking of taking a trip to London myself," the earl continued as he spurred his horse into an easy trot. Michael followed without hesitation.

"The whole family you mean. That is a dashed good idea."

"No. I was thinking of going alone."

Chesterfield turned to his brother, who stared straight ahead. Adrian had never left the family behind before. If there was one thing he could say about his brother, it was that his family came first. Despite any shenanigans with maids or mistresses.

"What gives, Adrian? Is everything as it should be?"

His brother heaved a sigh. "Everything is as it is expected to be."

"What does that mean?" Michael stared at his brother uncomfortably.

"I would give you advice that I am certain you will not follow. I for one would not have followed it if someone had given it to me," the earl turned to him with a sardonic smile. "Whatever you do Misha, marry for love. It is a dashed shore to marry for anything else."

Chesterfield stared speechlessly at his brother.

"I suppose I have taken a turn for the maudlin," the earl gave a self-deprecating laugh. "Come, let's return to the house and forget this serious talk. In any case I must meet with Mr. Mansford. You remember my steward?"

"Yes," Michael answered quietly. "I do remember him."

"Do you think you could find your own amusements," the earl continued lightheartedly.

"Yes, I suppose I could." An idea suddenly came to Michael. "I think perhaps I'll visit the children in their schoolroom. If that's alright?"

The earl raised a brow as he turned to his brother. Whatever his thoughts he did not speak to them but merely nodded. Still, Chesterfield wondered if his brother suspected anything. Had Lenora given any clues? Did his brother guess the affair he had had with his governess?

Whatever their thoughts, neither man spoke to them as they made their way back to the house.

CHAPTER 20

*I*t was madness to think she could sense his presence in the house. She of course could not. There had not been a shift in the fabric of space. The house had not betrayed his presence to her by suddenly springing to life. No, it was pure folly that led her to think any of those things.

That she suddenly needed to leave the schoolroom for a breath of fresh air was only due to nerves. Yes, she "n on pins and needles since Lizzie and Meg announced Michael's arrival.

"I shall return immediately," Lenora rose on unsteady feet.

The children barely looked up at her as they concentrated on their watercolors.

Lenora made her way to the door—suddenly certain her mind had deserted her. Perhaps she would take time to visit her mother. Yes, she must leave this house while he was here. If she could be gone by the morrow, perhaps she would avoid seeing him altogether.

She was all at once filled with the frenetic giddiness of a narrow escape. Yes, she would go to the countess immediately and ask for a few days holiday. She was not certain what reason she would give, but surely she could think of something.

She was barely out of the room when she immediately froze.

There he stood only steps away as though he had waited all morning in precisely that spot. Waiting for her to leave the room, like the patient spider waits for the fly.

She closed the door quietly behind her so the children wouldn't hear any of what they said.

"Why are you here?" She spoke sternly, bitterness seeping out like the flesh of overripe fruit. Did he not know what his presence at Waverly was doing to her? Did he not realize how hard won her current peace "n? How despondent it made her to have it unraveled so easily?

"I came only to see you," Michael spoke the words she did not want to hear. "You must know that."

"What can you hope to gain by coming here?" And why torment us both? She wanted to add.

"A brief audience with you," he spoke quietly. Earnestly.

They were both quiet when Lenora spotted Meg approaching with an armload of linens. The two women exchanged glances though neither said a word to the other. *She will know something is amiss,* Lenora told herself. *Why had he come?*

He had the good sense to wait until the maid had disappeared around the corner before continuing.

"Meet me this evening in the arbor," he continued though she shook her head. "After you have left the children for the day."

"Why are you doing this?" Her distress was beyond anything she could describe. It was evident to Lenora that if she had held on to even a small bit of hope to see him again, it was all in foolishness. What was there left for them? As much as she had missed him, she could not be his mistress.

"Will you meet me, Lenora?"

She looked into his eyes. So impossibly green. So vibrant.

They were framed by a face that was the most beautiful she had ever seen. She had thought him the devil once. She did so again. For he tempted her to leave behind her pride and her moral standards. He tempted her with his comeliness and gentle words to forget all that she was and all that she stood for. No, she could not give in. She could not capitulate on this point!

"You must go immediately, Michael," she said with all the fierceness she could muster. "You shouldn't have come!"

"I have every right to visit my own brother, Miss MacLeod," he answered her fire with cool reserve.

She stared at him. Yes, he had a right to be here. He had a right to be anywhere he wished. But she need not speak to him.

"Then enjoy your visit with your brother, Mr. Chesterfield. But please do not approach me again, sir." She turned to walk away, when she felt him grip her arm. Lenora opened her mouth to protest but his lips were suddenly on hers.

Lenora struggled in his arms only to have him hold her tighter against his hard body.

She wanted to scream. She wanted to fight. But lord in heaven did she want this kiss! She was like parched soil receiving its first bit of rain. She drank up this meager show of affection as if it were her last meal on earth. Her mind, her body remembered him. Remembered the feel of his solid form, his strong arms and soft lips. It remembered all of this in a brief kiss and hungered for more.

All those weeks, all that effort drained away with one thorough kiss.

He finally released her only when she had ceased fighting his embrace.

"I gave you fare warning what would happen should you ever call me sir again," he spoke in a cool tone. "Did I not?"

She slowly nodded no longer daring to look at him. Not trusting herself to keep from leaping back into his arms and begging him to take her away from this place. Oh, heavens, where were her morals now? Where were the ideals she once wore around her like a proud cloak?

She wanted to curse that damnable bargain.

"I shall wait for you in the arbor. The family still takes their tea at half past four?"

Lenora nodded meekly, still not daring to look at him.

"Then meet me at half past." He straightened his clothing as he watched her. She still did not look up at him. "I shall bid you a good day till then, Lenora."

"Good day si– Michael," she answered quietly staring at the floor.

Chesterfield looked at her. Truly looked at her. She wore a dull grey gown. Her hair was pulled back into a harsh bun erasing the softness of her face. She was all harsh lines and calculated coldness. She is far worse than before, he realized sadly.

With that he turned on his heels and continued down the hall.

For the first time in her employment at Waverly, Lenora did something she had never done; she left the children unattended as she fled to her room. She could barely see the hall before her, so drowned in tears were her eyes.

He had come to torment her—of this she was certain.

She reached her room, quietly closing the door behind her and locking it like the devil himself "n on her tail. Once secured she immediately crumpled to the floor and wept with a ferocity she had never felt before. She did not want to love him. Wrenched heart that beat in her bosom! If only she could rip it out and crush it in her fist. She did not want to love him!

But how was she to stop? How was she to fight against the onslaught of emotions that one kiss could bring? She had no power against it. She was a ship cast at sea, fighting ceaseless waves.

Lenora wept out her frustrations and unrealized hopes. She pounded at the floor with her balled fist, cursing their bargain, cursing his existence.

She didn't care when Lizzie's knock came at the door. Nor did she move when the sun began to set. She didn't care if her belly cried out for food. She wanted to starve, to die and disappear.

Cursed life!

What had it brought her but misery and pain? Since her earliest memories. And she "n fair with fate, had she not? She had made endless excuses why her portion was so meager when others grew fat with their happiness.

And where had it gotten her? Nowhere.

Lizzie came again with her tea, but Lenora did not answer the girl's knocks. She had quieted down by then, lying like a crumpled heap on the floor.

He would be waiting in the arbor for her. He had told her half past four, the usual time the family took their tea. He wanted to speak with her. More than likely lay siege on the last vestige of her sanity.

He must go. And if he would not, she must. There was no other choice.

She could picture him at that very moment, pacing the arbor, waiting for her to appear. Turning in anticipation at every sound, the rustle of the trees, the scurry of the cat through the rose bushes. He would turn around expecting her only to be disappointed time and again. That is until he grew tired and angry, waiting for a poor simple governess who would not show.

Lenora lay on the floor unmoving until the last golden rays of the sun flared to vibrant life than died quietly below the horizon.

She released a solitary sob. She had not gone to see him. Perhaps he would take this as a sign and leave her alone forever.

"Miss MacLeod?" This was the voice of the Countess of Walpole. The room had fallen into complete darkness now and the air took on a chill that sometimes came at night, even in summer.

Lenora sighed. She should open the door to her employer and be prepared to be sacked more than likely. She had left the children to their own devices. A foolish and silly thing to do. But this was what she had become. This was what loving him had made her, a fool.

With a gargantuan effort she managed to raise herself to a seated position. If only she could splash some cold water on her face before facing her employer. The countess was not a cruel woman, but she did not suffer fools lightly. She was an efficient hostess, a fair employer, and a product of her class. She would not take kindly to an inferior shirking her duties, no matter the reason.

Lenora made it to her feet quite aware that it was not a friend she would be letting in.

She opened the door hesitantly.

The countess stood in the hall, dressed in her favorite pale green silk. It was quite becoming with her dark hair. She was in her late thirties and a handsome woman, though not a great beauty. She wore a questioning look on her face, if at least not one of anger.

"Miss MacLeod?" The countess took in the dark room, Lenora's crumpled clothes and disheveled hair. She would have almost suspected the woman "n in the middle of an assignation if not for her puffy red eyes. "What on earth is the matter?"

"I am sorry my lady." Lenora tried to infuse her words with all the dignity her appearance lacked. "I did not feel at all well this afternoon."

"It would have done well for you to have told someone," the countess chastised hesitantly. She had never had trouble with the governess before. At least not until the woman had had to leave them so suddenly and for a whole month. But all "n forgiven. Truly Miss MacLeod "n an exemplary employee… until now.

"Will you be up for the children tomorrow?" She asked in concern.

Lenora could not believe her ears. She was certain after this blunder she would be let go. Perhaps something in her face gave evidence to her surprise.

"Miss MacLeod, you have been a wonderful governess and the earl, and I feel fortunate to have you," the countess explained quite sensibly. "But we really cannot have you leaving the children as you did today."

"No, my lady. I am sorry."

"Now, if you feel under the weather, please let us know, so that we may make other arrangements. We know Bertie and Sarah can be quite a handful."

"No, my lady. They are no grief to me at all."

"Very well," the countess answered, making it clear she did not quite believe her. "I am only saying if you need tomorrow off."

"No, my lady. I am quite fully recovered."

Both women knew Lenora's appearance belied her words, but the countess was never one to dig too deeply into an employee's life. She thus gave a simple nod, and the matter was considered forgotten.

"Very well, then. Tomorrow bright and early?"

"Yes, my lady."

Lenora gave a sigh of relief when the countess finally departed. She hardly knew what her employer must have thought of her, bedraggled as she was.

Lenora made quick work of lighting her lamps. Once that task was accomplished, she looked around at her surroundings and sighed—it was not a bad life she led. True her room was small and barren. She'd never tried to make it more inviting.

She had no complaints concerning her employers. She was safe, sound, fed and dry. What more could a woman in her position ask for?

It was then that she heard it. The quiet knock. She knew immediately who it must be and for a long moment she contemplated not answering. She waited quietly, like a mouse sensing a nearby hawk. The knock came again, this time a little louder. Her heart beat quickened. Her mind jumping forward to how this scene most likely would play out if she did not open the door. It would not end with him quietly leaving. She had no choice but to let him in and hope to speak sense into his stubborn brain.

Lenora quietly crept to the door and awaited a third knock. And as if summoning it by her mere thought, it came. She took a steeling breath and slowly opened the door. And indeed, it was Michael who stood there, eyes glowing with a mixture of fatigue and irritation.

They did not at first speak. Lenora merely stepped aside, her face a cold unreadable mask. Michael entered cautiously and with some amount of relief. His eyes scanned the drab room. For a moment, Lenora felt a sort of embarrassment. But then quickly shooed it away. She needed to focus on the message she had to deliver. She quietly closed the door.

"This is most inappropriate," she began in that familiar cold and clip manner.

"I think perhaps you and I are beyond impropriety, Lenora," Michael answered quietly.

"We were once, but we are no longer."

He approached her and she watched him suspiciously.

"We were also friends of sorts once," he continued. "Were we not?"

"Yes," came her simple answer.

"Could we not be so again?"

She made no answer to this.

"I can take you away from this life, Lenora. I can give you comfort. A house of your own. Servants. You were made for so much more than this work."

"What you speak of would be work... of sorts," she answered coolly.

"But there would be pleasure too." His words came out with a sadness she was unfamiliar with. She remained silent as she turned to look at him. It was then she finally noticed the dark circles beneath his eyes. He mistakenly took her silence as encouragement to continue pleading his case.

"You would have all the time in the world to spend with your family. I would be generous, Lenora. More generous with you than any woman I have ever known." There was a quiet desperation in his voice, and it confused her. Clouding her resolve.

"You know that I love you, do you not?" He finally spoke the words he should have spoken all those weeks ago, on the day she left Calais.

Lenora stared at him in disbelief, willing her heart to turn to stone. He loved her? But she could not care. She would not care. To care would be her undoing. Why on earth did he have to tell her this? Why now? It was a Herculean effort to force her face not to betray the turmoil wreaking havoc on her body. She must end this with him. She had to make him see reason.

"It does not matter," she finally said when she was certain her true feelings would not be given away by so much as a quiver in her voice.

"Does not matter?" Michael stared at her in disbelief. "Can you truly be so unfeeling?" He shook his head. "I have seen passion in you Lenora," he spoke fiercely. "Though you don't love me, I know that you care for me a little. You can't deny that."

Her silence was perhaps to tell him she didn't care for him at all. But he would not believe her. Just then a rumble sounded from outside.

"It's going to rain," she spoke quietly.

"Yes," Michael responded with some irritation. "It's forever raining it seems."

Lenora looked out the little window and the scene outside transported her to a time not so long ago.

"It was raining the first time you made love to me," she spoke as though her words were outside of herself. "Do you remember?"

Michael stared at her for one unbelieving moment. His gaze then followed hers to the window, which suddenly transformed into French doors. It was their little cottage again.

"Yes, I remember." And just like that something changed between them—something in the ether washed away all negative energy and left them calm and at peace.

They remained silent like this for an eternal moment. A moment so fragile and bittersweet.

"You told me I was lovely. Do you remember?" She turned to him. Her eyes filled with a remarkable innocence.

"Yes. Yes, I remember," his voice matched hers in quietude. Michael crept forward. Lenora returned her gaze to the window.

"I did not believe you," her voice quivered with the first evidence of tears.

Michael took her hand in his, gently stroking her soft skin with his thumb.

"Will the rain always haunt me?" She turned to him, her eyes begging for an answer. "Will it always remind me of you?"

"Lenora." He could not have helped himself, even if he had tried. His lips found hers and she did not fight him. They melted together proclaiming the rightness of their union.

It was only a matter of time before she returned his kisses with equal vehemence. Lenora could not remember such hunger. She wanted him. She wanted their bodies together. She wanted to tell him she would be his. She would be anything he desired as long as she was by his side. But the words would not come out. Some small pride in her would not allow it. And she cursed it now. Cursed it for not letting her play the fool completely.

"Michael," she whispered. "Michael."

"Yes, my love. Yes." His hands began exploring the familiar landscape of her body.

Lenora held him to her, wishing that somehow she could feel his skin against her body. She felt his hand reach under her skirt, and she leaned into him in welcome.

"Yes, yes…"

"Oh God, Lenora. You're a torment to me."

He moved them to her bed and laid her down. He then moved over her, recapturing her mouth with his.

She felt him reaching for the fastener to his pants and the anticipation was beyond maddening. She wanted him to fill her with a longing so acute that it bordered on pain.

"Michael, please."

"Yes, yes." His movements quickened.

"I need you inside me," she said with mindless desperation.

"Oh lord, save me."

Michael released himself and his erection sprang free, like a battering ram. He reached under her gown and roughly pulled at the material. Lenora lifted her bottom allowing the garment to slide free.

Michael covered her once again and their eyes met for a moment. Each saw their need reflected in the other. The want so deep. The desire so raw.

She opened her mouth, but her words were cut short as Michael pushed himself inside her. Lenora gasped with relief. Yes! This was what she wanted. He pushed in deeper, and her eyes shut tightly, squeezing out stubborn tears.

"Oh god," Michael groaned as her heat enveloped him. Was there any greater ecstasy than being buried inside this woman? Michael pulled out and pushed back in, beginning the sweet madness that was their mating.

Lenora wrapped her legs around him holding him tightly to her as if afraid he would vanish at any moment. They held onto each other as his speed increased. With each plunge she forgot more and more why she could not become his mistress. What did her morals matter? She had already sold her body to him. Why not give herself over completely?

Michael pumped into her as though each stroke was an argument for keeping her. Your body is mine. Your soul is mine. Your heart will be mine too!

Lenora whimpered as her pleasure began to build. Tears streamed down her eyes as she opened herself to him. Yes, my body is yours. My soul is yours.

And then she felt it, the beginning of her orgasm. She threw back her head and whimpered, trying so valiantly to remain quiet. The time apart and the effort to stay quiet conspired against her. She had never felt a more powerful climax! And he moved in her forcing her further. It was madness! But she kept climbing. Bursting even higher.

"Oh god," he groaned before reaching his own climax. And he poured himself deep within her. Pumping every last bit of his soul into her wet body.

They both landed back on the small bed weak and empty. Lenora's body went limp beneath his and Michael moved off of her, sliding to her side. There was suddenly an emptiness in her face.

"Goodbye Michael."

"No," Michael shook his head. But her expression did not change. He pulled her to him, and though she did not resist, neither did she return his embrace, but in fact turned her gaze away from him.

"Please." Michael held her to him, real fear filling his mind. She truly meant to leave him and there was nothing he could do to stop her.

Lenora spoke not a word. One thing was certain; she would have to resign from her post. She could no longer stay at Waverly.

CHAPTER 21

*L*ess than a week later, the Earl of Walpole looked down at the letter his wife had handed him just that morning over breakfast. It was an unexpected letter of resignation from Miss MacLeod. It was short, simple and to the point. She was leaving them due to a sudden illness in her family.

Adrian frowned over the letter. A look to the countess proved that she too thought the whole thing odd. Miss MacLeod had never been in the usual habit of lying to them. They had never had cause to suspect her of hiding anything. Something indeed was going on with their governess he agreed with his wife. It was now up to him to figure out just what that was.

A knock sounded at the door. The earl did not move from his position of leaning one elbow over the mantel of the fireplace. He knew who knocked on the door. He had summoned her directly after finishing his breakfast.

"Enter."

Lenora entered the room, closing the door quietly behind her. She wore one of her usual dull, serviceable gowns. Her hair, as always, pulled back mercilessly into a tight bun.

Adrian watched his governess's entrance immediately aware that something was not right. Her usual stoicism, though firmly there, was somehow overlaid with a fragility he had never known her to possess.

"Please take a seat, Miss MacLeod," Adrian indicated at a chair placed before his oversized Indian mahogany desk.

"I'd prefer to stand, my lord. If it's all the same to you." She spoke quietly, her voice possessing none of its usual crispness. It was as brittle as her demeanor. It spoke of a restless anguish and world weariness that only came after great heartache.

Adrian raised a brow but nodded. He himself decided to take a seat at his desk.

Lenora stared down at the dark green Persian rug waiting for the earl to speak further. She did not want to look at him and risk turning into a water pot.

But more than that, she did not look at the Earl of Walpole because she feared he would ferret out her secret if she gave him half a chance. The thought alone filled her with mortification.

Adrian examined the woman before him. His mind working methodically to solve this current puzzle. It was all so very odd.

"Her ladyship presented me with your letter of resignation this morning."

The statement sounded more like a question. Lenora nodded adding, "Yes, my Lord."

Adrian frowned. "Might I ask if there was something we have done to make your employment… unpleasant?"

"No, my Lord."

The woman was as tight-lipped as a prisoner of war.

"Perhaps something has happened to make your stay here unbearable?" Adrian continued his line of questioning. "Perhaps something that has escaped my notice."

She made no answer to this, almost as though she had not

heard him. Adrian leaned back in his chair examining her subtle movements. He was not mistaken. Something had happened to her. This caused him great concern. It was all well and good for him to tup a willing maid once in a long while, especially when his countess made it so clear she did not wish him in her bed. It was not something he relished, using an underling for his relief and he never sought them out, but occasionally accepted what they offered freely. But other than those few indiscretions he was fiercely protective of his staff. This thing that was worrying Miss MacLeod brought him great apprehension.

"Miss MacLeod, I sincerely wish to help you, but I cannot if you do not tell me what..."

"Please," came her sudden whispered entreaty. Adrian was startled to hear such desperation in her voice. What was this? What had happened to her?

"Miss MacLeod, look at me," he commanded and was further shocked when she shook her head. Adrian rose to his feet and in a few strides made his way around the desk.

Lenora took a step back wanting with every ounce of her body to escape the room, but he took hold of her arm pushing up her chin, forcing her to face him. And for an instant, a mere instant, she felt as if it were Michael standing before. Forcing her to face him. And her weak defenses crumbled like dust in the wind.

"What is it? What has happened to you?" Adrian stared down at her with growing concern.

"I must go! I must leave!" The tears were pouring now and her body shaking with the futile effort of holding back her sobs. She had not wanted this to happen! Not in front of the earl! Great heavens, what he must think of her!

She felt like a veritable fool—and she could not tell him the cause of her grief. She could not say that she was miserable with loving his brother. She could not confess that at least a hundred times a day she contemplated throwing caution and every ounce of dignity to the wind and running to Michael, begging to be his mistress! To be anything to him as long as she was in his arms. The feeling did not diminish with the passing days but instead grew stronger. She wanted him! How she wanted him with a burning hunger that would devour her whole!

"Has this to do with my brother?"

Her eyes flew wide, and Adrian knew he had hit his mark. It had only been a guess really, but a right guess. Michael had acted odd on his last visit. Odd first in that he had visited at all! But mostly because Adrian recalled his brother's desire to visit the nursery. He had thought it peculiar at the time but had not questioned Michael. And then he had fled the next day without explanation or warning.

"Can I not keep my staff safe from that man?!" Adrian spat out with some frustration. He then turned his attention again to Lenora. "How? You've shown nothing but contempt for him since your arrival?"

"I know."

"Then how?"

"I cannot say."

Adrian felt a sudden violent irritation. How had Michael broken through with Lenora? He never could have guessed this.

"Do you love him?" Adrian finally asked when the shock had settled a little.

"Yes." Her answer was filled with despair.

Adrian frowned. "Do you plan to go to him? Is that it?"

"No." Lenora's body heaved with the answer. It was the most miserable "no" Adrian had ever heard uttered in his life.

"And why not? Has the scoundrel abandoned you?" He could just wring his brother's neck. Miss MacLeod was not the sort of woman a man romanced and left high and dry. She was not a piece of fluff. She was a serious, religious woman. How on earth had this happened?

"He hasn't abandoned me."

"Then what has happened?" The earl asked in growing frustration. "It is apparent you are still miserably in love with him."

She lifted her eyes to him with such a look of stricken terror that it began to make more sense. She did not want to be in love with him. She loved his brother against her better judgment. Adrian shook his head. Why did people make their lives more miserable than necessary?

"Lenora," he tried to calm his voice as much as he could. He was not accustomed to speaking to a woman about her gentler feelings. Not even with the countess if he could help it. "Is it that you do not wish to love him?"

Lenora nodded, unable to stop a fresh flood of hot tears from rolling down her cheeks.

"But you do love him?"

"Terribly," she spoke with a shaky voice. It was a confession she had not wanted to make to anyone and yet was relieved to finally admit out loud.

"And he still desires you?"

"Yes. I believe he still does."

Adrian took her into his arms feeling as if his own heart would break. He so often forgot how very young she still was. She was always the capable, unflinching Miss MacLeod. He sometimes forgot she was still made of flesh and bone.

"Then you must go to him."

"I cannot."

"What is there to stop you? I'm certain Michael would take great care of you."

"But I can't be his mistress. I cannot!"

Was that it? Was it the morality? He did not intend on asking her if she had already been intimate with his brother. It was hardly his business. But he suspected she had.

"Lenora, I plan to leave for London in a few days."

"With the family?"

"No. Only myself. I, like you, have much to think about."

She looked at him not understanding what he could have to think about.

"Come with me to London. This thing between you and my brother can be settled easily."

"No. I intend to never see him again. I couldn't bear it."

"And what? You plan to live your life in this misery?"

"It will fade in time, I think. It must."

"If it does, it will not be for a very long time yet. I think you love him far too deeply."

Lenora shook her head, not wanting to hear his words.

"Does the pain lessen when you are away from him?"

"No," she replied plaintively. "It grows worse with each passing day. I sometimes think I'll go mad with it."

"Then come to London with me. Go to Michael. I suspect he is as miserable as you are."

"But what will people say?"

"To hell with what people say!" Adrian spoke from his own frustrations. "I've cared what people have said all my life and still do. Yet those same people have never lifted a single finger to make me happy."

"But the countess... the children."

"Yes, Bertie and Sarah bring me great happiness. But they are easy to please. As for my wife... well..." Adrian heaved a sigh. "Lenora, if Michael makes you happy, go to him. Do not be miserable for the sake of pride. Life is far too short."

It frightened her that he spoke just the words she wanted to hear. Though Lenora knew he spoke perhaps from his own failed dreams more than her best interest.

"And what do I do when he grows tired of me?"

"You must not think of that."

"I don't have the luxury to think of anything else. I must work for my living."

Adrian stared at her, studying her. It was in that moment

that he decided it was in his power to give his brother the happiness he himself did not have.

"Then come to me…"

Lenora inhaled sharply.

"No, I mean that I will settle an income on you should Michael leave you destitute—as I doubt he will."

Lenora's eyes widened as the full brunt of his words hit her. She need never worry over her finances again. She stood to lose nothing by accepting the earl's generous offer—except her heart perhaps. And maybe a little of her pride she reminded herself. But she could be with Michael. At last. It was a foolish hope, but she needed so little encouragement at this point. Anything would have pushed her toward this decision. But why would the earl help them? Help her? This could not be the normal way of things.

"And why would you do this? Why would you support your brother's cast off?"

"Because I suspect you will not go to him if I do not make this promise. And as harsh as I am with Michael, he is still my brother."

"You love Misha too."

Adrian nodded with a wry smile, more at hearing his brother's pet name used by Lenora than by her question. She did indeed love his brother. And it was good to know that at least one of the Chesterfield brothers would experience love.

"Do you agree to our bargain?"

Lenora hesitated. Another bargain. But this time it was different. This time it was for love. She would go to Michael and offer herself to him. She would be his at last.

CHAPTER 22

The air was cool and heavy with the scent of the ocean. The wind chased the sand along the abandoned shore, forming swirls and mystical shapes before wiping it clean again.

Michael stood by the sea's edge, his bare feet sinking into the moist dark sand. Two weeks. That was the length of time it "n since he last saw her.

He stood, a lone figure like an actor upon a stage—the endless ocean, with its cresting waves, his only audience. He stared out into the water, his face placid and his eyes unfocused. His hair had grown impossibly long and was in dire need of cutting.

He took in a deep breath filling his lungs with the chilled salty air. His shirtsleeves unbuttoned almost to his breeches. It felt good to feel the cool air against his hot skin. It felt good to be alone. To think.

Seagulls called overhead on their flight out to sea. It was a grey, haunting day. Unusually cloudy for this time of year.

He heard the sound of a carriage making its lonely way along the road. Michael did not turn. There "n a handful of farmers making their journeys to market or people heading to the town center. They did not bother him and he in turn did not bother them.

Because he did not turn around, he could not see the woman alighting from the plain hired carriage when it came to a stop. He did not see her making her way toward him.

But he sensed her.

At first thinking he was going a little mad. She was not here. It was perhaps a tourist. Maybe someone he knew. It could not be her. It could not be Lenora.

And yet he did not dare turn. Not even when he could finally hear the stranger's approach. The distinct crunch of the sand. The hesitancy in the steps as they drew closer. It could not be her. He would not allow himself to hope.

"Michael."

She spoke that one word and his world was knocked off center. He was either mad and hearing voices or she had come to him. Michael feared turning around, he feared not seeing her if he did so.

She saved him the effort by stepping around to face him. He stared at her like he had seen a ghost.

Lenora returned his gaze, her own emotions roiling within her. It "n two weeks since she had seen him, since she had said goodbye after their lovemaking, and he looked the worse for wear. He could not know the torment she had endured to find him. The heartache she had felt upon her arrival in London to be told Michael had only made a brief stop and had gone on to God knew where. No one on his staff knew his whereabouts. It "n days of enquiring before she even thought to return to Calais. But she was here. With the earl's help she had made her way back to Michael. To the man she loved.

But he didn't look pleased to find her here. After all her searching he appeared quite miserable to see her.

"Michael, are you not happy to see me?"

Michael swallowed hard, finding his throat suddenly parched. "Lenora?"

"I've come to you Michael. I've come to tell you I'll be your mistress. I'll be anything you wish me to be so long as I can be with you."

His eyes glazed with his unshed tears. She had come to him willing to be his mistress. Lenora MacLeod had come to him, giving herself to him. It was beyond wonderful.

"Do you recall that evening in Lille, after our dinner with the Bennetts." Lenora continued to speak. There was suddenly so much to say to him. So much of her true feelings to confess. "You asked me why you. Do you recall what I answered?"

Michael's brows furrowed. He barely remembered that conversation so long ago. He had wanted to know why she had chosen him, why she had not asked someone else for the money.

"As I recall it was I and not you who answered."

"Yes. And to salvage my pride I allowed you to think something that was not completely true," came her admission.

"And what is the truth?" Something in Michael tightened, wondering and fearing all in one moment what she would tell him.

"It was you because it has always been you," Lenora began her confession, tears sparkling in her eyes. "Since the very first moment I laid eyes on you, five years ago. You were a young vain cockerel, and I desired you. When I dreamed of a lover, he always bore your face. When I thought of what lay between a man and woman, I always thought of you. I chose you Misha because it was the only way I could have you."

Michael stared at her in disbelief. It could not be possible!

"A part of me always knew this, though I hated it and hated you for this desire you inspired. Loving you was like a thirst I could never quench."

"But why have you said nothing of this?" His mind recalled the countless times she spurned him.

"I never wished to be your lover, Michael. I never wished to be a plaything like all the others. I'm far too greedy to have you only temporarily. I wished to be your wife. Had I never been in such a great need for the money I would never have come to you."

"But you did come to me. And what you proposed put you in a far less favorable position."

"In some ways. But our bargain allowed me to hide my desire and save my pride. In this way I could convince myself I went to your bed because I had no choice."

Michael nodded in understanding. All this time she had desired him, and he had desired her. But perhaps her denying him was precisely the thing they had both needed. For, had she caved to her desires and allowed him to bed her when he first approached her, she would have meant nothing to him. She would have simply been another easy conquest in a list of many.

"I think I still held some foolish hope that I would be more to you. But now I see it all too clearly. I love you beyond reason. And if I can't be your wife, I'll be your mistress. I'll be your servant. I'll be anything you wish me to be!"

She stared at him, that glorious flame burning in her eyes. She was a goddess though she did not know it. She meant the world to him, this woman. For her he would die a thousand deaths. He loved her, and there was only one way to show her.

"I no longer want you as my mistress, Lenora," he finally spoke.

Her face looked stricken. "Michael, please!"

"I no longer want you as my mistress because I want you as my wife. You are my soulmate. My divine counterpart. And I want you at my side for all time, until death do us part."

"Misha!"

It was now her turn to stare at him in disbelief. In all her dreams—the ones she dared to allow herself—she never would have imagined such a blessing. She still could not imagine it even as he stood before her. Life did not work this way. At least not for her.

"You can't mean this."

"Yes, yes. I mean this and so much more." He held his arms out to her. "Say you will be my wife and make me the happiest man on earth."

"Yes! Yes!"

She threw herself into his arms, tears of joy flowing unabated. Tears of pure ecstasy. She would be his, mind, body and soul. And he would be hers from this day forward. Till death did them part.

"I have never dared dream of such happiness," she confessed as she let the warmth of his body seep into hers.

"Then I'll dream it for the both of us."

Michael and Lenora's lips met, and they drank in each other's joy, reveling in the happiness they had found at last.

There was joy in the world Lenora discovered. There was love and sunshine and great hope. And every other sort of delight she had never dared hope for. She would have his children. They would share their days and their nights together. And she would never again know the feeling of loneliness that had plagued her early days. In time, she would forget that there ever was a world without Michael. And Michael in turn would forget there was ever a day he existed without his Lenora.

BOOK CLUB QUESTIONS

CHARACTER DYNAMICS & DEVELOPMENT

Motivations and Intentions:

1. What drives Lenora MacLeod to offer herself to Michael Chesterfield in the first place?

2. How do her intentions shift as their arrangement evolves?

The Rake's Transformation:

3. How does Michael Chesterfield change over the course of the story?

4. What insights into his character emerge through his interactions with Lenora?

Loneliness & Connection:

5. Both protagonists confront deep loneliness—how does this shared experience affect their dynamic and emotional journey?

THEMES OF DUTY, DESIRE & IDENTITY

Status vs Self-Worth:

6. In what ways does the novel explore how societal status influences one's sense of self-worth?

7. How do Lenora and Michael each navigate this?

Obligation vs Desire:

8. Does their arrangement remain transactional, or does genuine desire and emotional need blur the lines?

9. How does Vincent portray this distinction?

SETTING & ATMOSPHERE

Regency-Era Influence:

10. How does the backdrop of Regency-era France and England shape the characters' decisions, freedoms, and constraints?

Culture Clash:

11. Does the dual setting amplify cultural or social contrasts?

12. How do these enhance the narrative tension or characterizations?

STYLE & TONE

Slow-Burn Romance:

13. How does the pacing of the romance, slow-building and simmering, affect your reading experience?

14. Does it heighten the tension or the emotional stakes?

Sharp-Tongued Banter:

15. Vincent is noted for her intelligent and witty dialogue. Which exchanges stood out most to you, and how do they deepen character connection?

EMOTIONAL JOURNEY & REFLECTION

Emotional Stakes:

16. Beyond the initial financial transaction, what deeper emotional journeys do Lenora and Michael undertake?

17. How convincing is their transformation?

Conclusion Satisfaction:

18. Are you satisfied with the ending?

19. Does it feel earned based on their development?

20. What alternatives, if any, would you have preferred?

BROADER CONTEXT & DISCUSSION

Genre Conventions:

21. How does The Bargain both embrace and subvert traditional tropes of historical romance?Modern Resonance:

22. Despite its historical setting, what themes (e.g., autonomy, negotiation of desire, self-identity) feel especially relevant today?

Room for Debate:

23. Were there moments or character choices you wanted to defend or criticize?

24. Which ones sparked the most interesting discussions among your group?